the *Forgotten* PEARL

BOOKS BY BELINDA MURRELL

The Locket of Dreams
The Ruby Talisman
The Ivory Rose
The Forgotten Pearl
The River Charm
The Sequin Star

The Sun Sword Trilogy

Book 1: The Quest for the Sun Gem
Book 2: The Voyage of the Owl
Book 3: The Snowy Tower

For Younger Readers

Lulu Bell and the Birthday Unicorn
Lulu Bell and the Fairy Penguin
Lulu Bell and the Cubby Fort
Lulu Bell and the Moon Dragon
Lulu Bell and the Circus Pup
Lulu Bell and the Sea Turtle
Lulu Bell and the Tiger Cub
Lulu Bell and the Pyjama Party
Lulu Bell and the Christmas Elf
Lulu Bell and the Koala Joey
Lulu Bell and the Arabian Nights

the *Forgotten* PEARL

BELINDA MURRELL

RANDOM HOUSE AUSTRALIA

This project has been assisted by the Australian Government through the Australia Council, its arts funding and advisory body.

 Australian Government

 **Australia Council for the Arts**

A Random House book
Published by Random House Australia Pty Ltd
Level 3, 100 Pacific Highway, North Sydney NSW 2060
www.randomhouse.com.au

First published by Random House Australia in 2012
This edition first published 2015

Addresses for companies within the Random House Group can be found at global.penguinrandomhouse.com

National Library of Australia
Cataloguing-in-Publication Entry

Author: Murrell, Belinda
Title: The forgotten pearl / Belinda Murrell
ISBN: 978 0 85798 696 2 (pbk)
Target Audience: For primary school age
Subjects: World War, 1939–1945 – Australia – Juvenile fiction
   Children and war – Australia – Juvenile fiction
   War and families – Australia – Juvenile fiction
Dewey Number: A823.4

Cover design by book design by saso
Cover images © iStockphoto.com
Internal design and typesetting by Midland Typesetters, Australia
Printed in Australia by Griffin Press, an accredited ISO AS/NZS 14001:2004 Environmental Management System printer

Random House Australia uses papers that are natural, renewable and recyclable products and made from wood grown in sustainable forests. The logging and manufacturing processes are expected to conform to the environmental regulations of the country of origin.

*For all the men, women and children who sacrificed
so much during the Second World War, and for my
husband, Rob, who shared my adventures in the
Top End and introduced me to its history.*

We Shall Keep the Faith
by Moina Michael, November 1918

Oh! you who sleep in Flanders Fields,
Sleep sweet — to rise anew!
We caught the torch you threw
And holding high, we keep the Faith
With All who died.

We cherish, too, the poppy red
That grows on fields where valour led;
It seems to signal to the skies
That blood of heroes never dies,
But lends a lustre to the red
Of the flower that blooms above the dead
In Flanders Fields.

And now the Torch and Poppy Red
We wear in honour of our dead.
Fear not that ye have died for naught;
We'll teach the lesson that ye wrought
In Flanders Fields.

Glossary of Japanese words and phrases

Arigato	Thank you
Chan	Affectionate term for a child, used after their name, as in Shinju-chan
Dou itashi mashite	It was my pleasure
Ogenki desuka?	How are you?
Ohayou gozaimasu	Good day
San	Term of respect, like Mr or Mrs, used after family name, as in Murata-San
Sayonara	Goodbye
Shinju	Pearl
Watashi wa genki desu	Very well

Prologue –
8 April 2012

It's hard to believe how completely your life can change in just a few minutes, thought Chloe. *Take friendship: one minute you have a group of friends to hang out with, gossip and laugh with. The next minute, something happens that changes everything.*

'Are you all right, Chloe?' asked her grandmother, gently stroking her forehead. 'You seem distracted.'

Normally, Chloe loved visiting her grandparents' apartment. It always seemed gracious and elegant – the polished, antique furniture; the vases of flowers; the paintings on the walls and the piles of books – but today she felt sad and dejected. It was the holidays, the weather was stunning, and yet everything was wrong.

Chloe mentally shook herself. 'I'm just thinking about my history assignment,' she fibbed. 'It's on the Second World War.'

'The war?' asked Nanna, frowning.

Chloe pushed her dark hair back and nodded. 'I have to interview a relative or friend about their experiences during the war in Australia and how it affected their lives,' she explained. 'We're supposed to create a video or a website about their experiences, including letters, photographs and relics — anything that brings the story to life.'

A shadow flitted over Nanna's face. She rubbed her left arm from shoulder to elbow as though it ached. 'That sounds terrifying,' she confessed. 'You kids are so clever with what you can do with technology these days.'

'Mum thought I should interview you,' continued Chloe, 'but I guess the war didn't really affect Australia. It was all fought in Europe, with Hitler and the Blitz and the concentration camps. I mean, I know you went to school here in Sydney during the war, but it's not like your dad was a soldier or anything.'

Nanna shut her eyes and pressed her fingers into the bridge of her nose. She was silent for a few moments.

'The war years . . .' mused her grandmother. 'Such a long time ago . . . So many things that we've tried to forget . . .'

Chloe looked at her grandmother with concern. 'Are you all right, Nanna? You don't have to help me — I could always ask Brianna's grandfather. His father fought in Tobruk.'

Nanna smiled — a smile that was loving and warm and somehow wise. 'No, my darling, I'd like to help you with your assignment. Perhaps it is time to talk about it all.'

Nanna stood up from her armchair, dropping her knitting needles on the sideboard. She was teaching Chloe how to knit a soft, pale-blue, mohair scarf. 'But before I tell you about the war, I think we need a cup of tea and a slice of my famous Belgian lemon cake.'

Nanna bustled into the tiny galley kitchen to put the kettle on. 'While the kettle's boiling, come and help me look for an old box of letters and photos I have hidden away in my bedroom somewhere. I haven't looked at them for years.'

Chloe followed her grandmother into her bedroom, with its handmade quilt on the bed, a cedar dressing table and a tall bookcase crowded with books and framed family photos. There were photos of Chloe's own mother, Margie, as a child, with Margie's big sister Daisy and brother Charlie. There were photos of weddings and graduations, birthday parties and newborn babies. There was a photo of her dressed as a mermaid on her sixth birthday, surrounded by all her mermaid friends.

As she looked at the mermaid party she was sharply reminded of the last week of school. For no apparent reason, her best friend, Brianna, had stopped talking to her, and so had everyone else. Chloe had no idea why, and no one would tell her. In English, her usual seat beside Brianna was taken by Stella, so she'd sat up the back by herself. At lunchtime, the girls were not sitting in their favourite place under the apple tree. They had moved lunch spots without telling her. When she'd said hi to Brianna in the locker room, Brianna had completely ignored her, and Chloe had scuttled away, alone and friendless, to spend lunchtime in the library. Chloe felt a fat tear roll down her cheek. Angrily she brushed it away before Nanna could see it.

Nanna was searching the drawers in her wardrobe. 'Where did I put it? Oh, I think it's right on the top shelf. There it is — the blue-and-white tin at the back there. Can you reach it for me, please, Chloe?'

Chloe dragged over a chair to stand on, reached up and lifted down a round biscuit tin, covered with tiny blue roses.

'Is this it?' asked Chloe, offering it to her grandmother. 'It's not very big.'

Nanna turned away. 'Mmmm,' she replied. 'You take the box into the lounge room and I'll make the tea.'

Chloe carried the tin back into the lounge room and placed it on the coffee table. She gazed at it, curious about its contents. Nanna returned in a few minutes with a pot of tea, teacups and two slices of crumbly lemon cake.

Together, they looked at the tin on the table between them.

'Shall we open it?' asked Chloe.

Nanna took a deep breath, then reverently opened the lid. Inside was a fat bundle of yellowed letters tied together with red satin ribbon. There was a slim collection of black-and-white photos. Nanna untied the letters and stroked them with her finger. She lay the photos down on the coffee table, her hands trembling.

There were photos of old-fashioned cars, girls in floral dresses, beach picnics and a gracious-looking white house on stilts surrounded by tropical gardens.

'Was that your house in Darwin?' asked Chloe.

Nanna nodded. 'At Myilly Point.'

There was a photo of a young man in uniform squinting into the camera, his slouch hat at a jaunty angle. There was a photo of a young Aboriginal woman, looking self-conscious and shy, with a tousle-headed toddler on her knee. There was a photo of two pretty teenage girls at the beach, their hair salty and windblown, laughing into the camera with their arms around each other's necks.

'Who are they, Nanna?' asked Chloe.

'That's my brother, Edward, who went away to fight in Singapore,' explained Nanna. 'And that was Daisy and her son, Charlie — not your aunt and uncle, of course, but the original Daisy and Charlie, who lived with us in Darwin.'

Nanna swallowed as she continued to brush the long-ago faces with her fingertips.

'And that was me, with my best friend, Maude,' confided Nanna, with a smile. 'That photo was taken in 1942 by a handsome young man called Jack.'

'Oh,' said Chloe. 'That was exactly seventy years ago.'

'My goodness — could it be seventy years?' replied Nanna. 'Where on earth has the time gone? I still feel like a teenager inside.'

Nanna poured out two cups of tea and handed Chloe a slice of lemon cake on a matching plate. 'This lemon cake is absolutely delicious, if I do say so myself, and is guaranteed to make anyone feel a whole lot better. Do you know that most of the troubles of the world can be solved with a cup of tea, a good chat and lemon cake?'

Chloe bit into the cake. It was delicious. The centre was runny with bittersweet lemon curd, while the base was sweet shortcake.

'Let me tell you a story,' Nanna began invitingly. 'A story about friendship and sisters, about grief and love and danger, and about growing up . . .'

1

The House at Myilly Point

Darwin, October 1941

Poppy was sprawled along a branch of the old mango tree, her back against the gnarled grey trunk, reading a book. From the house she was completely invisible, cloaked by the thick, green leaves. Flopped at the base of the tree among the tangled roots lay her dog, Honey, tongue panting in the heat.

A piercing scream broke the muggy stillness. It stopped and then started again, louder than before.

Poppy looked up then dropped from the tree, lithe as a possum, to the muddy ground below.

'Poppy! Poppy! Where are you?' called her mother's voice. 'Come quickly.'

Poppy flew across the garden, along the verandah and into the drawing room, her curly black hair flying and her dress rumpled.

A middle-aged woman, her face red and perspiring, stood on the sofa, clutching a girl to her chest. The woman continued to scream at the top of her voice, her hair seemingly electrified with fear. The girl was frozen in horror, her mouth agape — but this might have been due to lack of oxygen because she was being squeezed so tightly.

Poppy glanced over at her mother, intrigued by the commotion.

Cecilia Trehearne was making low, soothing noises, trying to coax her guests down from their perch. 'There, there, Mrs Tibbets — it's nothing to be frightened of.'

She gestured at Poppy. 'It's Basil. He's under the sofa.'

Poppy repressed a grin and dropped to her knees, groping under the furniture. She slowly withdrew her arm, entwined with a thick, golden-green snake about two metres long, marked with striking black-and-white diamonds. She draped the heavy body around her neck, holding the snake's head in her palm, gently stroking his scaly skin. Mrs Tibbets screamed louder.

'You really shouldn't scream,' Poppy told Mrs Tibbets. 'Basil is lovely but he has a nasty bite if he gets upset.'

The woman stopped hurriedly, staring transfixed at the huge snake.

'Why don't you put Basil back outside, Poppy?' suggested Cecilia softly. 'And bring in some tea for Mrs Tibbets and Maude. Daisy should have it nearly ready. And I think you must have been just on your way to get changed?'

Poppy smiled — the humour of the scene in the sitting room just a few moments ago was too much to resist. She was grateful to her mother, giving her a chance to escape just so she could have a hearty chuckle on the way to the kitchen.

When Poppy returned a few minutes later, her face suitably composed and bearing the heavy tea tray, Mrs Tibbets was sitting on the sofa, huffing slightly, with Maude close beside her. Poppy set the tea tray down in front of her mother.

'Thank you, darling,' her mother said, lifting the china teapot and pouring out a cup. 'Mrs Tibbets, this is my daughter Poppy. I think she's about the same age as your daughter Maude, so perhaps they'll enjoy spending some time together while you are in Darwin. Poppy, the Tibbets have just moved in next door. I did *remind* you they were coming for tea.'

Mrs Tibbets glanced over Poppy, noting the hastily brushed curls, the fresh blue dress and streak of mud on the back of her calf.

Poppy plopped down onto a footstool, smiling at Maude. Maude smiled back rather shyly.

'What was that *thing?*' demanded Mrs Tibbets, fanning herself with her gloves.

'That's Basil, my pet diamond python,' explained Poppy. 'He's lovely. He lives in the rafters of the verandah and eats all the mice and rats and tree frogs, although I don't really like him eating the frogs. He usually only comes out at night, but perhaps something disturbed him.'

'Is he really your pet?' asked Maude, peeking up from under her eyelashes.

'Yes, he comes when I drum on the verandah post — well, sometimes. He's really very affectionate, although he doesn't like strangers.'

Mrs Tibbets shuddered at the memory.

'Poppy has quite an unusual menagerie of pets,' Cecilia explained, passing a teacup to Mrs Tibbets, then one to Maude. 'She can show you some of them after tea if you like, Maude. So, how are you enjoying Darwin so far, Mrs Tibbets?'

'It's unbearably hot — and the humidity! Not to mention the mosquitoes and sandflies!' Mrs Tibbets huffed again, delicately mopping her brow. 'I worry about Maude because she has such a delicate constitution. The tropical climate is not suited to her at all, but her father wouldn't listen to me. He insisted we all come up to Darwin with him. I just hope it's not the death of one of us.'

Cecilia nodded politely, passing over a plate of egg sandwiches. Poppy squirmed.

'Sandwich? The eggs are from our own chickens,' offered Cecilia. 'It's the start of the wet season, but you do get used to it. And you came up from Sydney? My eldest daughter, Phoebe, is training to be a nurse down in Sydney. She says spirits are generally high down there, despite the war.'

Poppy jiggled her knee, nearly upsetting the half-full teacup.

'Thank you. The sea journey was dreadful, simply dreadful . . .' Mrs Tibbets replied, helping herself to a dainty finger sandwich. 'And we do miss our friends in Sydney. I am also frightfully concerned about Maude's education — she has no hope of a decent schooling up here. How is it possible there is not even *one* high school in Darwin? But her father insisted it wouldn't hurt her for a few months.'

Cecilia poured some more tea. 'I'm sure Maude will learn lots up here. Perhaps she could join Poppy for some of her lessons?'

Mrs Tibbets studied Poppy carefully. Poppy had the feeling that Mrs Tibbets found her wanting compared to Maude's sophisticated friends in Sydney.

'I'm surprised you haven't sent your daughter down south to boarding school,' said Mrs Tibbets.

Cecilia glanced fondly at Poppy. 'Edward and Phoebe went to boarding school in Adelaide,' she explained. 'Bryony went for a while but she absolutely hated it. We decided the younger children should attend school here, and we've employed a governess to teach them for the last year or so.

'Now, Poppy, why don't you take Maude and show her your room and some of the animals?'

Poppy leapt to her feet with relief.

'Come on, Maude,' invited Poppy with a generous smile. 'I have two orphan baby possums that I'm rearing at the moment, and my dog, Honey, and the most beautiful little wallaby called Christabel. She lives in a sugar sack on the kitchen door . . . And there are the chooks and a cat and two pet turtles named Tabitha and Tobias . . .'

Maude stood up, smoothing out her flared skirt. She was dressed in the height of fashion — a white cotton dress with short puffed sleeves, fitted bodice, a simple ruffle at the neckline, short socks and patent-leather Mary Jane shoes.

'Is that all right, Mother?' she asked.

Mrs Tibbets wrinkled her brow doubtfully. 'Perhaps you'd better stay here, Maude. You know you're allergic to cats. And that snake looked positively evil —'

'Basil is perfectly harmless, and I'm sure the girls would enjoy some fresh air,' Cecilia assured her. 'Poppy will look after her.'

Maude escaped after Poppy, before her mother could say more.

Poppy led the way out onto the deep verandah, which wrapped completely around the large white timber house. The house was set up high to catch the sea breezes, and she paused to look out over the view. It never ceased to make her catch her breath in awe at its beauty.

The Trehearne house sat on Myilly Point, just north of Darwin township, with views north-west over the turquoise Arafura Sea and east to the white sand and breakers of palm-fringed Mindil Beach. The garden was filled with bougainvillea and frangipanis, banana and paw-paw trees, and lush tropical plants, which grew so quickly that it was a losing battle to keep them tamed.

Poppy set off around the corner, leading the way towards the back of the house, chattering to Maude. Maude caught a glimpse of various spacious rooms through the windows — the sitting room, dining room and bedrooms — all stirred by the lazy whir of ceiling fans.

'That's my room — I share it with my sister Bryony. She's sixteen,' whispered Poppy. Maude peeked through the window. One half of the room was spotlessly tidy; the other half was cluttered with overflowing baskets and tottering towers of books. A girl sat at the dressing table, carefully applying crimson lipstick. Her black hair was meticulously curled, and she wore a fashionable navy dress with padded shoulders and a nipped-in waist.

'She looks like a film star,' Maude sighed, flicking her fringe out of her eyes.

'She tries!' replied Poppy, rolling her eyes. 'She's sweet on a young officer named George, who's started hanging around the house like a bad smell. She's turned completely dopey. He's always asking her to dances and picnics and the cinema, but Mum and Dad are quite strict.'

Poppy slid her fingers under the partially opened window and opened it a crack.

'You'll catch it if Dad sees you wearing bright-red lipstick like that!' Poppy called through the opening.

Bryony did not deign to answer, preferring to throw Poppy's pillow at the window instead.

Poppy continued along the verandah with Maude.

'My brother, Edward, ran away to be a soldier — he's only nineteen, and Mum and Dad didn't want him to join up. Dad was furious when he received the letter, but by then it was too late.'

A small white-and-caramel dog bounded up and began licking Poppy vigorously, tail wagging. Maude held out her hand to be sniffed.

'This is Honey.' Poppy stroked the dog's head. 'Isn't she beautiful? Watch — she can do tricks.' Poppy clicked her fingers and Honey jumped up on her hind legs. Poppy made a circular motion with her hand and Honey twirled around, pirouetting daintily.

'Oh, she's gorgeous,' cried Maude. 'How did she learn to do that?'

Poppy lowered her hand and Honey dropped, then sat up and begged. Poppy laughed, fished a dried biscuit from her pocket and fed it to Honey.

'I trained her. She can dance on her hind legs, roll over, play dead, beg and fetch, although Daisy says she drives her crazy constantly begging for snacks in the kitchen. I've had her since she was a tiny puppy. She loves to come everywhere with me.'

'Would she do it for me?' asked Maude.

'Maybe — give it a try.'

Maude copied Poppy's gestures but Honey ignored her.

Poppy laughed. 'She'll take her time to get to know you. Come on.'

Poppy and Maude continued walking along the verandah towards the back of the house.

'We have to be careful with our animals. Dad's last dog, Poncho, was eaten by a crocodile.'

'Nooo,' exclaimed Maude. 'You're teasing me!'

'True as anything,' Poppy retorted. She spat on her palm and crossed her heart. 'The butcher's horse was badly mauled drinking at the creek just a couple of weeks ago. It had to be shot. Sometimes they get people, too. Dad used to bring his shotgun down to the beach when we went swimming, just in case.

'They normally stay in the rivers and estuaries, but sometimes they swim out to sea for miles. Once, a huge croc tipped over Dad's boat while he was fishing. Dad thought he was going to be croc dinner, but the stupid reptile ate Dad's canvas tackle bag instead — Dad says he's never swum so fast in his life.'

Maude looked sceptical but didn't argue.

'The bag probably stank to high heaven of rotten fish!' suggested Poppy, pinching her nose comically.

Poppy clattered down the verandah steps towards the garden, Honey at her heels. At the very back of the house, at ground level, was a smaller stone outhouse, including kitchen, storerooms and laundry. The building was attached to the main house by a covered walkway.

'There's Basil,' said Poppy, pointing up into the rafters at a large golden-green coil. 'And here's Christabel.'

A bulging hessian sack hung from the kitchen doorknob. Poppy scooped inside and brought out an armful of soft, grey fur, curled in a ball.

Maude tentatively stroked the fur. Christabel's ears flickered back and forth, but she kept her eyes firmly shut.

'Would you like to feed her?'

'Yes, please.' Maude's eyes shone.

Poppy pushed her way into the kitchen, where a young Aboriginal woman was peeling potatoes at the kitchen sink. A dark-skinned child played at her feet, springing a peel of potato skin up and down. He stared solemnly at Maude through thick-lashed chocolate eyes.

'Thanks for the sandwiches, Daisy – they were delicious.'

Daisy smiled back, her teeth startlingly white against her dark skin. 'A pleasure, Miss Poppy. I know how hungry you get.'

'Daisy, this is Maude, our new neighbour,' Poppy said, fetching a baby bottle of milk from the refrigerator. 'And this is Daisy's son, Charlie.'

Poppy bent down and tickled the child on his tummy. Charlie squealed with delight and raised his arms. 'Charlie up,' he demanded. Poppy obliged, swooping him off his feet.

Daisy grinned. 'Hello, Miss Maude. That naughty Miss Poppy is always bringing animals into my clean kitchen. Sometimes I think I should feed them all to that hungry snake.'

Maude sat at the table cuddling the wallaby, who greedily guzzled and headbutted the bottle.

'You wouldn't be so cruel, would you, Daisy-dear?' Poppy teased. 'You love them as much as I do.'

Daisy plopped the peeled potatoes into a saucepan of water on the range. Drops of water hissed and sizzled as they splattered on the hot stovetop.

'Get along with you, Miss Poppy,' Daisy mock-scolded. 'That's enough of your tomfoolery. I have to make dinner, and I have enough to do without more children and animals under my feet.'

After feeding Christabel, the animal menagerie tour continued from the two turtles swimming lazily around the fish tank on the kitchen sideboard and the possums in a dark storeroom fruit box to Coco the elegant cat, the chooks in the fowl yard, Lola the cow and Angel the draught horse, grazing in a small paddock.

Poppy gave Maude a leg-up onto Angel's back. Angel continued to graze, unperturbed.

'Have you ever tasted a mango?' Poppy asked suddenly.

'No, what's a mango?'

'Follow me,' ordered Poppy, running through the long grass. 'You are in for one of the best treats of your life.'

Overhanging the stable was the huge old tree. Poppy scaled the thick trunk effortlessly, showing Maude which footholds to use. She wriggled out along a branch and picked two oval, orange-green, speckled fruits. Poppy used her teeth and fingers to tear the skin.

'They're messy,' Poppy warned Maude, handing one over. 'The best way to eat them is hanging upside down like a fruit bat.'

Poppy demonstrated, hooking her feet under a bough and swinging upside down from the knees. She sucked on the sweet mango flesh, its juice dripping down onto the ground below. Maude tentatively followed her example.

'Wow — that's so good,' Maude enthused, her mouth and fingers sticky with juice. 'That's the best fruit I've ever tasted in my life — and it grows in your back garden!'

'How long are you going to be in Darwin?' asked Poppy.

'My father works for the government,' explained Maude. 'A public servant. He was transferred to Darwin a few months ago — something to do with the war. Mother and I followed him up here and arrived last week, although Mother would much rather have stayed behind in Sydney. She thinks Darwin is far too dangerous.'

'Dangerous? What could possibly be dangerous about Darwin?'

Maude grinned and ticked the list off on her fingers. 'Crocodiles, snakes, venomous spiders, mosquitoes, malaria, dengue fever, villainous criminals and soldiers — not necessarily in that order.'

Poppy snorted in derision. 'Rubbish. Darwin is paradise.' She swung down from the tree. 'Would you like to see something quite amazing?'

'What?'

'A two-headed calf.'

Maude once more looked bemused, but obediently followed in Poppy's wake. This time Poppy led Maude to the western side of the house.

'This is my father's study,' explained Poppy, creaking open the French door. 'He's a doctor and works at the hospital in the afternoons, but he sees patients here in the mornings.'

The room was clinically white with a huge timber desk in the centre, facing the view. Bookshelves, crowded with journals and large jars, covered two walls. The third wall was occupied by an observation couch, medical charts and storage cupboards.

'Dad collects medical curios,' continued Poppy, gesturing to a human skeleton standing guard in the corner of the room. 'That's Hippocrates.'

Poppy shook hands with Hippocrates, making Maude giggle.

Two shelves of the bookcase were devoted to slimy, white specimens preserved in formaldehyde and a collection of skulls. Maude peered into each jar, her face a mixture of curiosity and revulsion. The collection included various floating organs, a soggy brain, a variety of animal foetuses, a dissected possum and a wrinkled human hand.

'Look, this one's a diseased liver,' explained Poppy.

'Dad saves it to show the miners and stockmen what will happen to them if they drink all their earnings in rum.'

'Eeeewww,' replied Maude. 'Do they stop drinking rum?'

'No — well, maybe for a day or two.'

In the very centre, in pride of place, was a glass tank containing the preserved remains of two calf heads, joined together at the neck.

Maude reeled back, swallowing nervously. 'Is it real?'

'Yes, of course. Isn't it fascinating?' asked Poppy, stroking the side of the tank, as though she was stroking the animal's face. 'The calf was born out on one of the stations. It had no chance of surviving, but they put the head in the icebox and saved it for Dad. He keeps it here to remind him of the peculiarities of Mother Nature.'

The girls poked around the exhibits, marvelling at the massive skull of a crocodile, big enough to encase a child in its jaws.

'Feel his teeth,' Poppy suggested, running her fingers over the powerful jaw. 'Dad snared this croc on his fishing line. It completely swallowed a prize barramundi he had just caught. I was only eight and was fishing with Dad down near the creek. The croc thought I looked more delicious than the barramundi and started paddling towards me, licking his chops and dragging Dad's fishing line behind him. He yelled at me to run. Next thing I knew, I was being chased up the mudflat by this enormous, pre-historic beast, who was gaining on me fast. It took Dad six shots to bring it down. Boy, was Dad in trouble when he brought it home and had to confess to Mum that the croc nearly snapped me up.'

A bell jangled from the front sitting room.

'Come on,' urged Poppy, 'I think Mum wants us back.'

The girls returned to the sitting room, where the two mothers were still chatting.

'Perhaps you'd like to join us at the weekly Red Cross meetings, Mrs Tibbets?' suggested Cecilia. 'Mrs Abbott, the Administrator's wife, is our patron. We do lots of work for the war effort: rolling bandages, knitting socks and rugs, and making care parcels for the soldiers. It would be a nice way for you to meet some of the other ladies of Darwin.'

'Thank you, that's very kind, Mrs Trehearne.' Mrs Tibbets nodded, smiling, and then caught sight of her daughter. 'Oh goodness gracious me, Maude Cordelia Tibbets — what on *earth* have you been doing?'

Poppy glanced at Maude and realised that she did not look the same as she had when they left the room half an hour before. Her white dress was rumpled and streaked with horsehair and dirt. Her mouth and hands were sticky with mango juice and grime, and there was a twig tangled in her hair.

Maude tried to straighten her skirt with her palm, but that only succeeded in further staining the once-white fabric.

'Oh, Mama, we have had the most lovely time,' explained Maude, her cheeks pink with excitement. 'Poppy showed me her orphan possums, and her dog Honey, and I fed the baby wallaby with a bottle, and I rode on Angel the horse, and we climbed a tree and ate a mango, and Poppy showed me a two-headed calf, and the skull of a crocodile that nearly ate her! I think I'm going to love living in Darwin.'

Mrs Tibbets's eyes widened. Poppy swallowed. Cecilia glanced up, alarmed.

Mrs Tibbets took a deep breath. 'Why, darling, I'm so thrilled that you've made a friend.' Mrs Tibbets smiled at Maude and then at Poppy. 'Perhaps tomorrow Poppy can come to our house. But now we've stayed too long and must get home to unpack the silver.'

2

A Surprise Visitor

The bell rang for dinner. Poppy pulled a brush through her tangled hair and straightened her ribbon. Doctor Trehearne liked the family to dress for dinner.

When she hurried into the dining room, her parents were already seated, her father at the head, her mother, elegantly dressed in a green silk sheath, at his right-hand side.

'Here she is, my darling girl,' greeted Doctor Mark Trehearne. 'How was your day? Did you enjoy meeting the new neighbours?'

Poppy stooped to kiss his cheek, inhaling the lingering smell of disinfectant and tobacco. Mark was dressed in a dark-brown suit, starched white shirt and tie.

'Yes, I met Maude and she seems like a lovely girl,' agreed Poppy, 'although you should have heard her mother scream when she sat on the sofa and found Basil curled up under the cushion.'

Mark chuckled at the thought.

Bryony sashayed into the room, her dark hair pulled back into a pompadour roll, her lips conspicuously bare of make-up. She slipped into the seat at her father's left.

'And here's my beautiful Bryony. She looks just as gorgeous as her mother did when I first laid eyes on her in England twenty-three years ago. I thought she was a dark-haired angel welcoming me to heaven.'

'An angel with a hypodermic syringe and a bedpan!' joked Cecilia.

'Well, I still maintain that if it wasn't for your uncanny nursing skills, I wouldn't be here today, and neither would either of you!'

Cecilia smiled at her two daughters and began to serve the baked potatoes. Mark carved into the butt of roast beef in front of him, releasing a mouth-watering aroma.

'I bet Mama didn't have so many freckles, though,' added Poppy, raising her eyebrows innocently at her sister.

Bryony screwed up her nose, which was really only lightly sprinkled with freckles.

'No, she didn't have freckles, but that's because she grew up in misty Cornwall instead of the tropics,' agreed Mark, serving Poppy some meat. 'I think Bryony's freckles are charming.'

While her parents were distracted with serving dinner, Bryony took the opportunity to poke her tongue out at her sister.

Cecilia, who seemed to have eyes in the back of her head, frowned warningly at both girls as she poured out the gravy.

A noise sounded from the hallway. Honey barked in warning, then woofed a joyous chorus.

'I wonder who would be dropping in at this hour?' asked Mark. 'I hope it isn't a patient in the middle of dinner.'

Cecilia flung her hand to her throat and half-rose expectantly.

'It's probably just dearest George,' suggested Poppy, darting a mischievous glance at Bryony. 'Perhaps he's come to sing arias under Bryony's window.'

Bryony ignored Poppy but straightened her back and tucked a wayward curl behind her ear.

The dining room door flung open and a tall, handsome young man in army uniform strolled in, a broad grin lighting his face. He held his hat in his hands.

'Edward,' shrieked Poppy, sending her chair flying backwards.

'Edward,' cried Cecilia, rushing forward to fling her arms around him.

'What *are* you doing here?' asked Bryony, crowding around him. 'Why are you in Darwin?'

'Can you stay?' begged his mother. 'Have you had dinner?'

'It's *sooo* good to see you,' shrieked Poppy.

Edward embraced his mother and sisters, and shook hands with his father. 'I'm on leave for a few days,' he explained. 'We finished our army training down in Sydney, and we're heading overseas — to Europe, I guess. Our ship's refuelling in Darwin, so I received permission to come and see my family and beg their forgiveness.' He shot an apologetic look at his father. 'I didn't want to leave the country without asking for your blessing.'

His father sat down heavily. Cecilia squeezed his arm.

'Poppy, run and get a plate and some cutlery for your brother,' suggested Cecilia. 'Bryony, can you please tell Daisy that Edward will be staying?'

In a few moments, the family was all seated around the table, enjoying their meal of roast beef, gravy and baked vegetables. Cecilia kept touching Edward's arm, as though she expected him to disappear like a forgotten dream.

Edward kept them entertained with stories from army training, everything he had seen and done since he left them six months ago, and the characters he had met.

'It's funny how quickly you get used to things,' Edward said. 'I can't believe how hot it is up here in Darwin after living down south for so long. I must be getting soft.'

'You look well,' decided Cecilia. 'Though I doubt you eat as well at army camp as you did here.'

'Nothing beats my mum's cooking,' Edward boasted. 'That is one of the many things I've missed; that and Poppy's never-ending mischief!'

Mark had been very quiet during much of the meal, listening to Edward's chatter.

'There's nothing soft about army life, my boy,' Mark began grimly. 'I know you think it's all fun and travel and adventure, but I wish you'd never signed up. There are so many things you could have done to help the war effort without using your body to stop bullets.'

Mark stopped himself with an effort, biting his lip.

Edward flushed and pushed his chair back. 'But Dad, *you* did,' he blurted. 'You ran away from the farm when you were younger than me and signed up for the Great War in 1916. You were seventeen years old. You served

25

your country on the Western Front and defeated the Hun. You were a hero.'

Mark choked, shaking his head. 'I was an ignorant, idiotic farm boy,' he contradicted forcefully. 'I broke my mother's heart by running away. On the Western Front I watched so many of my mates get slaughtered, one after another, or die of disease or infection.

'More than sixty thousand Australian men were killed in that war. If it wasn't for your mother's magical nursing skills, I wouldn't have survived.' Mark took a deep breath, making his voice steady again. 'On the battlefield I saw many men die who could have been saved with proper hospitals and medicines. That's what made me decide to study medicine and become a doctor. I wanted to devote my talents to *saving* lives, not taking them.'

Edward scowled, his eyes down and shoulders hunched. Mark rose to his feet and strode up and down the room, hands dug deep in his pockets. He sighed deeply, then stood behind Edward's chair with his hands on his son's shoulders.

'Edward, I know you are a man now, and must make your own decisions.' Mark spoke softly. 'I wish you weren't going, but of course you have my blessing. Of course I forgive you. You're my son, and I'll always be proud of you.'

Edward scuffed his feet and nodded with embarrassment. Cecilia brushed her hand across her eyes and patted Edward's hand.

'Come on, girls,' Cecilia said, 'why don't you help me whip up a quick pudding to celebrate Edward's homecoming. I have a little sugar saved, we can use the last of the cream, and Poppy can scoot up the tree and find us some mangoes.'

The special dessert made everyone ignore the earlier tension. While they laughed and joked, and made much of Edward, Poppy felt there was something forced about the atmosphere. No one could forget he was soon sailing off to war.

❧

Edward had four days' leave before his ship departed, and he was determined to fill the days with fun and frivolity. He organised picnics and outings to nearby waterfalls and swimming holes. He planned bicycle races and cricket matches and dancing on the sand under the moonlight. He invited Bryony and George, and a few of the other young people of Darwin, including a pretty girl called Iris, whose parents ran the post office. Poppy caught Edward gazing at Iris with what she suspected was adoration, although nothing was said. What was it with her siblings going dopey with love?

Cecilia stretched her resources to provide lavish picnic baskets and suppers. On the morning of the fifth day, Edward packed his kit bag, hugged them all and said his goodbyes.

'Look after yourself, Poppykins,' Edward urged her. 'Promise you'll write? I want to know all the details of life at home, no matter how boring! And look after Mum for me — I don't want her to worry.'

Poppy hugged him tightly, her throat thick with emotion. Edward picked up his kit bag, moved his hat to a jauntier angle and whistled cheerfully as he swaggered up the gangway.

I wonder where he's going? thought Poppy. *I wonder when I will see Edward again?*

❧

Poppy was sitting on the verandah, feeding Christabel, when she spied a huge wicker basket of linen tottering up the garden path on a pair of thin legs. Poppy put the young wallaby down, leapt to her feet and ran towards it.

'*Ohayou gozaimasu, Murata-san*,' Poppy greeted the basket carrier.

The figure carefully lowered the basket to the ground, revealing herself as a small Japanese woman, her hair almost white and her face creased into hundreds of wrinkles. She smiled and bowed. From behind her skirts peeked a small girl, with long, glossy black hair pulled neatly into two plaits.

'*Ohayou gozaimasu*,' replied the woman. '*Ogenki desuka?*'

'*Watashi wa genki desu, Murata-san*,' replied Poppy, returning a half-bow. '*Arigato.*'

'Very good, Miss Poppy,' said Mrs Murata. 'Your Japanese is coming along very well.'

'*Arigato*,' Poppy thanked her.

Poppy dropped down on her haunches and solemnly said, '*Ohayou gozaimasu*,' to the little girl. 'And what's your name?' The child was too shy to respond.

'This is my granddaughter, Shinju — it means "Pearl" in English,' explained Mrs Murata. 'She is my son's daughter.'

28

'Pearl — that's a very beautiful name,' replied Poppy. 'A perfect name for a beautiful girl.'

Mrs Murata smiled lovingly at the girl, stroking the fringe out of her eyes.

'The pearl is a magic jewel of good luck to the Japanese,' explained Mrs Murata. 'It was the pearls and the pearl shell that brought us to your country. My family have been pearl divers for generations — first in Japan, now in Darwin. My father came to Australia in 1880, and I was born in Broome. Pearls have been good to us.'

Mrs Murata bent down to pick up her load of washing.

'Can I help you?' asked Poppy.

'*Arigato*, Miss Poppy,' replied Mrs Murata. 'It's heavy.'

Poppy took one handle, and together the two carried the basket of washing towards the house, with young Shinju following.

'How are your family, Mrs Murata?' asked Poppy. 'Is your son feeling better?'

'Yes.' Mrs Murata's face beamed. 'Your father is a clever doctor.'

Several weeks before, Poppy had been with her father when he had been called to the Murata's house to treat Mrs Murata's son. The pearl diver had contracted a severe chest infection while out at sea and had been critically ill by the time the pearl lugger had returned to port. Poppy's father had treated Mr Murata and saved his life.

Mrs Murata delivered the linen basket to Daisy in the kitchen and bowed goodbye to Poppy.

'*Sayonara*, Miss Poppy.'

Poppy returned the salutation and then raided the bread box, taking a heel of stale bread and stuffing it in her pocket.

'Here's your picnic lunch, Miss Poppy,' said Daisy. 'I made enough to keep even you from being hungry — beef and tomato sandwiches, lemon cake and paw-paw.'

Poppy gave Daisy a quick hug. 'Thanks, Daisy. You're wonderful.'

Poppy picked up a laden picnic basket from the table and ran next door to collect Maude. From the kitchen doorway, she was watched by the little girl Shinju.

'Have you got your bathers on?' Poppy asked Maude. 'Daisy has packed us a picnic to have down at Kahlin Bay. I can't wait to go swimming — it's so hot.'

'There aren't any crocodiles at Kahlin Bay, are there?' asked Maude, jumping down the steps with her towel over her shoulder.

'No, you silly,' replied Poppy, 'but there are lots of fish. I've brought some stale bread so we can feed them. The mullet and catfish take the bread straight from your fingers.'

The girls ran along the rutted track, between the palm trees, down to the bay.

The track suddenly opened out, revealing a stunning vista over the turquoise sea south-west towards Darwin port.

'Wow,' said Maude, 'it's gorgeous.'

'It's gorgeous now at high tide, but at low tide the water drops about twenty feet so you can walk out on the mud-flats for miles. It's good then for mud-crabbing and gathering oysters, but you have to be careful because the tide rushes in again super-fast, which can be really dangerous if you're not watching.'

Maude shaded her eyes and looked to the north.

'Race you in!' challenged Poppy.

Dropping the picnic basket and towel on the sand, Poppy dragged her dress over her head, kicked off her shoes and sprinted to the water. Maude was only seconds behind, squealing in delight.

The water was cool and silky against their skin, washing away the clinging fug of the tropical heat.

Maude was an excellent swimmer and struck out for the deeper water. Poppy gave chase, grabbing Maude by the ankle. Maude tried to kick free but Poppy was too strong. The two girls paused momentarily, treading water and laughing.

'Where did you learn to swim like that?' asked Poppy, releasing Maude's ankle. 'I thought you were a city slicker!'

Maude floated on her back, lapped by the gentle swell, closing her eyes to the sun.

'In Sydney, we live right near the beach at Manly. We swim all the time — but there we don't need to worry about man eating crocodiles or poisonous jellyfish!'

Poppy grabbed Maude's ankle again, dragging her under. Maude spluttered to the surface.

'The crocs mostly stick to the rivers, and it's a bit early for box jellyfish, but did I tell you about the sharks?' cried Poppy, glancing around with a worried frown. Maude's head jerked around, searching for fins.

Poppy splashed her. 'Only kidding!'

Poppy glanced back towards the shore, where something unexpected caught her eye: a dark shape breaking the water, then disappearing. Poppy frowned. The dark shadow broke the surface again, then subsided, sinking without a trace.

Without pausing to explain, Poppy raced towards the beach, showering Maude with a powerful kick. Maude waited a moment, then chased after her friend.

Close to shore, Poppy dived under water momentarily, then her sleek, dark head reappeared. She dived again and again. Poppy resurfaced with a gasp, flipped on her back and swam to shore, hugging something to her chest with one arm. She kicked urgently, powering to the beach.

By the time Maude reached the sand, Poppy had dragged a small, limp body from the water.

'Hello, can you hear me?' Poppy begged, squeezing the child's hand. 'Are you all right?'

Poppy took a few seconds, checking for breath and a pulse.

It was a child — a girl about five years old — and she wasn't breathing. Poppy ran her fingers through the girl's mouth, searching for any obstructions, such as seaweed or mud. Poppy thought back to the resuscitation instructions her parents had taught her. First, she lifted the girl by the waist to drain the seawater from her throat.

Then she lay the girl face-down on the sand, head resting on her forearm. Poppy straddled the limp body, placing both of her own hands in the middle of the girl's back, then concentrated on rocking herself back and forth, pushing all her weight down on the patient and then releasing rhythmically.

Poppy could feel the panic welling up inside her. *The girl might die! What if I can't save her? What if I'm pushing too hard or not hard enough? Why isn't Mum here?*

Poppy took a deep breath and willed herself to be calm.

Focus, Poppy told herself sternly. *Okay, breathe in. Breathe out. Breathe in. Breathe out.*

'What are you doing, Poppy?' demanded Maude, panicking.

'She's not breathing, Maude,' replied Poppy, continuing to rock back and forth on her palms. 'I'm pushing the air out of her lungs with my weight, then releasing the lungs so they can drag in air. My father taught me how to do it — the Schaefer method.'

'Is it working?' asked Maude.

'I don't know,' admitted Poppy. 'Mum says it can take hours — sometimes it works, sometimes it doesn't.'

'Is there something I can do?'

'Get help,' gasped Poppy, continuing her rhythmic pumping. 'Get my mum.'

Maude picked up her towel and sprinted up the beach. 'Shinju!' screamed a voice from the path. 'Shinju!'

Mrs Murata ran down the beach, her face creased in fear. Poppy paused to check the girl's chest — nothing. Maude stopped and turned back towards them all, reluctant to leave.

Mrs Murata collapsed in the sand beside the inert body. Poppy kept rocking, forcing air into Shinju's lungs.

'Poppy pulled her from the water —' Maude began to explain.

'Doctor Trehearne,' Mrs Murata gasped, clutching at

her shirt, tears rolling down her face. 'We need Doctor Trehearne.'

'I'm on my way,' Maude assured her. She took off again, her feet kicking up puffs of soft sand as she raced towards the path to Myilly Point.

Poppy continued rocking back and forth for a few more minutes when suddenly Shinju began to choke and splutter, coughing up seawater. She took a huge gulp of air, then started to wail.

By the time Maude returned with Cecilia, Mrs Murata was cuddling a wet, bedraggled Shinju to her chest, alternately kissing and murmuring to her in Japanese. Poppy was sitting beside them, shivering with shock despite the oppressive heat.

'Well done, Poppy,' murmured Cecilia, stroking a strand of Poppy's wet hair off her face.

Poppy smiled wanly, relief and horror flooding through her in equal measure. *I saved her. Shinju's alive, but it was so close. I thought she was going to die.*

Cecilia checked Shinju over carefully, checking her pupils, pulse rate and breathing, then helped Mrs Murata carry Shinju back to the house. Maude carried the still-full picnic basket, while Poppy trailed behind, her legs wobbly beneath her.

3

The Dragon Pearl

Back at the house, Shinju was given a warm bath and
dressed in one of Poppy's old cotton nightgowns,
which was far too big for her. Poppy thought she looked
like an exquisite porcelain doll, with her pale complexion
and lustrous black hair. Shinju was then propped up on the
sofa and fed bread and milk.

The others gathered around to drink restorative tea and
eat Daisy's famous lemon cake.

'Thank you, Miss Poppy,' said Mrs Murata solemnly.
'You saved Shinju's life. You're very brave.'

She took Poppy's hand and pressed it warmly.

Poppy shook her head.

'I didn't see her go,' confessed Mrs Murata. 'I sorted the
linen with Daisy and collected the dirty washing, and all
the time I thought Shinju was playing with little Charlie.
When I turned around, she was gone. Daisy and I called
out everywhere, then Daisy remembered you and Miss

Maude had gone down to the bay for a swim, and perhaps she had followed you.

'When I ran onto the beach and saw her lying there . . . I thought . . . I thought . . . I have seen too many people taken by the sea.' Mrs Murata bowed her head, tears spilling down her cheeks.

Cecilia took her hand and squeezed it. 'Everything's all right,' she murmured. 'Shinju is safe. It was a miracle that Poppy saw her when she did.'

Poppy sat silently with her thoughts. *What if I hadn't seen her? What if I'd turned around just a minute later? Shinju could be dead . . .*

'I didn't notice her,' Maude admitted. 'Poppy and I were quite far out, then Poppy just started racing for the shore. I thought she'd seen a shark. Then I turned around and saw a splash and a small black head sinking under the water. It wasn't until I saw Mrs Murata calling that I realised it was Shinju.'

Everyone turned and smiled at the little girl, looking so old-fashioned in her oversized nightgown.

Shinju smiled at Poppy. '*Arigato*,' she said, her voice croaky and hoarse.

'*Dou itashi mashite*,' replied Poppy, taking a sip of tea, its warmth spreading through her, making her feel strong again. 'It was my pleasure.'

❧

The next morning, Poppy was feeding the hens in the chookyard when she heard Daisy calling her name. She wandered back to the house and found Mrs Murata waiting in the shade of the verandah.

'*Ohayou gozaimasu, Murata-san*,' called Poppy, climbing the steps to the verandah.

'*Ohayou gozaimasu*,' replied Mrs Murata with a bow. 'Miss Poppy, I have come to formally thank you for saving my granddaughter yesterday.'

Poppy flushed with embarrassment. 'Oh no, Mrs Murata, it was nothing, really. It was just lucky that I saw her.'

'Miss Poppy, it means a great deal; our Shinju is very precious to us. She is the third generation of our family to be born in this country.'

Mrs Murata sat down in a wicker chair on the verandah. Poppy sat down in the chair opposite.

'I have brought you something as a token of our thanks — from my son Oshiro and my daughter-in-law Masuko.'

From her pocket, Mrs Murata pulled out a delicate red silk bag embroidered with pale-pink flowers. She offered the bag reverently to Poppy with both hands.

'No — I couldn't . . . I mean . . . you mustn't . . . you don't need to give me anything — I was just happy I could help,' spluttered Poppy.

'My family would be honoured if you would accept this gift, Miss Poppy,' insisted Mrs Murata, still holding out the bag. 'It would hurt Shinju if you did not accept our thanks.'

Poppy swallowed. *What would Mum want me to do?*

Poppy smiled at Mrs Murata and took the tiny bag. She loosened the ribbon and opened the mouth.

A teardrop pearl rolled from the bag onto her palm, trailing a fine gold chain.

'Oooohh,' sighed Poppy. 'It's beautiful, but I can't.'

'My son Oshiro found the pearl just before Shinju was born,' explained Mrs Murata. 'It is a teardrop — an angel's tear.'

Mrs Murata closed her own hand over Poppy's, encasing the pearl.

'Pearls are the jewel of good fortune,' explained Mrs Murata. 'It is the jewel of wisdom, wealth and healing — but most of all, pearls have the power to keep children safe. The pearl helped you keep Shinju safe, so now it is yours, to keep you safe.'

Poppy didn't know what to say.

Mrs Murata patted her hand. 'Pearls are the essence of the Moon Goddess, which have fallen to earth as tears and lie forgotten under the sea.' Mrs Murata had adopted a sing-song storyteller's tone. 'These forgotten tears, with their supernatural powers, are the most prized possession of the sea gods and water spirits.'

Poppy stroked the perfect smoothness of the jewel.

Mrs Murata stared out over the garden to the distant Arafura Sea and continued her story. 'Ryo-jin, the noble and wise dragon-king of the sea people, lived in a beautiful palace of crystal and coral, built deep under the ocean. There he lived with his dragon-queen and his daughters, the Naga maidens, who were half-human and half-serpent. His greatest treasure was the Pearl Which Grants All Desires, which he wore around his neck when he flew. This treasure was guarded by the Naga maidens.

'One day the Naga maidens, frightened by a great fire-dragon, lost the pearl, and though Ryo-jin searched far and wide for the treasure, he could not find it. For many years, the great pearl lay forgotten under the sea, until one day it was found by a young man called Hoori. He soon married his heart's desire — the Pearl Princess Toyotama-hime, the daughter of the Ryo-jin, and they lived happily for many years.

'Hoori was very happy because his wife, the Pearl Princess, was expecting their first child. Toyotama-hime sent Hoori from the house and ordered him not to watch while she gave birth. Of course Hoori, being a man, was overcome by curiosity and could not help peeking through a crack in the wall. To his great horror, he saw that at the moment of birth his wife transformed into a great dragon. Hoori was terrified and ran away, while the Pearl Princess, devastated by her husband's betrayal, fled back to her father's coral palace under the ocean. Sick with remorse, Hoori was doomed to dive to the bottom of the ocean floor forever more, facing sharks and serpents and dragons, searching for the pearl tears shed by his beloved.'

Mrs Murata stopped, still staring dreamily out to sea as though she expected to see a great dragon swooping over the waves, breathing fire.

'That's a beautiful story, Mrs Murata,' said Cecilia, who had appeared unnoticed in the doorway. 'And it is a precious gift you have given Poppy. Thank you and your family so much — Poppy will always treasure her pearl and remember what it means.'

Poppy opened her hand and gazed at the luminous pearl. It gleamed pale-golden in the sunlight.

'Would you like Mrs Murata to help you put it on, Poppy?' Cecilia asked.

Poppy nodded and Mrs Murata draped the chain around her neck, fastening the delicate catch. The pearl nestled, cool and pale and magical, against her skin — a mystical jewel of protection.

'*Arigato, Murata-san,*' murmured Poppy, twisting the pearl in her fingers. 'It is beautiful.'

'Shinju would love you to come visit us one day and have tea,' offered Mrs Murata. 'Perhaps your friend Maude would like to come as well?'

'I would love to,' replied Poppy. 'I'm sure Maude would enjoy it, too.'

'*Arigato.*'

❦

The streets of Darwin were crowded in the cool morning air. Bicycles jostled for space beside horsedrawn carts, pedestrians and the occasional car on unsealed roads. Since the war had begun, petrol was rationed, so many people had garaged their cars and turned to other transportation. As a doctor, Poppy's father had greater access to fuel so he could still use the family car to do his rounds.

The crowds of people swarming the pavement were a striking mixture of colours, cultures and races. Chinese shopkeepers arranged their shining piles of fruit and vegetables. Japanese pearl divers and Malay crewmen mingled with Greek fishermen and Aboriginal stockmen.

On the appointed day, Cecilia dropped Poppy and Maude outside the ramshackle house where the Murata family lived, four generations under one roof.

It was a typical Darwin house, built of timber. Two small rooms were surrounded by a wide verandah where most of the family slept on mattresses, which they rolled away during the day.

Mrs Murata met them at the front door. Instead of her usual Western clothes, she was dressed in an elaborate kimono of pale-green silk with long, trailing sleeves. The kimono was intricately detailed with embroidered flowers. A wide obi sash was gathered at the back into a stiff knot and she wore white split-toed socks on her feet. Her white hair was piled on top of her head. The traditional dress made her look far more graceful and exotic than her usual work clothes.

'*Ohayou gozaimasu*, Miss Poppy and Miss Maude,' greeted Mrs Murata with a deep bow to each of them.

'*Ohayou gozaimasu, Murata-san*,' replied Poppy. 'You look so elegant, Mrs Murata. I love your kimono.'

She smiled, acknowledging the compliment. 'European dress is much more practical for everyday wear and easier to wash, but we do like to wear traditional kimonos for special occasions.'

She indicated a neat row of shoes by the door.

'We always take our shoes off when we come inside the house,' explained Mrs Murata. 'You may wear some of those house slippers. Come in when you're ready. I'll go and fetch the tea.'

While the girls took off their shoes and put slippers on, Maude whispered to Poppy.

'I didn't know you spoke Japanese. What does it mean? How did you learn?'

'*Ohayou gozaimasu*, means "good morning", and Murata-san is just a term of respect like "Mrs Murata",' Poppy translated. 'I don't speak a lot of Japanese, but I've learnt a few phrases from all the Japanese people I've met over the years. I can speak some Mandarin as well.

'Lots of people speak different languages up here. Dad says Darwin is really more a part of Asia than Australia. There are far more Aboriginals, Chinese, Malays and Japanese people up here than white Australians, like us.'

The girls struggled to find slippers big enough for their feet, which gave them the giggles. The Japanese women obviously had tiny feet.

Inside, the house was simple and uncluttered, with little sign that so many people lived there. There were straw tatami mats on the floor, and Mrs Murata ushered the girls towards a number of cushions scattered around the low table in the centre of the room. On the walls were parchments, decorated with paintings of fish, flowers and Japanese characters in thick black calligraphy.

Shinju was also dressed in a tiny pink kimono, long sleeves nearly to the ground, which made her look even more like a porcelain doll. She bowed elaborately and greeted the girls in Japanese. Shinju looked completely different from the small, limp child that Poppy had rescued from the sea.

Poppy returned a simple bow. Maude copied Poppy in both her bow and clumsy Japanese greetings to Mrs Murata and Shinju. Shinju's mother entered the room, carrying a black lacquer tray. She shuffled gracefully in her long, silk kimono, taking tiny steps.

Poppy felt underdressed in her summer skirt and blouse. She fingered her teardrop pearl, thinking that at least the jewel was elegant.

'Masuko, this is Poppy and her friend Maude,' said Mrs Murata.

Masuko took Poppy's hand, her eyes filled with tears. 'Thank you, Miss Poppy. I can never thank you enough for saving my little Shinju.'

Poppy blushed and stammered. 'No. No. It was my pleasure.'

Mrs Murata showed them where to sit. The Japanese women knelt on the floor, their feet tucked under their bottoms. Shinju's mother began to lay out the tea implements and food with precision, carefully folding back her long, wide sleeves to keep them out of the way. Black lacquer dishes held tiny cakes and sweetmeats. Bamboo vases contained delicate sprays of yellow and orange speckled orchids.

'The men are away diving for pearl shell,' explained Mrs Murata. 'My husband and three sons are usually out on the pearl luggers for a couple of weeks at a time.'

'You must miss them,' replied Poppy. 'And you must worry about them, too.'

'Yes — many divers die from paralysis, when they come up too quickly,' agreed Mrs Murata. 'You know, in Japan, it is the women who are pearl divers, but we're not allowed to dive for pearls in this country. So Masuko and I wash clothes instead.'

With great ritual, Masuko carefully wiped each porcelain bowl with a white linen cloth, holding up each precious article to be admired and examined. She opened the blue-and-white tea caddy, measuring out powdered green tea and then whisking it vigorously with hot water.

The porcelain bowls of tea were ceremoniously passed to each person around the table. Only when everyone had been served did Mrs Murata take a tiny sip.

'My mother brought this tea set with her from Japan as part of her dowry when she married my father. It belonged to her grandmother, so it is very old and valuable,' explained Mrs Murata. 'In Japan, taking tea is a very important ritual.'

Poppy and Maude sipped their tea. It tasted far stronger than the tea they usually drank with milk and sugar.

'Everything must be done in exactly the right order and with absolute grace,' said Mrs Murata. 'Shinju-chan must learn the ceremony from her mother, Masuko, just as I learnt it from my mother.'

Masuko smiled, covering her mouth with her hand.

'Would you like some cake, girls?' offered Masuko. 'Shinju-chan helped me bake them this morning, especially for you.'

'*Arigato*,' Poppy and Maude said in chorus.

The cakes were tiny and very sweet. The girls weren't sure if they liked them, but politely ate a couple.

Mrs Murata pointed out the paintings on the wall and explained their significance. Poppy's legs were aching and going to sleep in their uncomfortable kneeling position, so she had to wriggle into a different posture. Maude shifted too, rubbing her calf muscle gingerly.

'Now, Shinju-chan, I think our guests would like to see you dance?' Mrs Murata said. 'Will you fetch me my *shamisen*?'

'Yes, please, Shinju,' urged Poppy. 'That would be lovely.'

Shinju obediently left the room with the same tiny steps as her mother and returned with a long lute-like instrument, a bamboo flute and two fans.

Mrs Murata tuned the *shamisen*, plucking the strings with a tortoiseshell pick. Masuko accompanied her on the bamboo flute.

Shinju took up a position, kneeling on the tatami mat, the two fans spread open like wings on either side of her.

'This is the butterfly dance.' Mrs Murata began to play, slowly plucking the strings of the instrument. The music was strange and discordant to the girls' unaccustomed ears, but hauntingly beautiful.

Shinju took dainty steps, fluttering the fans up and down, left to right, in a shimmering semblance of a butterfly's flight. When she finally finished, gracefully swooning to the ground, both Poppy and Maude burst into applause.

'Bravo, Shinju,' cried Poppy. 'That was just beautiful.'

'You looked exactly like a pink-and-gold butterfly,' agreed Maude.

Shinju beamed with pleasure and quickly covered her face with one of the fans.

'Would you like to learn?' asked Masuko. 'Shinju can show you.'

'Yes, please,' agreed Maude, her eyes lighting up.

'That would be fun,' added Poppy, 'although I'm not much of a dancer.'

Mrs Murata shook her head gravely. 'But they cannot learn the butterfly dance dressed like that!'

'Oh.' Maude looked downcast. 'What a shame.'

Mrs Murata stood and went to a large oak chest in the corner of the room. She opened it and pulled out metres of crimson and cream fabric, neatly folded.

Together Mrs Murata and Masuko dressed Poppy and Maude, draping the silky fabric around them and fastening it with the wide obi sashes. Poppy wore the crimson kimono and Maude the cream. Masuko gathered their hair up into buns with mother-of-pearl clips, finished with scarlet hibiscus flowers.

Shinju giggled at the sight of the girls transformed into Japanese maidens. Maude curtsied.

'You are the Butterfly Princess, Miss Maude,' decided Masuko, giving Maude two open fans for her wings before turning to Poppy. 'And you, of course, are the Pearl Princess, daughter of the wise and noble dragon-king, Ryo-jin.'

Masuko smiled at Poppy, lifting her arms aloft so that the sleeves draped regally.

'Now, poised and elegant,' instructed Mrs Murata, plucking the *shamisen*. 'No, *tiny* steps. You'll trip if you take great, big man-steps like that, Miss Poppy. Yes, that's better Miss Maude.'

The girls laughed, trying hard to copy Shinju and Masuko's graceful movements. Poppy felt like she had been whisked to another country and another time.

Cecilia arrived later to collect the girls and found them giggling and dancing, fluttering their fans and swaying to the music.

Poppy felt oddly disappointed as she shed her borrowed robes and became her everyday self again. It had felt special being a Japanese princess for an afternoon. Poppy and Maude hugged Shinju.

At the door, they both bowed to Mrs Murata and Masuko.

'*Arigato*.'

'*Arigato*.'

'*Dou itashi mashite,*' replied Mrs Murata. '*Sayonara.*'

As they clattered down the stairs, Maude grinned at Poppy. 'That was such fun. You know, I've never met a Japanese person before the Muratas. They were nothing like what I'd expected. They were lovely.'

4

The Drover's Boy

Maude and Poppy sat at the kitchen table helping Daisy bake Anzac cookies to send to Edward. On the dresser against the wall, the two turtles, Tabitha and Tobias, swam around lazily. Charlie sat on the floor cuddling Coco the cat. Christabel hopped around on the floor, nuzzling up crumbs. Honey studiously ignored her, preferring to lie with her head on Poppy's feet.

'Now add one cup of brown sugar,' ordered Daisy as she stood by the stove frying mince for shepherd's pie. Maude measured out a cup of sugar and added it to the bowl of flour, rolled oats and coconut. Poppy added golden syrup, water and bicarb soda to a saucepan of melted butter and stirred them together.

'Daisy, tell Maude the story of when you were a drover's boy on the plains,' urged Poppy, pouring the liquid into the bowl of ingredients and mixing them vigorously with a wooden spoon.

Daisy laughed and shook her finger. 'Don't you ever get tired of that story, Miss Poppy?'

'No,' she replied, handing the gooey wooden spoon to Charlie, who crowed and began licking eagerly. In an instant, his face was a sticky mask of caramel biscuit dough. Christabel hopped over and licked him on the face. Charlie giggled with delight.

'Please, Daisy?' begged Maude with a beguiling smile, rolling the dough into balls between her fingers. Poppy flattened the balls with a fork and laid them on the baking tray.

Daisy pulled the mince from the stove and sat at the table, a bowl full of potatoes in front of her. She began to peel them expertly with a sharp knife, her long fingers flying.

'Before I came to work with Doctor and Missus Trehearne I was a drover's boy,' began Daisy with a shy smile. 'You see, I'm not originally from the bush — I was born on Never-Never Downs, a big cattle station down south. My mum and aunties worked in the kitchens at the homestead, and my dad was a stockman with all the other fellas. I had a great childhood, running wild and playing with the other kids.

'Gran taught us how to track goannas and find sugar bag — you know, bush honey — and discover water in the bush. She taught me how to find my way home from anywhere in our country, just by asking the birds.'

Daisy scraped the potato peelings in the chook pail and started chopping the spuds into chunks.

'When I was fifteen, I fell in love with one of the drovers, a white man called Charlie, and he asked me to come mustering with him. Those drovers worked hard, moving the cattle over hundreds of miles, following the feed and water, or taking them to market. They might be gone for months.

'Well, girls weren't allowed to be drovers, but I wanted to be with Charlie. So I cut my hair short, dressed in a chambray shirt and moleskins, and told everyone my name was Jackie.

'I became a drover's boy. For the next two years we drove those bullocks up and down the country, sleeping under the stars by the campfire and riding the horses all day. I cooked and scrubbed, branded cattle and mended tack. It was hard work but a good life.'

Daisy scraped the potato into a pot of boiling water.

'As I grew older, it became harder to pretend to be a boy. I wore a scarf bound around my chest to hide my sex.'

Daisy started stripping thyme leaves from a twig with her fingertips. Charlie junior put his arms up for a cuddle. Daisy swept him up in her arms and kissed the top of his dusky curls.

'One day, I started feeling sick. I could feel the spirit of a little piccaninny growing inside me. When Charlie found out, he was scared he'd get in trouble with the boss. He sent me to the missionary and told me not to come back or it would cause him big problems. When my time came, little Charlie didn't want to come out into the big, sad world. The missionary's wife helped me, but still Charlie didn't want to be born.

'Finally, they called the doctor to come flying down. Doctor Trehearne and Missus Trehearne came on the plane to help. Missus Trehearne talked to baby Charlie and told him everything would be all right, it was safe to come out. Charlie fought for a while, but then he turned around and came out, meek as a lamb.'

The thyme was scraped in with the mince, then Daisy began finely grating a block of cheese. Charlie licked the crumbs from his fingertips.

'Missus Trehearne was so kind and asked me about Charlie and his father. I told her the story of being a drover's boy for all those years, and she wrote a letter to Charlie senior, telling him about his baby boy. Then when Charlie up and left Never-Never Downs, Missus Trehearne asked me if I'd like to go back to the station, stay with the missionaries or come here to Darwin to work for her, with baby Charlie.'

Poppy smiled at Daisy. 'Of course Daisy-dear decided she'd much rather live with us.'

Daisy flashed Poppy a smile of affection.

'Poppy!' cried Charlie, blowing a bubble kiss at the girl.

'No, *Charlie-boy* decided he'd much rather live with you.'

Maude rolled the last few balls and added them to the tray. 'It's rather sad, that story,' she confessed.

'But it has a happy ending,' insisted Poppy. 'Daisy and Charlie live with us.'

Maude frowned. 'But Daisy, have you ever heard from Charlie's father?'

'No,' admitted Daisy. 'But I can't weep over him forever. I have Charlie and Miss Poppy and her sisters and brother. We all have to make the best life we can with what we have.'

'You're very brave, Daisy,' Maude said.

'Let's get those biscuits in the oven. I have to mash the potato.'

Charlie toddled over to Maude and raised his arms to her. 'Up. Up,' he ordered.

Maude obliged, sweeping him into her lap and kissing his cheek.

On Saturday night, Cecilia asked Bryony's swain, George, over for a family dinner, before joining them at the open-air cinema.

George arrived carrying a spray of orchids for Cecilia and a bouquet for Bryony. George wore his khaki army uniform, his hair slicked back with oil. Bryony had spent all afternoon curling her hair into graceful waves that fell to her shoulder. She wore her best floral dress, high heels and a slick of red lipstick.

'Mama, this is my friend, George Payne.' Bryony clutched onto George's arm, gazing up into his face.

'Good evening, Mrs Trehearne,' greeted George. 'I can see where Bryony gets her beautiful looks.'

Bryony blushed and became very interested in the pattern on the floor rug.

'Thank you, Mr Payne.' Cecilia repressed a smile. 'And thank you for the orchids. Would you like to take a seat? My husband will just be a moment.'

'Lovely, and this must be Bryony's baby sister, Poppy? I brought you a present, too.'

George handed Poppy a small parcel wrapped in brown

paper and string, which she tugged open with delight. Inside was a small rag doll. *A doll!* thought Poppy. *How old does he think I am? Bryony's 'baby sister' indeed.*

Poppy scowled. Cecilia glared at Poppy warningly, so she sighed and pasted on a bright, fake smile.

'Thank you, Mr Payne. I just *love* dolls.'

'Splendid.' George grinned broadly. 'When you smile, I think one day you might even be nearly as pretty as your sister.'

Poppy raised her eyebrows at her sister and rolled her eyes.

Dr Trehearne came in and shook hands with the young soldier, leading him into the sitting room where they all sat sipping on ice-cold soda water with lemon.

'How do you like Darwin?' asked Mark. 'Are they keeping you busy?'

'So far, it's been great. Some of the men find it boring and are disappointed to be missing out on the action, but I've enjoyed it.

'Of course we've been training, but there have also been excursions out to the Dripstone Caves, picnics and swimming at Rapid Creek, games of football and cricket, fishing for barramundi. I know I'd rather be here than hiding in a rat hole in the desert.'

'Sounds like quite a picnic,' replied Mark.

George flushed. 'Of course, sir, we're not here for a picnic,' George assured him. 'We're here as the front-line in Australia's defence, just in case we're needed — which of course we won't be.' He smiled at Bryony and squeezed her arm. 'You're safe with us here.'

Bryony simpered and gazed at him through her lashes.

'Bryony, perhaps you'd like to help me carry the meal through,' suggested Cecilia. 'I'd hate it to be overcooked.'

Bryony reluctantly left the side of her beau and followed her mother to the kitchen.

'Poppy, I'm going out to the Shanahans' station tomorrow to run the monthly clinic,' Doctor Trehearne said. 'Would you like to come with me?'

'Yes, please,' Poppy agreed.

'We'll be flying out at five am and staying the night, so make sure you pack tonight — and pack light.'

Poppy felt a flutter of excitement. She loved visiting the Shanahans' station, Alexandra Downs. It was always so much fun.

5

Alexandra Downs

Poppy woke the next morning in the dark and dressed hurriedly. Her father was already up, sipping a cup of tea. Honey wagged her tail hopefully when she saw Poppy, but it drooped when she saw Poppy's bag over her shoulder. She sat up on her hind legs and begged hopefully.

'Sorry, Honey old girl, you can't come today. Those big station dogs would eat you in one bite.'

Honey whined piteously at the kitchen door as they left.

Doctor Trehearne drove them out to the airport, dodging the potholes on the unpaved road.

The pilot, Bert, met them at the hangar. 'You riding up front with me, Miss Poppy?' he asked with a grin.

'Yes, please.'

Poppy scrambled up into the front seat of the four-seater de Havilland biplane. Her father threw her bag into the back with his own medical kit and duffel bag.

The sun was just rising as Bert fired the engine. Poppy held on tightly as they bumped over the runway, gathered speed, then soared into the air. In moments, the ground was far below. The pilot flew north-west over the town and the port, then swooped around in a semicircle and headed south.

To the east Poppy could see the golden-pink blush of sunrise on the horizon. The tiny buildings of the township clustered around the harbour soon gave way to thick scrub spreading as far as the eye could see. They followed the red dust of the winding track to the south for a while, then broke away, heading south-west. The scrub became sparser and the land increasingly parched. The wet season had not yet brought the transforming greenery and wildlife to the outback.

Poppy eagerly scanned the landscape below, watching for any signs of human habitation.

'Would you like to fly for a while?' asked Bert. 'Take the controls and just keep her steady.'

Poppy's face lit up. 'Absolutely! Is it safe?'

'I'll be right here to take over if anything goes wrong,' Bert assured her. 'Just fly straight.'

Poppy felt a surge of excitement and adrenaline as she took over the controls, trying to hold the plane on course. The plane shuddered a little until she became used to it. Bert let her steer the plane for fifteen minutes, chatting to her about some of the interesting flights he had done over the outback. Poppy reluctantly handed back the controls.

It was an amazing feeling, steering a tiny plane so high in the sky.

After about an hour, Bert recognised something on the featureless plain and circled lower. Poppy soon made out a straight strip of grass that looked different to the surrounding scrub. In the distance, she could see a cluster of buildings that she recognised as the Shanahan homestead.

Bert circled again, dropping altitude, then brought the biplane down for a bumpy landing over the tussocky grass strip. As the plane came to a stop, Poppy could see a horse-drawn dray parked in the shade of a large banyan tree.

Bert opened the doors to let them out.

A tall, thin youth of about sixteen jumped down from the dray to shake hands with Bert and Mark. He was dressed in a light-blue cotton shirt, pale moleskin trousers, elastic-sided riding boots and the ubiquitous bushman's Akubra hat pulled low over his eyes.

'Beautiful morning, Jack,' called Doctor Trehearne.

'Hello, Doctor Trehearne,' Jack replied. 'Thanks for coming. Good to see you, Bert. Hope you brought us some mail?'

'Oh no, Jack, I forgot — and I'm sure there was a big pile of valentines for you, too,' teased Bert. Jack punched him on the shoulder.

'Not for me. You must have me confused with the Dandy at Victoria Downs.'

Jack turned towards Poppy with a warm smile, lifting his hat to reveal dark-blond hair, damp with sweat.

'G'day, Midget. Long time no see. How're you going?'

Poppy suddenly felt shy. Jack seemed to have grown about eight centimetres since she had last seen him a few months ago. He suddenly looked so grown up. 'Hi, Jack.'

His blue eyes, creased at the corners from squinting against the sun, twinkled with humour. 'Cat got your tongue? That's not like you, Midget. Normally you could talk the back leg off a camel. Come on, let's get your gear onto the dray before that sun gets up any higher.'

Everyone helped unload the plane and pack the goods onto the dray. As well as the Trehearnes' baggage, there were mail, parcels for the station and a sack of sugar.

Poppy climbed up onto the front seat next to Jack, and Bert and Doctor Trehearne sat on top of the baggage in the back.

'Giddup, girl.' Jack clicked his tongue and flapped the reins, and the horse broke into a slow trot towards the homestead.

'Fuel is getting so scarce,' complained Jack. 'The old Ford is rusting away in the shed.'

The flight party was welcomed enthusiastically at the homestead. Jack's brothers and the other men who had been out working in the cattle yards had come back when the plane had been sighted. Jack's mother had prepared a late breakfast to celebrate the arrival of the visitors — bacon, eggs and slabs of home-baked bread with sweet, hot tea.

After breakfast, Doctor Trehearne set up a surgery in the dining room. A line of patients had gathered on the verandah — stockmen, station hands, the Chinese gardeners, the Aboriginal wives and their children. Some had ridden over from the neighbouring stations the day before. There were burns, broken limbs, sprains, cuts, viruses and eye infections. Most of the small injuries were handled by

Mrs Shanahan on a daily basis, with advice from one of the Darwin doctors by radio if required. In an emergency, a doctor would fly in and evacuate the patient back to Darwin.

Poppy was helping her father lay out some instruments on the white tablecloth when Jack poked his head around the door.

'Hey Midget, there's a mob of cattle we missed this morning. Do you want to come riding with me to muster them in?'

Poppy glanced at her father for permission. Doctor Trehearne looked stern, then smiled at her hopeful expression. 'I thought you were meant to be my nurse today?' he asked with an expression of mock hurt. 'Oh well — I guess if you're careful. Some of these Shanahan cattle can be a bit wild. I have enough patients to tend to today without *you* breaking anything.'

Poppy flew and gave him a quick kiss on the cheek. 'Thanks, Dad. I promise I'll help you when I get back.'

Poppy raced to get changed into her jodhpurs, riding boots and hat. When she emerged onto the verandah, Jack was saddling a black mare for her. His own chestnut stood tied to the gate, snuffling at the grass.

Poppy offered her hand to the black mare. 'Hello, Sheba. There's a good girl.'

Poppy swung herself up into the saddle and grasped the reins. Jack mounted his own horse and led the way. They rode in companionable silence, alternately walking and cantering.

Jack spotted a plume of dust up ahead and broke into a gallop. Poppy followed him up a rise, her eyes peeled for rabbit holes. They paused at the top of the hill, looking down into the gully below. A strange sight met their eyes: a string of eleven camels plodded through the dust, their humped backs laden with hessian sacks and boxes.

Leading the procession on a shaggy pony was a wrinkled, brown-skinned man, who looked like something straight out of *Arabian Nights*. He wore gold earrings, baggy pants, a loose cotton shirt and a turban, the loose tail covering the lower half of his face.

'Ali,' yelled Jack, galloping down the rise towards the exotic caravan. 'Welcome. They'll be glad to see you at the homestead.'

'Hello, Mister Jack.'

Jack and Poppy rode alongside Ali for a while, listening as he shared news from further down the track.

Ali the cameleer wandered the tracks of the outback for thousands of kilometres with his camel-back emporium. The hessian bags held all sorts of necessities that were hard to procure so far from civilisation — bolts of material, dresses, shirts, hats and boots, needles and thread, tools, cookware and outback gossip.

'Any news of the war?' asked Ali, dropping the wrapping from around his chin.

Jack nodded, frowning. 'A few days ago Prime Minister Curtin announced that HMAS *Sydney* was attacked by the German cruiser *Kormoran* just off the coast of Western Australia. The *Sydney* was sunk and everyone on board killed — a total of six hundred and forty-five men. The German cruiser went down, too, but most of the Germans survived and have been taken as prisoners-of-war. The government tried to keep it quiet but the information leaked out.'

'That's not good news,' replied Ali with a sigh. 'So many killed.'

Jack shook his head. 'It's a bit close to home. Apparently the Germans were pretending to be a Dutch merchant ship.'

Ali looked around at the featureless scrub. 'Can't imagine what the Germans would want with this place.'

'Oh, it's not so bad, Ali.' Jack flashed a grin. 'We quite like it, don't we, Midget?'

Poppy turned her head back to the conversation. She tended to tune out when people started talking about the war. It all seemed so far away.

'Oh, yes,' replied Poppy. 'It's beautiful.'

'We'll see you back at the homestead, Ali,' Jack finally said with a wave of his hand.

Ali covered his face again and trotted off, the animals raising a cloud of red dust.

'It must be a very lonely life,' Poppy commented as she watched the camel caravan disappear. 'No one to talk to but camels.'

'The Afghans are used to it, I think.' Jack shrugged his shoulders. 'Some of them travel with their wives and children. They know the deserts like you know the streets of Darwin. They follow the hidden springs across the desert from South Australia right through to the far north.'

Jack turned the head of his horse and trotted south.

'Look, there are my cattle! You take the left and I'll take the right. If any of them charge you, just get out of their way as fast as you can.'

The two friends worked together to round up the cattle, Jack using his stockwhip to get the beasts moving. Poppy's horse, Sheba, began to prance with delight, eager to get to work. When a cow and a calf made a break for the shelter of the scrub, Sheba leapt into a canter without being urged, racing to head them off.

A fiery young steer charged Jack, its horns down. Jack's horse, Meg, sidestepped to safety and Jack brought the steer back into the herd with a loud 'YAAA!' and a flick of his stockwhip.

At last, Poppy and Jack trotted the beasts in to join the rest of the herd in the dusty, steamy cattle yards. Flies buzzed and nipped. The sun beat down relentlessly, making humans, cattle and horses equally crotchety. The thermometer hanging in the shade crept up and up until it hit forty-six degrees — and still they worked.

Jack's dad was there, checking over the cattle for signs of disease and picking out the ones that would be walked by the drovers for hundreds of kilometres to the railway, for further transport to the meatworks in Darwin. The stockmen worked like a well-oiled machine. One by one, the cows and calves were directed through the race and into the crush to be examined, treated if necessary and released into one of two yards — those going to market and those staying.

Jack helped his father move the cattle through the race, using his hat to prod, urge and hasten them forward. Poppy helped where she could, cutting out calves, urging on recalcitrant steers, opening the crush. Jack passed around a leather-skinned water bottle. It tasted horrendous but Poppy was too thirsty to care, slurping the warm liquid down her throat.

Cows mooed. Calves bellowed. The bull stamped and snorted. Clouds of dust billowed up from stomping feet. It was early afternoon when the last cow was released and the herd had been divided into two.

'Well done, everyone,' said Jack's father, Mr Shanahan. 'Let's head back to the homestead for lunch. It's been a big morning.'

Poppy was too tired to talk as she mounted Sheba and rode her towards the homestead.

'All right, Midget?' asked Jack as he caught up to her, a weary smile across his dusty face.

She smiled and nodded, pushing the sticky strands of hair out of her eyes. 'It was fun.'

'You did well,' Jack offered with a cheeky grin, 'for a town girl! You'll feel better after a swim. We'll go down to the creek for a dip after lunch.'

Back at the homestead, the lawn had been turned into a bazaar by Ali the cameleer. Doctor Trehearne's patients queued patiently to see him and then celebrated their cures by browsing among Ali's piles of colourful merchandise, giving the homestead a festival air. The camels, meanwhile, lay by the fence chewing the cud.

Jack's mother, Mrs Shanahan, had spent the morning baking and cooking to feed the crowds of people from their own station, as well as the neighbours who had dropped by from the nearby stations — some as far as a hundred kilometres away. The Aboriginal women fluttered like bowerbirds among the bolts of cloth and household wares, their dark-skinned children running and hiding among the mounds of goods with squeals of excitement.

Poppy was not tempted to browse. She was exhausted after the early start, the excitement and the hard, dusty work of the muster in the intense Northern Territory heat. Plus, she had the familiar proximity to Darwin's best stores and suppliers.

After splashing their faces and hands under the water tank tap, the Shanahans and Trehearnes ate at a table set on the verandah. There were Jack, his parents and his two older brothers, Danny and Harry. Despite her exhaustion, Poppy was hungry.

Mrs Shanahan had baked a butt of home-grown beef with mustard, potatoes and pumpkin, served with a salad of tomatoes, cucumber and lettuce from the vegetable gardens and freshly baked bread. Another butt of beef had been served in the garden with bread and vegetables for the visitors.

Jack poured Poppy a large glass of water with lemon and mint. 'This tastes a lot better than the water bottle, Midget.'

The promised trip to the creek was delayed further when Doctor Trehearne begged for help in the surgery to examine the Aboriginal children, many of whom had nasty eye infections from the flies, heat and dust. Poppy's job was to chat to the children and keep them occupied while her father cleaned and anointed the infections. Poppy created a puppet out of one of Jack's socks, which she used to entertain some of the anxious children.

'*Got you!*' squealed Poppy, tickling a child with the sock puppet. 'I'm going to eat you up!'

'No,' giggled the young boy, swiping away the sock puppet. 'You can't hurt me!'

Like the people of the Mediterranean, those in the Top End often rested through the hottest hours of the day, from midday to three o'clock. The patients drifted away, the cameleer closed up shop and the men found a place to rest in the shade of the verandah or the surrounding outbuildings. Poppy, who rarely rested throughout the day, felt her eyelids and limbs growing heavy. She found a sofa in the corner of the surgery and closed her eyes, just for a moment.

When she woke, her father had finished for the day. Ali had moved on to camp in the scrub, on his way to the next station. Jack and the other stockmen had groomed and turned out all the horses. The Aboriginal stockmen, their wives and children had gathered their new purchases and drifted back to their own huts and cottages.

It was late afternoon when Jack poked his head through the door to say that he and some of the stockmen were heading down to the creek for a swim. Doctor Trehearne and Jack's parents eagerly agreed to join them. One of the stockmen harnessed up the draughthorse to the dray to carry people, towels and food down to the creek.

The Shanahans were blessed with a shallow, sandy swimming hole that was generally safe from dangerous saltwater crocodiles. The smaller, freshwater crocodiles were more timid and often hid from human interlopers. During the dry season, the creek leading to the waterhole evaporated, so it was impossible for the larger beasts to reach them from downstream. In addition, the waterhole was fed by a hot spring from deep underground. This water mingled with the icy water of the creek to form a bubbling warm bathing place. The bathers could then choose the perfect temperature to wallow in — boiling hot, warm, tepid or cold, depending on where they sat.

It was nearly dusk when the dray pulled up in a clearing near the swimming hole. Poppy ignored thoughts of freshwater crocs, snakes and bandicoots to jog down to the swimming hole through the tall paperbarks and shady river pandanus. The adults followed at a more leisurely pace, towels slung over their shoulders.

Poppy reached the creek first, throwing her towel and dress over a log and sinking luxuriously into the water, the chattering adults approaching in the distance. She sank under the water to block out the noise, lying flat on the pale sand, only her face sticking out from the warm water. The sky arched overhead, awash with reds, pinks, yellows, rose, peach and violet.

Flocks of yellow-and-white cockatoos screeched and swooped down to drink from the creek. A lone wedge-tailed eagle soared high in the sky. Tiny fish nibbled her toes. Poppy felt like she was the only person in the world, surrounded by this vibrant natural beauty.

A loud splash woke Poppy from her reverie. It was Jack, dive-bombing into the pool, spraying her and the birds with a shower of tepid water. The cockatoos swooped away with an indignant screech.

'It's too hot here, Midget,' complained Jack. 'Come downstream a little where it's cooler. It's more refreshing.'

Poppy groaned lazily but obeyed, crocodile-walking down to where the water was colder, raising goosebumps all over her arms. The adults and Jack's brothers stayed higher where the water was warm as a bath. Jack lay back, half-submerged, like a log.

'Look up,' he ordered. 'Keep your head under water so you can't hear anything.'

Poppy obeyed, staring into the vast, wide sky. The horizon had dimmed from crimson to mauve. The dome overhead was a deep purple, with the odd spangle of silver stars gleaming in the velvet. Poppy felt like she was floating in a peaceful, innocent vacuum.

Soon the adults drifted down to the cooler water. Finally, as it grew truly dark, Mrs Shanahan urged Jack and Poppy to dry off and help build a campfire. Jack's brothers had already collected and stacked a pile of firewood, so Jack soon had the fire roaring, sending sparks flying into the air and the silvery tree branches arching overhead.

Mr Shanahan and Doctor Trehearne sat back, chatting about old acquaintances and news of the war.

When the flames died down and the coals were red hot, Mrs Shanahan and Poppy mixed flour, salt and water in a large bowl to make a sticky dough. This was then shaped into four large loaves of damper that were buried directly in the hot coals to bake for half an hour.

When the damper was nearly ready, Jack cooked steaks over a hotplate, which they ate with mustard, fried onions and slices of hot damper.

'That was just delicious, thanks, Mrs Shanahan.' Poppy sat back, contented.

The billy can of water boiled and Jack threw in a handful of tea leaves. He then took the billy away from the shadowy figures seated around the fire and swung it over his head quickly in big circles three times. Poppy couldn't believe that the scalding water didn't pour over him. Mrs Shanahan and Jack passed around enamel mugs of black tea, which they drank with sugar or condensed milk. It was sweet and hot and heartwarming.

At last, it was time to pack up the cups and cookware, pour sand over the embers of the fire and climb onto the dray for the slow ride back to the homestead. It was the perfect end to a gorgeous day.

6

Pearl Harbor

8 December 1941

Poppy and Bryony were sitting at the dining room table, working on their lessons, when Cecilia ran into the room, her face white with fear.

'Girls, come quickly,' she ordered. 'There's just been an announcement on the radio. Japan has launched a surprise attack on Malaya, Thailand and the American naval base at Pearl Harbor in Hawaii.'

The girls followed their mother into the sitting room. Their father was there standing by the radio, listening intently.

'We repeat, the White House in Washington has announced a Japanese attack on Pearl Harbor this morning . . .' the radio crackled. The announcer's voice was urgent.

'It's happened,' said Mark, turning the radio down. He sat down heavily. 'This is a disaster — now we are fighting a war on two fronts. Australia may be in real danger; most of our troops are in Europe and we can't depend on Britain to defend us. They have their hands full with the Germans.'

'But surely Australia is too vast for the Japanese to invade,' objected Cecilia.

'It's certainly too vast for us to defend properly,' replied Mark. 'Only time will tell what the Japanese plan to do.'

❧

Later that afternoon, Poppy, Maude and Honey wandered down Cavenagh Street on their way home. Tantalising, exotic scents wafted from the Chinese cafes and stores.

Poppy wasn't sure if she was imagining it but there seemed to be an ominous energy in the air. Housewives huddled in groups, whispering about the Japanese attacks. Soldiers seemed to hurry with a sense of purpose, instead of their usual languorous swagger. A messenger boy raced past on a bicycle, jingling his bell and dodging the traffic.

The sky boiled with menacing, grey clouds. Thunder clapped on the horizon. The air was heavy with impending rain.

A truck roared down the street, loaded with uniformed soldiers, and pulled up near the girls, right outside the primary school. The soldiers leapt down, their bayonets at the ready, and marched through the school gate.

'What are soldiers doing at the school?' asked Poppy in disbelief. 'And why are they armed with bayonets?'

'I can't imagine,' replied Maude. 'Perhaps there's been some kind of trouble?'

Poppy and Maude hurried over towards the school fence to get a closer view.

The soldiers marched up the stairs of Darwin school and into one of the central classrooms, their rifles at the ready. Poppy and Maude could hear the raised voices from the children inside.

A few moments later, the soldiers came back out onto the verandah, leading a small group of frightened children huddled between them.

Poppy and Maude leant over the fence. As the soldiers marched down the stairs, Poppy realised that all the children were Japanese, aged between five and twelve. One of the smallest saw Poppy and turned towards her, terror written on her face.

'Poppy!' she called desperately, holding out her hands.

'Shinju?' replied Poppy. 'That's Shinju.'

Teachers and students in a range of nationalities had crowded onto the verandah, watching silently as the Japanese children were taken away.

Poppy ran towards the soldiers. She suddenly recognised one of them as Bryony's beau, George.

'George,' Poppy called. 'What are you doing? Where are you taking them?'

George glanced at Poppy and shook his head warningly. Shinju flung herself at Poppy, tears pouring down her face.

'Poppy!' cried Shinju again. 'Help me! I don't want to go with them. I want my mama.'

George put his hand gently on Shinju's shoulder. 'I'm sorry, Poppy.'

'That's Shinju,' Poppy tried to explain. 'She's my friend. She's just a child.'

'They're Japanese,' George explained, urging Shinju forward towards the truck. 'Our orders are that all Japanese men, women and children are to be detained and interned as prisoners-of-war.'

'But that's not fair,' insisted Poppy, running along beside him, trying to grab Shinju's hand. 'Shinju didn't do anything wrong. She was born here in Darwin. She's the fourth generation of her family to live in Australia.'

George stopped for a moment, and smiled sympathetically at Poppy. 'Poppy, there's nothing you can do. The adults have already been taken into custody. She'll be with her family. Today the Prime Minister has declared war on Japan, and all Japanese people must be interned for the national safety. The Japanese pearlers have been in a prime position to spy for their country for years. They know this coastline better than anyone. Who knows what information they may have given their Emperor about our defences?'

Poppy shook her head vehemently. She couldn't believe that Mrs Murata and her family were spies.

Poppy squatted down beside Shinju and hugged the child while she sobbed.

'Shinju, this man says he is going to take you to your mother and grandmother,' explained Poppy calmly. 'Everything will be all right. It must be a mistake; they'll let you go home soon.'

George put his hand on Poppy's shoulder. 'You and your friend better run along home, Poppy. Give my regards to your sister and your parents.'

Poppy shook off his hand, feelings of resentment burning inside her. Maude took Poppy's elbow and pulled her away gently.

'*Sayonara*, Poppy,' whispered Shinju.

'*Sayonara*, Shinju-chan,' replied Poppy.

George frowned at Poppy, dropping his voice to a whisper. 'I wouldn't be speaking Japanese if I were you, Poppy. I don't think you understand — we are now at war, and they are our enemies. You don't want anyone thinking you're on their side.'

Poppy looked at George helplessly. She could feel tears prickling her eyelids. What would become of Shinju, Mrs Murata, Masuko and Oshiro?

'Come on, Poppy,' whispered Maude gently. 'Let's go home. There's nothing we can do.'

Poppy began to follow Maude, then she turned and watched the group of Japanese children clamber onto the truck. She held her hand up in a salute to Shinju, and held it there until the truckload of children and soldiers disappeared around the corner.

'Let's go and check the Murata house,' suggested Poppy. 'Maybe someone's there. Maybe we can find out what's going on.'

Maude nodded in agreement. The girls ran the few blocks to the Murata's house, which was back near the pearling fleet anchorage. It was ominously quiet. The verandah floorboards creaked as they tiptoed up the stairs. The front door stood wide open.

'Mrs Murata?' called Maude, poking her head around the doorjamb.

'Murata-san?' called Poppy. 'Is anybody home?'

There was nothing but silence. Poppy slipped off her shoes and stepped inside the living room. Everything looked much like it had the day the girls had come to tea and dressed as Japanese princesses, except that one of Mrs Murata's precious teacups had smashed on the floor. On the table stood the other cups and the teapot. Poppy felt the pot; it was still warm.

'Murata-san?' called Poppy again, knocking on the door to the other room. There was obviously no one there, but there were signs of hurried packing — clothes spilling out of a chest, a basket overturned, papers dropped on the floor.

'Let's go, Poppy,' suggested Maude. 'There's no one here. George must have been right; they've all been taken away.'

Poppy smeared a hand across her stinging eyes. She turned and headed out the front door. Then she paused and ran back, picking up the teapot and the remaining cups, cradling them carefully in her hands.

'It belonged to Mrs Murata's great-grandmother and is very valuable to her,' explained Poppy. 'I'll keep it safe for her until she comes back.'

Maude looked around the house at all the other belongings that the Muratas had to leave behind. She carefully closed and locked the front door.

⋙⋘

That evening, Mark arrived home late from the hospital. Cecilia and the two girls were gathered in the sitting room, knitting squares to make rugs for soldiers, nervously listening to the radio for fresh news. Their cups of tea sat cold and forgotten on the side table. As Mark entered the room, Cecilia shushed him with her hand.

Prime Minister Curtin was making a broadcast to the nation: 'Men and women of Australia, we are at war with Japan . . . The leaders in Tokyo have ignored the convention of a formal declaration of war and struck like an assassin in the night.' The Prime Minister's voice boomed out ominously into the room.

Poppy twisted her pearl teardrop between her fingers. Bryony chewed on the quick of a fingernail.

'These wanton killings will be followed by attacks on the Netherlands, East Indies, on the Commonwealth of Australia, on the dominion of New Zealand, if Japan can get its brutal way . . .'

Mark sat down in his armchair, his hands over his eyes. Cecilia sat with her legs crossed, jiggling her foot.

'Each must take his or her place in the service of the nation, for the nation itself is in peril.'

Australia is in peril, Poppy thought. We *are in peril*.

'This is our darkest hour.'

Mark jumped up and turned off the radio with a deep sigh.

'In the last few hours, Japan has attacked Malaya, Thailand, the Philippines, Singapore, Hong Kong, Guam and Hawaii,' Cecilia informed him, her voice shaking. 'In Pearl Harbor alone, more than two thousand people have been killed.'

Bryony held Coco the cat on her lap. Poppy huddled into the sofa next to her sister, her arms crossed as though she was cold, despite the heat of the summer air. Honey sat at Poppy's feet, whimpering, sensing the stress in the air. Mark nodded.

'Sorry I'm late, darling,' he apologised to his wife. 'I've been in meetings all afternoon, discussing ways to protect the hospital and how to evacuate it in case of emergency. The hospital is in a dangerous position so close to the barracks, and the air-raid wardens are very jumpy about the town's defences.'

'They don't really think the Japanese will attack Darwin, do they?' asked Cecilia, jumping to her feet, hands clenched by her side.

Mark rubbed his forehead. 'There are rumours that they will start evacuating all civilians from Darwin any day now, starting with the women and children,' he explained, glancing over towards Poppy and Bryony and smiling reassuringly. The girls smiled back nervously. 'Only women in essential services will be allowed to stay.'

'That's ludicrous,' argued Cecilia. 'This is our home. Where would we go?'

She strode back and forth across the floor, biting her thumbnail. Mark took her hand, stilling her. 'I know this is our home, but we must think of the safety of you and the girls above all else. That's the most important thing.'

The ceiling fan whirred slowly overhead, stirring the muggy air.

'Of course, I would have to stay here,' continued Mark. 'I'm needed at the hospital and, if things start getting worse in the Pacific, Darwin will be an important base for treating injured troops. You could take the girls down to Sydney or Adelaide for a few months until we know what's happening.'

Cecilia frowned. 'I won't leave you. This war might drag on for years. If Darwin becomes an important medical centre, then I should be here, too. I've nursed countless of our patients over the last twenty years, including the Great War. I won't sit twiddling my thumbs in Sydney doing nothing when I'm needed here.'

Poppy glanced at her father.

Mark nodded, smiling ruefully. 'You are a wonderful nurse, and I could ask for none better,' he agreed, 'but what about the girls?'

Cecilia's eyes filled with tears. 'Perhaps they should go to boarding school down south,' she suggested after a pause. 'They'd be safe there, and I really should have sent them a couple of years ago. It was just with the war on, I didn't want them to be so far away . . .'

'No,' cried Poppy. 'I don't want to go to boarding school. I want to stay here with you.'

Cecilia and Mark exchanged worried glances.

'Phoebe and Edward enjoyed boarding school,' Cecilia reminded her, trying to be cheerful. 'They made some lovely friends and had lots of fun.'

Poppy crossed her arms and put on her mutinous face, which made Mark laugh. Her stomach was knotted with tension. She could sense the stress in the air as palpably as the humidity. Honey whined and rolled on her back. Absentmindedly, Poppy leant down and stroked her tummy.

'What about you, Bryony?' asked Mark.

'Of course she wants to stay here,' insisted Poppy. 'George is here!'

Bryony flushed and then tossed her head, not a curl out of place.

'Of course I love Darwin, but I think it would be wonderful to visit Sydney. Phoebe says it's a marvellous city — full of theatres, shops and dance halls . . .'

'Of course all you can think about is *shopping*!' snapped Poppy. Her fear made her want to strike out at something, anyone, but particularly her smug, gorgeous sister.

'Well, you might want to start thinking a little more about how *you* look, Poppy,' Bryony retorted. 'You can't spend your whole life looking like a ragamuffin hoyden.'

Cecilia could not help but smile.

'Poppy, Bryony — there's no need for sniping. Sisters should support each other, especially in troubled times.'

Poppy rolled her eyes. Bryony smirked back.

'Girls, listen to your mother,' Mark admonished impatiently. 'I can't believe you are baiting each other when we have to make life-changing decisions. We are trying to decide what is best — and safest — for you . . . what's best for us as a family.'

'What's best for us as a family is to stay right here,' maintained Poppy.

Cecilia put her hand on Poppy's shoulder and rubbed it soothingly. 'For the time being, Poppy's right,' she agreed. 'Who's to say that Sydney is any safer than Darwin? Surely the Japanese would be more interested in a big city than a tiny backwater? What on earth would they want with Darwin?'

Mark sighed, pinching the bridge of his nose. 'We don't

need to make a decision straightaway,' he suggested. 'The Japanese are a long way away. The British say that Singapore is impregnable, and now the Americans have declared war. If things get worse, we can make a decision then. In the meantime, we'll take as many precautions as we can.'

Cecilia nodded. 'They've asked us to tape up all the windows with masking tape in case of explosions, and pin up black material at night to block out any light that could show the bombers where to aim.'

'Poppy and I can get to work digging a shelter in the backyard,' suggested Mark with a quick grin at Poppy. 'We'll manage, darling.'

Poppy jumped up, relieved. *Good, Dad's not going to send us away. Everything will be fine.*

'I'm going to feed the animals. Christabel will be starving.'

7

Iris

Over the next few days, things changed rapidly in Darwin. Teams of soldiers laboured to improve Darwin's defences — bulldozing the trees around Fannie Bay, building gun emplacements on the headlands, digging air-raid trenches and barriers of barbed wire around the harbour. Trucks full of soldiers poured in from the south, while planes full of wharf labourers arrived to help unload the ships of supplies.

Poppy and Maude wandered into town to pick up the mail from the post office. Outside the old stone building, a pretty girl, about nineteen years old, waved at them. She was dressed fashionably in a floral dress with a nipped-in waist, her hair curled back in a pompadour roll, a slick of red across her lips.

'Hello, Poppy,' she called. 'How are you? Have you heard from Phoebe? And how's that handsome brother of yours?'

Poppy waved back and dragged Maude over. 'Hello, Iris,' replied Poppy. 'We're all fine. We're just visiting the post office to see if there are any letters from Phoebe or Edward. Iris, this is my friend Maude, from Sydney. Maude, this is Iris, she's one of Phoebe's friends. Her parents run the post office.'

'Hello, Maude. Welcome to Darwin. How're you enjoying it?' asked Iris. 'It's certainly a lot more fun now that the army's taking over.'

'I like it,' Maude replied, 'although I'm not sure I'll *ever* get used to the heat and humidity.'

Maude pulled at her limp skirt sticking to the back of her sweaty legs.

'Is Peter home for the holidays yet?' asked Poppy. She turned to Maude to explain. 'Iris's fifteen-year-old brother is down in Adelaide at boarding school.'

Iris wrinkled her nose. 'No! Mum is devastated. The military has commandeered his flight. They're not letting any civilians come north at the moment. Mum's convinced she can get him on another flight, but it looks like poor Peter is stuck in Adelaide for Christmas.'

'I'm so sorry to hear that,' Poppy sympathised. 'That's really rotten luck.'

Iris glanced at her watch. 'I have to get back to work. It's chaos there with everything happening. I was just popping in to tell Mum that I wouldn't be home for dinner — a handsome young man has asked me out to the cinema. Can't pass up a chance like that now, can I? Make sure you send my love to Phoebe and Edward next time you write to them — especially Edward. Tell him to hurry home or all the gorgeous girls will be snapped up!'

Poppy smiled. 'I will. Do you want me to tell your mum? We're going in there now.'

'Thanks, Poppy, that would be lovely. See you soon. Bye, Maude.'

Iris waved and darted across the road, her high heels clicking. A uniformed soldier passing by stopped and wolf-whistled in appreciation at the pretty girl. Iris tossed her head in disdain and kept going. Poppy laughed.

'Bryony says that Iris is having a wonderful time,' Poppy explained. 'She's always being asked to dances and picnics and the cinema. She's so lovely that she'll have half the Australian army chasing her.'

Maude grinned. 'I guess there's not a lot of competition up here. Most of the girls are hardly fashionable, compared to Sydney. It's hard to look glamorous when it's hot and raining all the time. I don't think gumboots count as a fashion statement.'

Poppy shrugged, pushing open the heavy door into the post office and heading to the wooden counter.

'Hello, Mrs Bald,' Poppy called. 'Anything for us?'

'Hello, Poppy,' said Mrs Bald with a smile. 'Can you believe how many soldiers there are everywhere? The army are flying them in by the thousands!'

'Sorry to hear about Peter,' Poppy offered. 'He'll hate being stuck down south for the holidays.'

A look of distress crossed Mrs Bald's usually cheery face.

'I've been so looking forward to seeing him,' she said. 'He hasn't been home for months. But I'm hoping the military will relent and put him on a flight. We miss him terribly. In the meantime, he's staying with my sister and she'll look after him.'

Mrs Bald turned away and searched through the stacks of mail on the shelves behind her. She turned back, smiling brightly once more.

'Here you go, Poppy.' Mrs Bald handed her a small pile of envelopes. 'A letter from Phoebe and one from overseas, from Edward. Your mother must be missing them, too.'

Poppy nodded. 'Especially Edward — she worries about him. Maybe this letter will tell us where he is?'

'We're all praying for him, love.'

A man came into the post office, carrying a large parcel.

'Good morning, Mr Lockwood. Just a moment,' called Mrs Bald. She turned back to the girls and spoke in a low voice. 'Nice young man — a journalist from Melbourne. Just married. And here are some letters for Mrs Tibbets as well, Maude.'

'Thanks, Mrs Bald,' replied Maude, taking the small pile of brown envelopes.

'By the way, we saw Iris outside and she said to tell you that a gorgeous young man has asked her to the cinema tonight, so she won't be home for dinner,' said Poppy.

Mrs Bald laughed. 'Thanks, Poppy. Well, you're only young once, and it's wartime, so I'm glad she's having fun. It's a shame that older brother of yours isn't around — we saw quite a bit of him when he was home on leave. I hope he's all right.'

Poppy gathered her mail, waved goodbye and headed outside.

'Give my regards to your mother, Poppy.'

⚭

Cecilia was beside herself with anticipation when Poppy handed her the two envelopes. She dithered over which one to open first, then tore at Edward's, her hands shaking. Two photos fell out — one showed Edward with two mates, Joe and Frank, all smiling at the camera under the brims of their slouch hats. Another grainier photo showed a group of soldiers, shirts off, lounging in the shade. Cecilia ran her finger over the smiling face of her son.

Poppy read over her shoulder.

Dear Mum, Dad, Bryony and Poppy,

Just a quick note to let you know I'm fine. Hope you're all well too and that Poppy hasn't brought home any baby salties or brown snakes. The sail was shorter than we expected. The powers-that-be diverted us from Europe, which I must say I was disappointed about. We're in Malaya, which reminds me of old Darwin — hot, sticky and wet. So we're all kitted out for desert country and here we are in jungle. Typical army disorganisation!

It seems old Churchill has caved in and let some of the Aussies stay a bit closer to home, which is good news. Don't worry about the Japs. We'll see them off quick smart. The jungle up here is impenetrable — and the mud! I must say I'm looking forward to seeing a bit of action after all these months of training. We've been doing lots of route marches — my muscles are aching after not doing much aboard ship. We get time for fun, too — rugby, soccer, cricket, and some leave in town to watch a movie.

I tried out my Malay on one of the locals but found they mostly speak really good English. Our new camp is near the beach, which gives some relief from the heat.

I'm with a great bunch of blokes, although I still feel a bit of a rookie. Here are a couple of snaps of me with some of the lads. Joe Callahan is a good mate and we have lots of jokes. He's a great rugby player — I think he could've played for Australia if it wasn't for the war. My other mate is Frank Bernard — a typical country boy from WA with a heart of gold. We all look out for each other.

I'll write you once a week so you know I'm okay. Please send my love to Phoebe, too, and everyone I know in good old Darwin. Look forward to hearing all the news from home.

Cheerio for now, and much love to you all.

Your son,
Edward

'Thank God, he's all right,' sighed Cecilia, clutching the letter to her chest. She tore open the envelope from Phoebe.

Dear Mum and Dad,

It's late so I'll just scribble off a few words to let you know how it's all going. I love the nursing but working and studying hard. There are some lovely girls training with me, from all over Australia, so we have a good laugh together. Some of them are quite young, not much older than Poppy.

It's up at 5.30 and often not to bed until midnight. We work sixty-three hours per week, then study at night for our exams. We're allowed two nights out a week to go to the cinema. I went with a group of girls last night to see Humphrey Bogart in _The Maltese Falcon_, but am ashamed to say I fell asleep within the first few minutes. I'm just so tired. The girls gave me a real ribbing.

Discipline is strict. The Matron is an absolute dragon. Heaven help the girl whose veil is crooked or who misses the ten o'clock curfew. We all have to wear stiff, starched uniforms with long sleeves and big cuffs that must be kept pristine – or else! We all joke that the Australian Army should send Matron up to Malaya – she'd terrify the Japanese into surrendering in no time at all!

I miss you all but know I'm doing the right thing. I'm learning so much and am glad to be doing something useful. I guess you both know what a good feeling it is to know that every day you could be helping to save someone's life. Sorry I won't be home for Christmas.

Love and kisses to you both, and to Bryony and Poppy, too. Sweet dreams.

Phoebe

Poppy felt a wave of longing and love wash over her for her absent siblings. *I hope they'll be all right. I wonder when I'll see them again. It could be months. It might even be years. I just wish we could all be together at home.*

8

In the Mood

The next day a welcome visitor turned up on the
Trehearnes' verandah, his best town hat in hand.
Honey wagged her tail madly, jumping up into a show-off
pirouette. Coco stalked across the verandah, nose and tail
firmly in the air, to check out the interloper.

'Jack,' cried Poppy, tucking a wayward curl behind her
ear. 'What are you doing here?'

'Hello, Midget,' replied Jack with a warm grin. 'Mum,
Dad and I have come up to Darwin to see off my brothers.
Danny and Harry have joined up, now that Japan is in
the war. So have most of our stockmen. We're staying
at the Hotel Darwin — it's pretty swish.'

Jack stood on the verandah, dangling his hat in his
hands. He was tanned a deep brown, which enhanced
the startling blue of his eyes beneath his fair fringe. He
wore a white open-necked shirt and cream moleskins with
polished brown riding boots.

'Come and sit down,' offered Poppy. 'When do they leave?'

Poppy and Jack sat side by side in the cane chairs facing out over the view. Jack stooped and picked up a fallen pink frangipani flower and handed it to Poppy with a smile.

'Their ship leaves for Fremantle tomorrow.'

Honey had rolled over, four paws in the air, exposing her belly for a rub, and Jack obliged.

'What are you going to do at Alexandra Downs?' asked Poppy. 'If all the stockmen have joined up, how will you run the cattle?'

'It'll be just Mum, Dad, me and some of our Aboriginal stockmen. It'll be hard work. The only good thing is that Dad says cattle prices will surge with the army needing all that meat.'

The two sat in silence for a while, Jack rubbing Honey's tummy.

'How do you feel about Danny and Harry joining up?' asked Poppy, thinking of her own siblings far away.

Jack pulled a face and shrugged his shoulders, slouching down into his chair.

'Oh, it'll be good to be rid of them for a while,' Jack claimed with false bravado. He paused a moment. 'Actually, I feel pretty rotten. It'll be lonely without them on the property. To tell you the truth, I'm jealous. They're sailing off tomorrow to new places and adventures, and I'll be stuck at home doing all their chores, as well as mine.'

Poppy giggled, her nose wrinkling up. 'But not today,' she suggested. 'What are you doing? Do you want to come fishing with us? I promised to take my friend Maude barra fishing today. She's never seen a croc, so hopefully there'll be a few big reptiles lazing around.'

Jack sat up straighter. 'Sounds good. Do you have enough gear? By the way, before I forget, Mum told me to ask all of you to come and dine with us tonight at the Hotel Darwin. She wants to give Danny and Harry a proper send-off. Mum's pretty cut up about the boys going so she needs some cheering up.'

Poppy nodded. 'My mum, too, about Edward. I'm sure we'd love to come. I'll check with my parents and let you know.

'Why don't we bike over and pick you up in an hour?' Poppy continued. 'You'd better get changed, though — we don't want to get your good town duds all muddy.'

Jack smiled. 'You'd better get there sooner than that if we want to catch the top of the incoming tide. How about asking Daisy if she'll pack us some of her special lemon cake, too?'

Poppy rode to the Hotel Darwin with three fishing rods over her shoulder and a bucket over the handlebars, while Maude carried a thermos of tea, some picnic supplies and pack of lemon cake in a canvas knapsack on her back. Honey ran along behind, her short legs struggling to keep up.

Jack had changed into shorts and an old shirt and borrowed a bike from the bellboy at the hotel. Together they rode out of town towards Frances Bay, bumping off the road and over the fields.

They stacked the bikes together and Poppy tied Honey up to the handlebars. Honey whined pitifully, looking up at Poppy and Maude with round, liquid eyes. Jack bent and scratched between her eyebrows.

'It's not safe for her to come closer to the water,' explained Poppy. 'A croc would gobble her up in no time.'

Maude looked nervous, scanning the mangroves for dog-and-girl-eating crocodiles.

'We'll be okay if we're careful,' Jack assured her. 'Every year, someone gets taken by a croc, but it's usually out-of-towners or young kids who don't know what they're doing. Just don't wade out into the water, and don't crouch down.'

They hoicked their rods, bucket and knapsack, and picked their way through the mangroves. They forced their way through to where the trees were thickest, a gnarled forest of twisted, writhing roots and salty branches. From the knapsack, Poppy took a folded throw net.

'First we have to catch some bait,' Poppy explained to Maude. 'Then we bait up the hooks and see if we can catch some big barramundi. It's the best fish you'll ever taste.'

The three took off their shoes and socks and stood on the bank.

'There *are* crocs around,' observed Jack, pointing to a wide slide mark in the muddy sand. 'Crocs are hard to see in this muddy estuary water. They love to hide out of sight, then jump when you get too close. I reckon they'd think you were a perfect, tasty mouthful, Maude.'

'Thanks a lot! I'll take that as a compliment!'

'I don't think crocs are that fussy,' Poppy joked, pushing Maude in the side.

'Who's going to have a go with the throw net first?' asked Jack. 'Midget, why don't you show Maude how to throw like a true Territorian?'

Poppy rose to the challenge, hurling the net out over the water and hauling it in. In her first cast she collected a baby stingray, a collection of mullet and a small barramundi. The net thrashed and jerked with its catch.

'Watch out for the stingray's tail, Maude,' warned Poppy as she carefully opened the net to examine her haul. 'They have a nasty barb.'

'Not bad, Midget,' observed Jack. 'We'll keep the mullet but let the other two go to grow up.'

Jack had a throw, catching some more mullet for their bait bucket, then helped Maude try. Her first two attempts were clumsy, but in her third throw she also hauled in a few small fish. When the bait bucket was full of wriggling mullet, they baited up the hooks and cast out.

Maude was first to have a bite, the fish nearly ripping the rod out of her hand. Jack had to help her reel it in slowly and carefully, a little at a time. Finally, Maude hauled it up on the bank — a perfect barramundi, nearly a metre in length, its scales sparkling silver in the sunlight. Maude held it up by its jaw, admiring it proudly.

Jack whistled. 'It's a beauty.'

'Well done, Maude,' Poppy congratulated her. 'It's nearly as big as you!'

Half an hour later, Poppy's rod jerked violently as a barramundi swallowed the bait whole. Poppy pulled back, regaining her balance, then concentrated on reeling the fish in slowly. Poppy was just about to haul the fish onto the bank when it jumped out of the bay, followed by the huge body of a saltwater crocodile. The reptile was massive — nearly six metres long — and it leapt clear out of the water, crunching the barramundi in its jaws.

Maude screamed and jumped backwards. Poppy was jerked forward by the line and nearly dragged into the water after the beast. Jack lurched forward, grabbing her by the arm and hauling her back up the slippery bank.

The prehistoric reptile thrashed and rolled, taking Poppy's fishing line with it.

'That was *my* barramundi,' Poppy complained loudly. 'And *my* fishing line.'

Jack laughed. 'Better he eats your barra and line than *you*, Midget!'

The crocodile sank below the muddy water, just a flick of his knobbly tail showing where he lurked.

'My heart is thumping like crazy,' confessed Maude. 'That's one of the scariest things I've ever seen! I think I've had enough fishing for one day. Can we get out of here?'

The others agreed, letting the rest of the bait fish go and packing up the remaining rods, all the while keeping one eye out for the huge predator.

'I was thinking we should go to Mindil Beach for a swim and a picnic,' suggested Poppy as they picked their way back through the mangroves. 'It's much prettier on the ocean side.'

'Great idea,' agreed Jack. 'Did you bring the lemon cake?'

'Yeees,' Poppy replied, smacking Jack on the shoulder. 'I'm sure the only reason you came today was to get your hands on Daisy's lemon cake.'

'Nooo,' said Jack in mock horror. 'How could I refuse the invitation to go fishing with two gorgeous girls and a fish-stealing croc?'

Poppy tossed her head and then busied herself making a great fuss of Honey, who was jumping up and down as though she thought she'd never see any of them again.

Jack rode his bike through the potholed streets of Darwin, carrying the metre-long barramundi by its jaw with one hand. They received plenty of jokes and calls of congratulation. A Chinese cafe proprietor offered to buy it from them.

At the beach, they gathered a pile of firewood, which they set alight on the sand under the shade of the palms. While the fire was burning down to form hot coals, they all dived into the water to wash away the sweat of the muggy afternoon. They jumped, chased and tackled each other, splashing and falling in the small waves. Honey raced back and forth along the water's edge, barking.

Exhausted, they swam in to check the fire. In the knapsack was a bag of flour that Poppy and Maude mixed with water to form a dough, then Jack carved the big fish into thick fillets. Poppy laid them straight on the coals, together with the damper. The fish charred, filling the air with its fragrant aroma. They had to go for another swim to take their mind away from the food while it cooked.

When Jack and Poppy agreed it was ready, they sat cross-legged in the sand around the fire in their swimming costumes. Each one took a hunk of damper and a chunk of fish, scraping the ash and coals off it, then squeezing a slice of fresh lemon over the top before tucking in.

Maude looked at it doubtfully, trying to flick tiny grey ash out of her bread with her fingernail.

'Stop fussing, Maude,' advised Poppy, when she'd swallowed a large bit of fish. 'It's delicious, I promise you.'

Maude wrinkled her nose and then took a tiny, tentative nibble. Honey came over and sat up on her hind legs, begging, her pink tongue hanging out. Maude laughed and fed her a chunk.

'Mmmm, that is good.' Maude took another bite. 'How did you learn to cook that?'

'Daisy showed me,' said Poppy, feeding Honey another morsel, 'although Daisy normally stuffs hers with leaves she picks from the swamp.'

Jack lay back in the sand, hands behind his head.

'You just can't beat swimming in the sea and eating outdoors, can you? That was great, thank you. I'm full.'

'Aaaah,' teased Poppy, leaning over to the knapsack. 'Then you won't want any lemon cake? I'll feed yours to Honey.'

'Not so fast, young lady,' Jack retorted, grabbing her hand to steal the cake. 'Honey's not getting any of *my* cake. I didn't come all the way to Darwin to miss out on that.'

After the sticky, bittersweet dessert, they all lay back in the sand resting, then had another swim to wash off the crumbs, sand and ash. Finally, they dressed, covered the fire with sand, and packed up for the short bike ride back to Myilly Point.

⊗

In the evening, the Trehearnes were to meet the Shanahans at the Hotel Darwin for cocktails at six o'clock, followed by dinner and dancing. At four o'clock, Maude arrived at Poppy's house, freshly showered, hair damp and carrying a big bag. She found Poppy feeding a bottle to Christabel on the kitchen step, Honey eagerly licking up any stray drips that were spilled.

'Come on, it's time to get ready,' Maude suggested.

'Ready for what?' asked Poppy, checking her watch.

'Ready for the party, silly,' Maude said, dragging Poppy to her feet.

'It's only four o'clock — we've got ages,' argued Poppy, making sure Christabel finished the last drops of the bottle. 'Plus, it's not a party; it's just dinner with the Shanahans.'

The milk finished, Christabel hopped away to browse for some fresh green grass. Poppy wiped her sticky fingers on her shorts.

'Yes, but it's at the Hotel Darwin, which is supposed to be very ritzy, and I've never been. There'll be music and dancing and fun! So we should get dressed up.'

Maude skipped along up to the verandah, Poppy following reluctantly.

'So, what do you have in your bag?' asked Poppy.

'Dresses and rollers and bobby pins and brushes and make-up and all sorts of goodies,' Maude said, counting on her fingers. 'Now, have a bath and wash the salt off, while I start getting ready. I'll meet you in your room in a few minutes.'

Poppy obediently went to have a bath and wash her hair. When she returned to her room, a towel wrapped around her head, she found Bryony and Maude deep in conversation, poring over nail polishes and lipsticks. Both girls had their hair curled up in rollers and were wearing slips.

'No,' said Poppy, 'you're not doing that to me.'

'Stop making a fuss, Poppy,' chided Bryony with a grin. 'Sit down here at my dressing table. Maude and I have a lot of work to do.'

Maude giggled and started pulling all the beauty paraphernalia out of her bag. Bryony pushed Poppy down onto the frilled stool in front of the dressing table.

'What do you think, Maude?' asked Bryony. 'Up or down?'

Maude looked critically at Poppy in the mirror. 'Half up, half down,' she decided, pulling the towel turban from Poppy's head. Bryony nodded, filing her nails.

Poppy thought she looked like a drowned rat with limp, wet hair and a grubby, stained bathrobe on over her underwear. Maude set to work, combing the tangles out of Poppy's hair. Poppy winced as the comb snagged a big knot at the back of her head.

'Sorry about that,' Maude apologised, working quickly and efficiently. First, she parted Poppy's hair over her left eyebrow, then she sectioned off segments of hair, which she carefully curled onto a fat roller and pinned into place. Within fifteen minutes, Poppy looked a bit like a hedgehog, with rollers and pins all over her scalp.

'Gorgeous!' Poppy said sarcastically, rolling her eyes. 'This is ridiculous.'

'Give me your hand,' ordered Bryony. She examined Poppy's hands — the chapped fingers covered in cuts and scratches, fingernails torn and broken. 'Awful . . . I think clear polish?' Maude nodded.

Bryony rubbed cream into Poppy's hands, then she used an emery board to file her nails until they were short but even. Lastly, she painted them with clear nail polish. Maude did her own nails at the same time, painting them pale pink.

'Now, close your eyes, Poppy, and turn this way,' ordered Maude with a giggle. Poppy could feel Maude powdering her face and brushing make-up about her eyes, cheeks and lips. Poppy relaxed and let herself enjoy the sensation of being fussed over.

'No peeking,' warned Bryony as Poppy's eyelids fluttered open. 'Now, stand up and put your arms in the air.'

Poppy felt the old, damp bathrobe being tugged away and a silky fabric being slipped over her head and tweaked into place. Then the girls began unrolling the curlers and fluffing out her hair, pulling back segments and pinning them. She was enveloped in a cloud of sticky hairspray, which made her cough, then a puff of sweet-smelling perfume.

'Just be patient a moment,' Maude instructed. 'We're nearly ready.'

Poppy sat fidgeting, impatient to peek after all this time. She could hear the other girls getting dressed.

'Now, pucker up for the final touch,' ordered Bryony, colouring in her lips with lipstick.

'Tada!' squealed Maude. 'Open your eyes.'

Poppy opened her eyes and stared. In the mirror were three faces: two with dark hair, one with fair. Each girl had her hair elaborately coiffed on top of her head, twisted into rolls, then falling in soft waves over her shoulders, a flower pinned in a different spot. Their faces were flawless with pale powder. Dark eyeliner and mascara rimmed their eyes, and their lips pouted with bright-red lipstick.

'We . . . we look beautiful,' stammered Poppy.

Bryony and Maude grinned at each other.

'We do, don't we?' crowed Maude.

'I don't think Dad is going to like the lipstick,' Poppy muttered.

'We'll see,' Bryony said. 'It *is* a special occasion.'

Maude twirled around the room, the soft drapes of her skirt swirling out. Bryony wore a long pale-green dress with sheer, capped sleeves, gathered at the waist with a narrow belt of the same material. The colour made her green eyes gleam like a cat's. She posed in the mirror, tucking a stray curl behind her ear and pinning a red hibiscus firmly into place.

The younger girls wore Maude's knee-length dresses of soft chiffon — Maude's blue and Poppy's cream, sprigged with tiny flowers. Poppy had a cream frangipani pinned above her right ear, which glowed against her dark hair.

Bryony tossed Poppy some sheer stockings. 'Put these on — roll them up gently and please don't put a hole in them. Then you can try on some of my shoes — I don't think your flat Mary Janes are quite the right look for tonight.'

Bryony handed her a pair of black velvet evening shoes with silver straps around the ankle and across the top of her foot, like the rays of a setting sun. The heel was mid-height but sturdy for dancing.

Poppy felt glamorous and grown-up — something she had never felt before. She sashayed across the floor in Bryony's shoes. Maude tweaked her skirt, ensuring it draped perfectly.

'Ready to go, girls?' Cecilia called from the hall, before sticking her head around the doorway. 'Oh, my goodness,' she exclaimed. 'Don't you all look so *gorgeous*. Poppy, I would never have recognised you.'

The girls followed Cecilia out to the hall and into the sitting room. Mark was there, listening to the radio, wearing a white dinner jacket and shirt with a black bow tie and trousers. He switched it off when the girls came in and started in surprise. 'Poppy, Bryony, you look —'

'Gorgeous,' Cecilia finished firmly.

Mark nodded. 'Just what I was going to say.'

The Hotel Darwin was only a little more than a mile away on the Esplanade, so the family strolled together. It was a lovely walk in the relative cool of the evening air, straight down Mitchell Street, past the new hospital, the Larrakeyah Barracks, the old hospital and the parkland along the foreshore. Maude, Bryony and Poppy were conscious of a group of young soldiers elbowing each other, whispering and admiring the girls as they walked past.

The opulent Hotel Darwin was considered to be the Raffles of the north. It was a two-storey white building surrounded by lush, tropical gardens of palms and poinsettias overlooking the oval to the harbour. Mark and Cecilia led the way through the garden courtyard towards the terrace.

A waiter showed them to where the Shanahans were sitting, enjoying the view and evening sea breezes. Jack stood up with his brothers, Danny and Harry, all wearing the formal attire of the tropics: white dinner jackets and shirts, black bow ties and trousers. Everyone stood up to shake hands and exchange greetings.

Jack took Poppy's hand, his eyes twinkling. 'Hello, Miss Trehearne, I don't think we've had the pleasure of meeting before. I hope you're enjoying your visit to Darwin.'

Poppy blushed and held her head high. 'Lovely to see you again, Jack.'

The adults had gin and tonics with lemon and bitters, or beer, while the young people had lemonades. Mrs Shanahan was determined to be bright and cheerful, encouraging everyone to have fun. Jack's brother Danny flirted with Bryony. She blushed and lowered her eyes.

After an hour or so of chatting and admiring the view, they moved inside to the dining room, a decadent room with starched white tablecloths, gleaming silver and glassware, and potted palms. Despite the war restrictions, the Hotel Darwin still managed to serve a fine feast: steamed mud crab, roast chicken with gravy, boiled potatoes with sour cream, and roast beef and mustard, all with minted carrots and peas. These courses were followed by creamy, whipped mango parfaits that melted on the tongue.

For the final stage of the evening, everyone moved into the Green Room, the famous Hotel Darwin ballroom decorated with palms in brass pots, comfortable cane chairs, round tables and a polished timber floor. A brass jazz band was playing in the corner around the piano. Ceiling fans whirred overhead. The gay lights spilled out through the French doors into the gardens beyond.

A stirring swing tune played. The oldies chatted about the war and traded opinions on how Prime Minister Curtin was dealing with the problems of the wharfies' union. The younger set tapped their feet, humming and smiling, until Danny asked Bryony to dance — they were soon joined by Maude and Harry. Outside, the sun had set and stars blazed in the deep night sky.

'Would you like to dance too, Poppy?' asked Jack. 'I'm not much of a dancer but it seems like a good night to try.'

The band played a jazzy swing tune popularised by Glenn Miller called 'In the Mood', which soon filled the dance floor with motion and laughter. Saxophones, trumpets and trombones duelled and harmonised to keep the dancers swinging in and out, round and round, accompanied by the piano, double bass and drums.

For a moment, Poppy felt awkward as Jack led her onto the floor, but then her borrowed dress and Bryony's silver shoes seemed to make her skim above the dance floor. She smiled at Bryony and Danny, then Maude and Harry, then Cecilia and Mark as they floated past, then she smiled at Jack. She smiled until her cheeks were aching.

Jack laughed and swung her out and around, then pulled her back in close.

'I love this tune,' Poppy said. 'It makes me feel like the whole world is happy.'

It was a feeling she never wanted to end.

9

The Warning

Two days later, Poppy was asleep in her room when she was woken by a dreadful wailing. It took her a few moments to realise that the piercing sound was real and not just part of her dream.

Poppy's heart pounded; her mouth was dry with fear. Her cotton nightdress and sheets stuck to her sweaty skin.

'Bryony? Bryony? Are you awake? What's that?'

'Wha —?' Bryony raised herself on her elbow and pulled aside her mosquito netting.

Honey whined from her basket at the foot of Poppy's bed. She crept over and licked Poppy's hand reassuringly.

'Girls,' Cecilia hissed from the doorway, 'get up quickly. It's the air-raid alarm.'

'Air raid?' asked Poppy. The alarm wailed on, rising and falling urgently.

'Grab your pillow and a blanket and meet me at the

back door,' urged Cecilia. 'Hurry. And be careful not to put on any lights! Don't go outside without me.'

Only that morning the girls had helped their mother and Daisy tack black fabric over all the windows to block out any chinks of light that might guide enemy planes towards their house.

Poppy jumped out of bed obediently, grabbed her bedding and ran to the back door in bare feet, following Bryony. Cecilia met them a moment later, also carrying an armful of bedding.

'Where's Dad?' asked Bryony fearfully.

'He's gone to help Daisy carry Charlie to the air-raid slit trench and get some water,' explained Cecilia. 'He'll meet us there. Now, when I open the door, *walk* as fast as you can to the trench — don't run — and stay down low.'

Cecilia opened the door and ushered the girls out onto the verandah. 'Go. Go,' she shouted.

There was no moon, so the garden was pitch black. Poppy and Bryony hurried down the steps and across the lawn. Poppy stubbed her bare toes on the edge of the stone path. It was impossible to see the trench in the darkness, and Poppy tumbled down into it, twisting her ankle. Bryony dropped down behind her, followed by Honey and Cecilia.

'The animals!' exclaimed Poppy, scrambling to her feet. 'I've got to get Christabel and the possums.'

'You will do no such thing, Poppy Trehearne,' ordered her mother in a tone that Poppy had never heard before. 'You will stay in this trench until the all clear sounds. Honey's here and the others will just have to fend for themselves.'

Cecilia set to work making the air-raid shelter as comfortable as possible, spreading out the blankets and pillows, and draping a mosquito net over them to keep away the vicious mosquitoes and sandflies. A couple of minutes later Mark arrived carrying a grizzling Charlie, while Daisy brought two bottles of water and a jar of biscuits.

'Are you all right, Daisy?' asked Cecilia. 'Is Charlie okay?'

'He's scared. He doesn't like the noise.'

'I think we all are,' Cecilia agreed, spreading out a blanket for Daisy.

'Well, we're lucky we spent all day yesterday digging this funk-hole,' joked Mark, handing Charlie down to his mother. 'I didn't think we'd need it quite so soon. If I'd known I'd have made it a little more comfortable.'

The girls smiled wanly at Mark's feeble attempts at humour. Daisy squatted down on a blanket, cradling Charlie in her arms and crooning softly. His sobs gradually quietened. Poppy sat with Honey cuddled on her lap, her round eyes straining up into the darkness to see if she could see any planes.

'Now that you're all safe out here, I need to go to the hospital to make sure the patients are evacuated,' said Mark.

'No, Mark,' Cecilia said, her voice rising in fear. 'It's too dangerous. Everyone is supposed to stay undercover until the all clear sounds.'

'There are wounded men at the hospital who can't walk,' he explained. 'It's a huge job for the nurses and orderlies to get them all down to the beach. They'll need help. You stay here and look after the girls.'

Mark kissed her, then both of the girls.

'Stay safe, my darlings. I'll see you afterwards.' He clambered out of the trench and disappeared into the darkness. Cecilia put an arm around each of the girls and hugged them to her.

They could hear sounds of panic on the still night air. An air-raid warden shouted, 'Turn off those bleedin' lights.' Glass smashed. A woman screamed.

For nearly two hours, the family crouched in the bottom of the slit trench under the mosquito net, ears straining for the sound of planes or gunfire, legs cramping in agony. Poppy thought it seemed like an eternity. Charlie fell asleep on a pillow.

'Would you like some biscuits?' asked Daisy, offering around a jar. 'I baked them this morning.'

Poppy felt sick, her stomach knotted with anxiety. 'No thanks, Daisy. I couldn't eat a thing.'

At last the all-clear siren sounded.

'It's over,' murmured Cecilia, folding up the mosquito net. 'We can go back to bed.'

'Did anything happen? Did any planes come?' asked Bryony, stretching.

Poppy struggled to her feet, stretching out her numb legs, and lifted Honey out of the hole.

'I don't know,' Cecilia said. 'I didn't hear any. I guess we'll find out in the morning.'

They slowly folded up the blankets and pillows and went back to bed.

Poppy couldn't sleep; her ears strained for sirens or planes or bombs. At last, she dropped off to sleep as dawn's faint grey light shone through the black-out curtains.

'Wake up, sleepyhead,' called Maude's voice from the hallway. 'You've slept half the morning away.' Maude walked in and perched on the end of Poppy's bed.

Poppy yawned and stretched. 'What a night! Wasn't it scary? What did you do?'

'Dad hasn't finished our trench, so we had to go down to the beach,' explained Maude. 'We were absolutely gobbled by mosquitoes and sandflies. It was horrible.' Maude stretched out her pale legs to show the dozens of nasty red bites. She scratched one irritably.

'We huddled in the bottom of our trench, but at least we had a mozzie net. Is there any news on the raid? Has anyone been hurt?'

'Apparently, according to Berlin radio, Darwin was wiped off the map,' explained Maude, bouncing up and down on the bed.

Poppy sat up, her eyes wide with horror.

'It hasn't been,' Maude assured her. 'That was just the usual Nazi propaganda. There weren't any bombs dropped at all — maybe it was just a reconnaissance flight — but the air-raid wardens smashed a few windows to put out any lights that were left on.

'Dad says that the Administrator is pushing forward with plans to evacuate two thousand women and children. Mother is packing up, getting ready to go. Dad says the orders will come through at any time and there won't be much notice.'

Poppy nodded. 'Mum says she won't leave. She wants

to stay here and work at the hospital as a nurse. We're all going to stay.'

'But you can't — you have to go,' Maude insisted with a frown. 'It's crazy to stay here.'

Poppy put on her mutinous face and crossed her arms.

'I was hoping we'd go together,' coaxed Maude. 'You could come to Sydney with us. You could come and stay with us in Manly. I could show you everything in Sydney — it's a beautiful place.'

Poppy took Maude's hand. '*This* is my home, Maude. Everything I love is here. I don't want to run away.'

'It's nice in Manly, too.' Maude pouted and crossed her arms. 'And there're no crocs or sandflies.'

'So you keep telling me,' Poppy snapped, her stomach twisting in fear and irritation. 'I'm sick of hearing how nice Manly is. I don't want to go there.'

'I beg your pardon,' retorted Maude, her face revealing her hurt. 'Sorry for caring.'

Maude stood up and stormed out. Poppy lay back in bed and pulled a pillow over her eyes. *Why is everything going wrong? Why is everything falling apart? It isn't fair!*

❦

Rumours abounded of the town's imminent evacuation; however, the details were still unclear, like whether it would be by road, sea or air.

On Tuesday, Cecilia and Poppy walked into town to collect the mail and gather some news. Near the courthouse, they bumped into Iris, who was on her way back to work.

'Have you seen the newspaper?' asked Iris, brandishing a copy of the *Northern Standard*. 'They've announced details of the evacuation. All women and children will be compulsorily evacuated, with the first party leaving within forty-eight hours.'

'Can they do this?' asked Poppy. 'Can they make us go?'

'They say they can — only women in essential services are to stay,' replied Iris.

'We won't be going,' Cecilia said staunchly. 'They can say what they like, but I won't be forced out of my home town by the Administrator. I'll wait till the Japanese do that.'

Iris nodded fervently in agreement.

'What about you, Iris? Are you and your mother going?' asked Poppy. 'Will you go back to Adelaide?'

Iris shook her head. 'My boss told me I should get out as soon as I can,' she admitted. 'The post office has also given mum and the other female telephonists the opportunity to leave, but we've all decided to stay. The communications at the post office are absolutely vital, so we think we'd be letting everyone down if we evacuated just because the Japanese are threatening to bomb us. Think about the English — they've been braving German bombs and aeroplanes for months.'

Cecilia squeezed Iris's hand.

'That's how we feel,' confessed Cecilia. 'I just can't walk away from everything here. I feel like that's inviting the Japanese to take it away from us. What hope would we have then?'

'They wouldn't dare,' cried Iris. 'I'd rather die than let that happen.'

Poppy gazed over Darwin Harbour, which was crowded with troop carriers, warships and barges. Dozens of men scurried along the long L-shaped wharf, unloading and moving supplies. The scene was so different to what it had been just a few short weeks before.

'Do you know, I was just talking to my friend Audrey at the State Shipping Company,' said Iris. 'She's having a nightmare trying to organise who's going, where and when. She's been inundated with men, begging, bribing, bullying her to get them on a ship out of Darwin.

'One threw a wad of money on the counter and ordered her to get him a place. She asked him if he didn't think that place should be given to a child or a mother. He said no, so she threw the money back at him.'

'Fear does strange things to people,' Cecilia admitted. 'It brings out the very best and the very worst.'

The first spits of an afternoon tropical storm began to hit. In moments, the rain was pouring down in torrents. The road turned to thick, churned mud. Pedestrians scattered for cover. Poppy could feel warm rivulets of water on her forehead, running down her cheeks and dripping off her chin. She stood still, letting the water drench her hair, hoping the rain could wash away the sick, cold feeling in the pit of her stomach.

'Come on, Poppy,' urged Cecilia, taking her daughter's hand and squeezing it. 'Let's go home.'

10

Farewell

Aloud rapping on the front door announced the arrival of a harried warden, his uniform already drenched in sweat. He carried an officious-looking list several pages long that was crisscrossed with pencil marks. Honey barked loudly in warning, her hackles raised.

'Is your mother home, Poppy?' asked the warden.

'I'll just fetch her,' she replied, feeling a sudden headache coming on. 'She's in the kitchen.'

Honey stood guard over the warden until Poppy and her mother returned. The dog ran to Poppy, her tail wagging enthusiastically now that her job protecting the family was done. Poppy leant against the verandah post, anxious to know what the man had to say.

'Good morning, Mr Anderson,' Cecilia said. 'What can I do for you?'

'G'day, Mrs Trehearne,' the warden replied, tipping his helmet at her. 'As you know, we've begun evacuating the women and children. Two hundred odd left yesterday on the *Koolinda*. Tomorrow, more than five hundred leave on the *Zealandia*, and you and your daughters are on the list.'

Poppy breathed in deeply. This was the news she had been dreading.

'Each person can take one calico bag of toiletries, plus a small suitcase of clothing weighing no more than thirty-five pounds, two blankets and a waterbag,' explained the warden. 'You can't take any other personal effects. I also need to remind you that all domestic pets are to be destroyed before you leave. We don't have the food or the manpower to feed them after you've gone.'

'No!' Poppy wailed, dropping to her knees and burying her head on Honey's back. Tears streamed down her face and into Honey's fur. *Destroy Honey and Coco and Christabel and all the other animals? That's impossible. I could never let them do that.*

'I'm sorry, Poppy,' apologised the warden, 'but those are the orders. It's war and we have to do what's best for the country.'

How could destroying Honey be good for my country? thought Poppy.

Cecilia squeezed Poppy's shoulder gently to give her courage. 'Thank you, Mr Anderson, but my daughters and I won't be requiring those places on the ship tomorrow,' she replied firmly. 'We are happy to give them up to other evacuees who have a greater need to leave.'

The warden frowned, tapping his pencil against his clipboard. 'You'll have to go at some stage, Mrs Trehearne. The top brass want all civilians out of Darwin to free up supplies and infrastructure for the military.'

'I thought it was a noble gesture to save women and children first?' asked Cecilia with a wry smile.

'That too,' he said, pushing his helmet back on his head.

'Don't worry,' Cecilia assured him. 'I'm a trained nurse and will be working in an essential service at the hospital.'

'What about your daughters?' he challenged. 'All children *have* to go.'

'My daughters are no longer children, thanks to the war,' Cecilia replied. 'They are budding young women and have a right and a responsibility to help their country, too.'

Cecilia smiled at the warden warmly. 'I know you're just doing your job, Mr Anderson, but surely there are pregnant women, mothers with young children and people who are old and sick who should go before us?'

The warden sighed in defeat and reluctantly crossed out their names. 'All right,' he conceded. 'I'll put you down on one of the later ships.'

The warden trudged next door to the Tibbets's house.

Cecilia gave Poppy a huge hug. Poppy relaxed against her mother's chest, breathing in her soft, familiar scent.

'Don't worry, Poppy darling,' her mother soothed. 'We'll find a way to stay as long as we can.'

✥

That evening, Poppy found her father sitting on the verandah in his favourite white wicker chair, staring out north over the Arafura Sea. Thick, grey clouds boiled on the horizon, bloodied by the setting sun. Lightning crackled and flashed. A pile of medical reports lay unread on the table beside him. Her father looked tired and suddenly much older, with dark circles under his eyes and streaks of grey in his hair that she hadn't noticed before.

'Come and join me, Poppy,' he invited, gesturing to the chair next to him. 'I'm taking a break from my paperwork. How have you been? I don't feel like I've spoken to you for days. It's been so busy at the hospital.'

The cheerful voices of the Andrews Sisters crooning 'Boogie Woogie Bugle Boy' drifted out from the record player in the sitting room. Basil the diamond python slithered down the verandah post and set off across the floorboards, searching for a tasty meal.

'I'm fine,' replied Poppy, sitting down. Honey flopped at her feet, panting.

'I heard that Maude and her mother are leaving on the *Zealandia* tomorrow, sailing back to Sydney,' Mark said.

'Hmmm.' Poppy scuffed her shoe back and forth on the floorboards.

'Shouldn't you be over there helping Maude pack?' asked Mark, raising his eyebrow.

Poppy examined the toe of her shoe, streaked with mud. 'Perhaps,' she replied.

'Did you have a fight with Maude or something?' asked Mark. 'I haven't seen her around for a few days. Not since just after the air-raid alarm.'

'No, well — sort of.' Poppy leant down to stroke Honey. 'Maude said she was hoping we'd be evacuated together. She wanted me to go and stay with her in Sydney. She said she was looking forward to showing me everything in Manly. I told her I didn't want to go . . . Actually, I told her I was sick of hearing how beautiful everything is in Manly.'

Poppy flushed. She felt ashamed of snapping at her friend.

'Ah, I see,' replied Mark. 'So, how do you feel about that?'

'Well, kind of stupid really.'

Mark leant over and kissed Poppy on the forehead. 'Why don't you pop across and see how Maude is going with that packing?' he suggested. 'She can't take much, so she may need help working out what to leave behind. It might make both of you feel better to have a chat before the ship leaves tomorrow.'

Mark smiled at her.

Poppy thought a moment, then jumped up from her chair and raced to the stairs, Honey chasing.

❦

Next door, she found Maude sitting in the middle of her bedroom floor, surrounded by clothes, books, papers and shoes. A small suitcase lay open with a few items folded neatly in the bottom.

'Oh.' Maude tossed her head and busied herself with folding a navy dress.

'Hi, Maude.' Poppy twisted her pearl nervously. 'I just wanted to come by and say sorry . . . I'm sorry about what I said the other day.'

Maude bit her lip and shook out the dress, folding it again more precisely.

'I just didn't want to think about leaving

Darwin . . . leaving home,' Poppy confessed. 'I didn't mean what I said about Sydney. I guess I'm scared . . . '

Maude nodded, placing the dress in the bag. 'Me too. I guess we're all scared.'

Poppy made a space on the floor among the clothing and plopped down next to Maude.

'Of course I'd love to come and visit you in perfect Manly sometime,' joked Poppy, pulling a comic face. 'Just so long as you're not embarrassed to introduce me to all your city-slicker friends.'

Maude grinned. 'Apology accepted. My friends would love you — as long as you don't wear those horrible gumboots of yours.'

Poppy leant over and gave Maude a quick hug. 'Now, what are you going to take? We don't want all your fancy city friends to think you've lost your sense of fashion up here in the wilderness — you'd be ostracised!'

Poppy picked up one of Maude's straw hats and perched it on top of her own unruly curls, pouting as though she was a sultry film star.

'Good point,' agreed Maude. 'I'll take that, but I don't think I'll be needing my gumboots anymore.'

Poppy laughed, tossing the hat in the suitcase.

The girls chatted about film and music and what they'd like for Christmas as they sorted through Maude's clothes.

'I guess you'll be having Christmas on the ship?' asked Poppy. 'That won't be much fun.'

'Mmmm,' agreed Maude. 'Look at this.' She held up a soiled white dress. 'It's the dress I wore the very first time I met you. Mrs Murata could never get the mud stains out of it!'

'What a shame. Leave that behind.'

'No.' Maude folded the dress up carefully and lowered it into the rapidly filling suitcase. 'I'll keep it — it'll remind me of you and all the adventures we've had together in Darwin.'

Poppy grinned and squeezed Maude's hand.

'By the way, Poppy, Dad mentioned something today. The Japanese internees are being sent south tomorrow on the *Zealandia* as well. The Muratas should be on that ship. I thought you'd like to know.'

Poppy winced at the reminder of the Murata family, who had been arrested just eleven days ago. 'Where are they going?'

Maude shrugged. 'An internment camp somewhere down south — probably New South Wales.'

Poppy tried to close the now overflowing suitcase. Maude sat on top of the case, squashing it down. It still wouldn't fasten. Poppy pushed Maude off.

'Sorry, old girl,' Poppy sighed, 'I think we're going to have to unpack and start again.'

❧

At dinner that night, Bryony made an announcement. She stood inside the dining room door, wearing a floral cotton dress, her hair pulled back into a green velvet snood. She looked pale and determined, her hands twisted together nervously.

'Mum and Dad, there's something I want to tell you,' she declared. 'I've decided that I'm going to sail on the *Zealandia* tomorrow.'

'What?' cried Poppy. 'Are you insane?'

Cecilia breathed deeply.

'Are you sure, Bryony?' asked Mark. 'What are you planning to do?'

Bryony stood up and squared her shoulders.

'I've decided I want to go to Sydney and train to help in the war effort.'

'But you're only sixteen,' Cecilia objected. 'Sydney is thousands of miles away. And you can't stay with Phoebe — she's living in the nurses' quarters.'

Bryony swallowed hard and stood firm. 'I've talked to Mrs Tibbets and she said I can stay with them until I get organised. Phoebe says there are lots of girls even younger than me, training to be mechanics, telegraph operators, drivers or munition factory workers.'

Poppy thought of her glamorous sister in filthy, oil-stained overalls, her head inside the bonnet of a car, wielding a wrench. 'A mechanic?' asked Poppy with a chuckle. 'You might break a fingernail!'

Bryony flushed. Cecilia frowned at Poppy.

'I'd like to try to join the Australian Women's Army Service,' Bryony said.

'You have to be eighteen to join the AWAS,' objected Cecilia. 'Why don't you stay here and help at the hospital? That would be assisting the war effort, and you could stay at home with us?'

'I don't want to be a nurse,' Bryony insisted. 'I know I come from a long line of Cornish healers, but I can't stomach the blood and gore and seeing people in pain. No, I've made up my mind. I could use Phoebe's birth date and say I'm eighteen. People always say I look older than I am.'

Cecilia searched Bryony's face carefully. Mark glanced between his wife and daughter, noting the tension thick in the air.

'What about George?' asked Poppy. 'I thought you were madly in love?'

'George is great fun, but I'm too young to get married just yet,' replied Bryony. 'I want to do some things for myself before I spend the rest of my life married and having children.'

Poppy felt surprised. She thought she knew her sister but Bryony seemed to have changed.

'Bryony, I think you're too young to go to —' Mark began.

'No.' Cecilia interrupted him. 'She's not too young. Wars mean everyone has to grow up sooner than in peacetime. We know that from the last war.'

Cecilia smiled at her husband, her eyes brimming with tears. She blinked rapidly.

'Bryony, if you really want to do this, then I think you should go,' decided Cecilia. 'I'll talk to Mrs Tibbets tonight and work out the details. You'll need to get packing if you're going on that ship tomorrow. It'll be quick — you can't take very much. Poppy, perhaps you'd like to help your sister?'

Poppy stared down at her half-eaten plate of shepherd's pie. She suddenly felt sick in her stomach. Images of disaster tumbled through her head.

Bryony is leaving too. Bryony . . . Maude . . . Shinju . . . Mrs Murata . . . Mrs Tibbets. All these neighbours and friends on board the Zealandia. *What if the Japanese bomb it? What if it is torpedoed by the Germans like HMAS* Sydney *just a few weeks ago? What if I never see any of them again?*

❧

The next day the Darwin wharf was a chaotic scene as hundreds of women and children of many different nationalities were farewelled by husbands and fathers. Soldiers patrolled, supervising the embarkation. There were wails of grief, tears, hugs, lost children and scolding officials.

Poppy searched the crowd frantically. She waved and nodded to many neighbours and school friends. Beside her, Cecilia was giving Bryony last-minute instructions and advice in a brave, bright voice. Mark checked once more that her bags were properly secured.

At last, Poppy spied Maude and her parents. Mrs Tibbets was struggling along, carrying what appeared to be a heavy suitcase that could hardly be described as small. Mr Tibbets carried Maude's bag, while Maude carried the pile of blankets and calico bags.

'Hurry up, Harold,' urged Mrs Tibbets. 'We want to make sure we secure a good cabin.'

'You seem to be having trouble with that bag, dear,' replied Mr Tibbets. 'Would you like me to take it for you?'

'No, no,' insisted Mrs Tibbets, hefting the bag higher. 'It's not heavy at all.' She jammed her oversized hat down on her head to stop it blowing away.

'Maude! Maude!' shouted Poppy. 'I've come to wave you all off.'

Maude rushed forward, dropping all of her parcels on the wharf.

'Maude, pick those up,' scolded Mrs Tibbets. 'The blankets will get dirty.'

Maude ignored her mother and flung her arms around Poppy's neck. 'I wish you were coming with us,' Maude cried. 'Are you sure you won't come?'

Poppy shook her head, her voice choked with tears. The crowd ebbed and flowed around them. Mark shook hands with Mr Tibbets and traded news about the war.

'Come on, we need to get on board,' Mrs Tibbets said, hefting her bag. 'Hurry *up*, Harold.'

'Keep moving, ladies,' instructed a nearby soldier.

'Make sure you write *lots*,' begged Maude.

'Make sure you don't cause any trouble for the Tibbets,' Cecilia reminded Bryony for the tenth time. 'Give Phoebe a big kiss from me.'

'Let me know if you need any more money, Bryony,' said Mark. 'Don't rush into anything. Make sure it's what you really want to do before you sign up.'

Bryony nodded, fighting back tears as she hugged her mother. 'I love you,' she said, breaking into a sob. 'I'll miss you.'

'Be careful of strangers in the city,' warned Cecilia, brushing the hair back from her daughter's forehead. 'It's not like Darwin. Did you remember to pack your tooth-brush?'

'I love you, too, sugar pea,' croaked Mark, hugging Bryony in turn. 'Thank you, Mrs Tibbets, for looking after our Bryony. I hope she's not any trouble.'

'Goodbye. Goodbye,' said Bryony.

Bryony hugged Poppy, and then she was swept away with the Tibbets up the gangplank.

'Love you, darling,' called Cecilia, waving frantically. 'Write as soon as you can.'

Poppy stood bereft in the surging river of humanity. Belatedly, she waved up at the ship.

'Bye. Take care. I'll miss you . . .' she whispered.

11

Letters

8 April 2012

Nanna paused, a tear trickling down her wrinkled cheek as she remembered that long-ago parting.

Chloe sat forward, hands clasped together, mesmerised by Nanna's story.

Nanna pulled a tissue from her pocket and blew her nose. She smiled wanly at Chloe. 'Sorry, darling,' she apologised. 'I can see it all as though it were right in front of me. I felt like a little part of me shrivelled up when Bryony and Maude sailed away on that ship.'

'Oh, Nanna,' sighed Chloe. 'I had no idea. I've never heard you talk about any of this. It must have been terrifying.'

Nanna shook herself and rose to her feet, pushing on the arms of the chair. 'I'm getting stiff and cold sitting here. Why don't we go out into the autumn sunshine and get some fresh air?'

Chloe obediently stood up and stretched. She hadn't realised how tense she had been, sitting while Nanna told her story.

Nanna picked up the photos and yellowed letters and packed them away in the biscuit tin. Chloe was itching to read them.

'Would you mind bringing down some cushions for us, please, Chloe?'

'Sure, Nanna. Would you like a rug or anything?'

'No, no. I'll be fine.' Nanna led the way down the stairs and into the garden to a love seat under a large gum tree. Chloe placed down the cushions she had brought, tucking one behind Nanna's back.

'Are you feeling better, Nanna?' asked Chloe.

Nanna smiled and squeezed Chloe's hand. 'I'm absolutely fine, thanks darling. Let's take a look at those letters now, shall we, Chloe?'

Nanna set the opened tin on the bench between them. She picked up the letters, flicked through them and pulled out a few.

'Can you read the handwriting, Chloe? That looks like my messy handwriting, speckled with ink splotches and written in a hurry, as always! It has faded somewhat and my eyes aren't quite what they used to be.'

Chloe took the letter that Nanna handed her and started to read it out loud.

Sydney

January 1, 1942

Dear Mum, Dad and Poppy,

Happy New Year! How are you all? As you can see, we made it safely to Sydney this morning. The journey so far has been terrible. The ship was crowded and filthy, with not enough food or lifeboats – or even water. There were eleven people in our cabin that was only designed for four. At least we had a cabin – the Chinese women and children were crowded on the open deck, while the Japanese internees were kept locked in the hold. So many people were seasick, and we were constantly terrified that we'd run into Japanese submarines. It has been a total nightmare.

Maude and I managed to see the Muratas down in the hold. They are all right and sent their best wishes to you all. I felt so sorry for Shinju and all the other Japanese children locked in that stinking hold with nowhere to play or run.

Mrs Tibbets was devastated because one of the soldiers threw her silverware overboard. We were only supposed to have clothing in it up to a maximum of thirty-five pounds, and they checked each bag. Mrs Tibbets tried to argue that the notice had said we could take eating utensils and hers just happened to be silver, but the soldier threw it all over the side anyway. She has been very seasick and miserable but is much happier now that we are on dry land once more.

We were shocked to hear that Hong Kong fell to the Japanese on Christmas Day. Who would have imagined that a British colony would be taken so easily, but apparently they were vastly outnumbered. Did you hear that the first American troops arrived in Brisbane on Christmas Eve? I laughed because we were told that the first question some of the soldiers asked was, 'Do you speak English here?'

It was a beautiful sight sailing into Sydney Harbour this morning — and a great relief to feel that we are finally safe. I had my first glimpse of the famous Sydney Harbour Bridge. It certainly is impressive! We cruised the harbour twice today. Once coming in on the Zealandia, then again on the ferry to Manly.

Tomorrow Maude has promised to take me into the city to explore, which will be fun. Anyway, I'll post this now and write again soon.

Much love to you all,
Bryony xxx

Myilly Point, Darwin

January 2, 1942

Dear Bryony,

Merry Christmas. I hope your Christmas was more cheerful than ours.

There were no presents. The dining room table seemed lonely with just Mum and Dad and me. Mum and I tried to cheer the place up with frangipani flowers and the best china and silverware. But it didn't work. Mum roasted a chook with a few vegies and everyone tried to be cheery. Dad has been mooching around, looking worried. I think he really misses you and Edward and Phoebe.

Mum has thrown herself into nursing at the hospital. She's working long days — I think she's trying to forget things by keeping busy. I've been helping at the hospital, too — making beds, emptying bedpans (yick), feeding patients and running errands for the nurses. Poor Daisy has had to work harder without us to help around the house.

Dad is thrilled because the new hospital is nearly finished at Myilly Point. He says the operating theatres and obstetrics wards will be the best in Australia. It will certainly be a change from the ramshackle old hospital at Doctors Gully. He can't wait for the move.

You wouldn't recognise the view from the verandah now. I don't like it. All the trees have been bulldozed along Fannie Bay, and hundreds of soldiers spent Christmas and New Year's laying down rolls of barbed wire entanglements along the beachfront. They've built machine-gun emplacements everywhere and dug lots of funk-holes, super-funk-holes and super-duper-funk-holes! The place is full of American troops — they seem friendly but there has been some antagonism between the American and Aussie soldiers.

There have been shortages of both beer and petrol

which, as you can imagine, has made the locals very cranky. Food is getting scarce, so soldiers have been banned from the cafes and restaurants, which led to a fight where nearly all the windows in the main street were smashed <u>again</u>. There've been more problems at the wharves with strikes, and on top of that all the air-raid wardens have resigned after fighting with the Administrator. Darwin's a mess!

We had another air-raid warning on New Year's Eve and spent two hours squelching in the mud of our own super-funk-hole. Apparently, a Japanese sub was detected in Darwin Harbour on New Year's Day — scary to think they came so close! Dad says he's going to build another shelter under the house with sandbags so at least we can stay dry. There's no doubt everyone is getting jumpy about whether or not we might be invaded.

Hope you enjoy your stay with the Tibbets. Give Phoebe and Maude a big hug from me.

Much love, your sister,
Poppy xxx

January 9, 1942

Malaya

Dear Mum, Dad, Bryony and Poppy,

Thanks for all your letters filled with wonderful, ordinary news from home. Thanks, too, for the care package. The Christmas cake and biscuits were very welcome. Poppy, did you really knit those socks??

We received a Christmas present from the Red Cross, too, with chocolate, biscuits, barley sugar, chewing gum and cards — amazing how small things can make such a difference over here.

Well, it's happened — we have finally partaken in face-to-face combat with the enemy. They are like wraiths — eating nothing, disappearing in the jungle, then attacking us from nowhere. They are riding thousands of bicycles, if you can imagine it, so they cover vast distances quite quickly and silently. The cheeky chaps captured the radio station in Penang and have been broadcasting messages urging us not to fight. The monsoon is in full swing now, so it's muddy, swampy, hot and damp. The mosquitoes are vicious but morale is still high.

The food is good. The local population has been evacuated to Singapore, so we've been eating roast poultry every night. Certainly beats boring army rations! I'd be happy if I never saw bully beef again.

One of our men made good use of the Indian shops. The captain received a huge account from the principal storekeeper — it had been signed off by Ned Kelly!! Of course, the captain was furious and made all the men sign their names to see if he could recognise the handwriting, but it seems as though the wily 'Ned' signed with his left hand to disguise himself.

We have to be careful of our stuff. The jungle is full of mischievous monkeys that will steal anything, as quick as lightning, especially food. My mate Joe Callahan had his camera pinched, and the thieving monkey sat up on the branch of a tree pointing it at Joey as though he was taking his portrait. Joey coaxed and cajoled, swore and hollered, chased and climbed, but couldn't get his camera back. Soon there were a dozen monkeys fighting over it. Eventually, the wretched animal threw the camera at Joey and it smashed on the ground, absolutely ruined. Joey was furious but the rest of us couldn't help but laugh at the antics. It was like watching a circus.

Hope everyone is well. Sounds like Darwin has been overrun with Yanks. Please send my love to Phoebe and Iris and everyone else. Look forward to hearing more news from home.

Cheerio for now, and much love to you all.

Edward

January 15, 1942

Manly

Dear Poppy,

I miss you and I miss Darwin! Though it is lovely to be home again. Sydney has changed so much in just a few months. Food is much scarcer than it is in Darwin, and it is almost impossible to get some grocery items, like Vegemite and Blue, which Mother thinks is very annoying. We have to queue for meat and ice, and there are soldiers everywhere. The streets of Manly seem to have gone back to the olden days with deliveries by horse and cart and bicycle instead of cars and trucks. Mother is even talking about putting in a vegetable garden like the one you have in Darwin. I can't imagine Mother out there hoeing the vegies!

I will start back at school in a couple of weeks, which will be hard after such a lovely long holiday. It will be nice to see some of my old friends – although none of them are as special as you. I doubt they will believe my stories of life up in the far, wild Never-Never.

Give my love to Honey and Christabel and Daisy and Charlie and your parents. Watch out for crocs and handsome American soldiers.

Take care, all my love,
Maude xxxxx

Singapore

February 2, 1942

Dear Mum, Dad and Poppy,

Thanks for your letters filled with all your news and the package. I read them over and over again, imagining you all in good ol' Darwin. We've had two weeks right in the thick of the action, being bombed and gunned. It's been tough, but on the whole I think we're coming out on top.

I am very sad to write that my mate Joey Callahan copped it last week in a run-in with the Japanese while we were out on patrol. It was his nineteenth birthday. I have written to his mother to let her know what a true and brave friend he was.

No doubt you've read in the papers that we have withdrawn to Singapore Island. We were one of the last units to cross the causeway from the mainland, as we were covering the withdrawal of other troops. There were quite a few anxious moments, but we've all arrived safely now. As they say, Singapore is the Gibraltar of the East, so we should be sitting here safely for a while.

There's no doubt we will have a hard fight ahead of us, but I'm sure we will prevail. Our men and artillery are better in every respect. All of us are confident that we will beat the Japanese, and we have the thoughts of our loved ones at home to keep us strong.

Please don't worry about me.

Thinking of you all with much love, your son,
Edward

12

Singapore

14 February 1942

Poppy was in bed, tossing and turning, the mosquito net draped around her stopping the cooling breeze blowing through the louvres. She could hear the muffled sound of her parents talking in the sitting room. She felt lonely.

Finally, she decided to get up and fetch a glass of water, slipping her feet into the cotton slippers by her bed. She tiptoed out into the hall. Something in her mother's tone alerted her that her parents were discussing serious issues. On impulse, Poppy crept down the hall towards the front of the house. She paused in the hallway near the open doorway.

'The Japanese advance has been incredible,' Mark said grimly. 'The Allies have seriously underestimated their ability as fighters, and that every Japanese soldier is prepared to commit suicide missions for the glory of their country. Their push south to take over the oilfields has been relentless. In only five weeks they have captured a huge part of the Pacific. '

'But do you think they plan to invade Australia?' asked Cecilia.

'I don't know,' Mark confessed. 'From a strategic perspective, Australia provides the Allies with the ideal base to attack the Japanese in the Pacific. In just a few weeks, Darwin has really become the front-line of defence. So the Japanese will either want to invade and control Australia, or completely cut it off from the United States.'

'So there is a good chance the Japanese will attack,' Cecilia surmised.

'Australia is a vast continent,' Mark replied. 'It would take a massive Japanese army to invade and hold the country.'

'The nurses were talking today about carrying cyanide pills with them in case the Japanese invade . . .' Cecilia said quietly. 'They have been told it would be better to take poison than to be captured by the enemy . . .'

There was the sound of a muffled sob.

Poppy had to strain to hear Mark's response. 'The rumours of Japanese atrocities have been horrific. Wounded men in hospitals, women, nurses — even children — have been massacred. If they invade Australia, we can expect nothing else.'

Poppy could hear Cecilia collapse on the couch. 'But we have defences, guns, submarines, warships . . .' Cecilia said hopefully.

'From everything I've heard, our defences in Darwin are woeful,' Mark said. 'We don't have enough fighter aircraft or guns — or even ammunition. One of the gunners told me that most of their ammunition is left over from the last war twenty years ago!'

Cecilia began to cry.

'What do we do?' Mark asked, his voice gaining in urgency. 'We have a choice: we either stay and fight for our homes and our families, or we run and let the Japanese have them. We have no choice. We have to fight. But if things get really bad, you and Poppy could disappear into the bush. You could take the car, or Angel and the buggy, and just head south-west as far as you can go.'

'What if we get no warning? What if they just overrun us like they have everywhere else?'

'If worst comes to the worst, Cecilia . . . I have my old rifle. I will protect you all with my life.'

Poppy imagined her parents hugging and whispering as their voices dropped to a murmur. She felt totally despondent. She forgot all about her thirst, or anything else. She just crawled into bed and lay there, staring through the dark towards the ceiling. Hours seemed to pass until she eventually fell into a deep sleep.

❧

Poppy was awoken suddenly by a scream — a scream of indescribable terror. A scream of grief.

She lay still for a moment, trying to get her bearings, before hearing a muffled sound. Her heart pounded and she froze. The room felt very empty without Bryony in the bed opposite.

She slipped from beneath her sheet, through the netting

and padded to her parents' room. She nearly bumped into her mother, who was pacing up and down the hallway, ghostly in her pale nightgown.

'Oh, Poppy, did I wake you?' Cecilia's voice sounded thick.

'Mama,' Poppy whispered, 'are you all right? I thought I heard a scream?'

Cecilia hugged Poppy tightly. 'Sorry, darling. I had a nightmare. I thought something had happened to ... . It was just a nightmare. It means nothing. I'm sure Edward is fine ...'

Cecilia shuddered, her voice constricting with unshed tears.

Mark came in with a glass of water for Cecilia. 'It's all right, Poppy. Go back to bed. Everything is all right.'

Poppy went back to bed, but she couldn't go back to sleep. She kept remembering the sound of her mother's scream. She could feel her own terror bubbling just below the surface, threatening to erupt.

❧

'Cecilia?' Mark called from the kitchen doorway. Cecilia stood at the bench pouring out tea, ready for work in her white nurse's uniform, black hair tucked beneath a starched veil. She looked pale, except for around her puffy eyes, dark from lack of sleep. Poppy was sitting at the kitchen table eating a piece of toast, while Daisy washed up in the sink.

'You'd better sit down,' Mark suggested, taking Cecilia by the elbow.

Cecilia began to tremble. 'Edward?'

'Singapore has fallen,' he said gently. 'General Percival surrendered to the Japanese last night. One hundred thousand Allied troops have been taken as prisoners-of-war, including fifteen thousand Australians.'

'No . . . No,' Cecilia stammered, bunching her fists together and grinding them into her eyes. 'My boy. My Edward!' she cried, rocking back and forth.

Mark stood behind Cecilia, rubbing her shoulders, trying to provide some comfort.

'They've managed to evacuate the nurses, civilians and some of the wounded soldiers,' he continued. 'I was warned that we'll soon be inundated with the wounded. Thank goodness we're now settled in the new hospital.'

Cecilia nodded shakily, pulling herself together.

'But they said Singapore was impregnable,' insisted Poppy, her jaw clenched tightly. 'They said Singapore would never fall!'

'They were wrong,' replied Mark grimly. 'The Japanese forces seem unbeatable. Who could have imagined that they would sweep through most of Asia in just a few short weeks?'

Mark paused.

Poppy shuddered with horror, her thoughts churning. *They said Singapore would never fall and they were wrong . . . They said Singapore would protect Australia . . . If the Japanese have invaded most of Asia in a few short weeks, how long before they target us? How long before they invade Darwin?*

'The Administrator is urging the last of the women and children to leave Darwin,' Mark continued, as though reading her thoughts. 'The *Koolinda* left yesterday with more evacuees, and he wants the remainder to be flown out by plane over the next few days, leaving just the single nurses at the hospitals. There has been some talk that the Allies could have evacuated more wounded soldiers from Singapore if there hadn't been so many civilians who had refused to leave earlier because they thought they were safe. I think the time has come for you both to be evacuated down south with Daisy and Charlie. It's not safe for you to be here anymore.'

Cecilia looked around, bereft, taking in the details of her home. 'You're right — I'd never forgive myself if something happened to Poppy, or Daisy, or Charlie. We'll go to Sydney so we can be close to Phoebe and Bryony.'

Poppy buried her head in Honey's silky fur, her eyes brimming with tears.

Mark glanced at Daisy, still standing beside the sink. 'Daisy, do you and Charlie want to go and stay in Sydney with Mrs Trehearne?' he asked. 'Or would you prefer to go back to your family at Never-Never Downs? Or you could go to Adelaide and look for work there?'

Daisy wiped her wet hands on a tea towel. She glanced through to her own room, where Charlie was playing on the floor with some mixing bowls, then nodded.

'Charlie and I will go to Sydney, too,' decided Daisy. 'Missus Trehearne needs me, and someone has to keep Miss Poppy out of trouble.'

'Thanks, Daisy,' Cecilia said. 'You are a gem.'

Cecilia picked up a sheet of paper and a pen from the dresser and jotted down a couple of notes.

'I'd just like a couple of days to get organised,' she suggested. 'We can't take much, so I'd like to pack away some of my silver and china and bury it in the garden. Plus, I'm needed at the hospital today. We'll need to get organised if there's going to be a big influx of wounded men.'

'I'll book seats on a plane for you all as soon as we can,' Mark promised. 'You'll probably fly to Adelaide, then catch a train to Sydney. We'll also need to get permission to evacuate Daisy and Charlie.'

Cecilia smiled at Poppy reassuringly. 'We'll be okay. Edward's not dead — I'd know if he was dead. He's hurt, but he's not dead.'

'I pray you're right, Cecilia,' Mark said. 'I pray you're right.'

Poppy glanced at her mother, sitting composed, her face weary but set with determination.

Poppy remembered her mother's scream in the night. *Did Mum somehow know? Did she sense something terrible happening to Edward?*

'Well, we'd better get to work then,' announced Cecilia. 'Come on, Poppy — we've got a lot to do.'

13

The Hospital

19 February 1942

Four days later, Poppy, Cecilia and Mark sat out on the verandah on the white cane chairs, having breakfast. The table was set with a big pot of tea, boiled eggs, a bowl of sliced paw-paw, marmalade and toast.

For the first time in days, the rain and grey clouds had been replaced by mostly blue sky and sunshine — a rare sight at this time of year. It was already hot and humid. Poppy sat trying to memorise her favourite view: the garden below with its lush greenery, hot-pink bougainvillea and fragrant frangipani, the vast turquoise-blue sea stretching north towards Asia.

The scene was tranquil and picturesque. Cecilia and Mark chatted about the plans for the evacuation. Mark had finally managed to book Cecilia, Poppy, Daisy and Charlie on a small plane flying to Adelaide the next day. He would stay behind to continue his work at the hospital.

Poppy had carefully avoided asking what would happen to all her animals. She couldn't bear to know.

Just before nine o'clock, Mark and Cecilia left on their short walk to the hospital. Poppy stayed behind to help Daisy with some household chores — hanging out the washing to make the most of the sunshine, clearing the table, washing up the dishes and feeding the chickens. At 9.45 she followed her parents to the hospital.

Sister Minnie Scott, a friend of Cecilia's, was standing out front, enjoying the change in weather and chatting to one of the doctors. Her white uniform was already wilting in the heat.

'Hello, Poppy,' Sister Scott called out. 'I heard you and your mum are flying south tomorrow?'

'Yes,' Poppy replied. 'Has it been a busy morning?'

'No, love,' Sister Scott said with a smile. 'We have an appendix operation booked for ten o'clock, otherwise it's been as quiet as the grave.'

Poppy felt a shiver of apprehension run up her spine. 'Well, I'll just head inside and start making some beds,' she replied, nodding to the doctor.

At two minutes to ten, Poppy was propping the pillows up behind a young sailor and chatting to him. Cecilia had always told her that the best medicine for wounded servicemen was a cheery smile on a pretty face, and some friendly chatter.

'There — is that better, sir?' she asked, straightening his sheets.

'Bless you, love.'

Poppy heard a distant thunderclap, followed by the sound of an explosion. The eerie sound of the air-raid siren blared out over Darwin.

'It's a bombing raid!' yelled Sister Scott, running past her. 'It's the Japanese!'

Poppy froze, unsure what to do. She could hear yelling and shouting from all parts of the hospital, and then the sound of explosions coming closer. Her mouth was dry with fear, her stomach in knots.

'Poppy! Poppy, where are you?' her mother yelled from the corridor.

'Mum, I'm here!' Poppy replied, running out of the ward breathless with relief to hear that familiar voice.

'Poppy, I want you to stay with me at all times, understand? We need to get these men evacuated down to the beach if they can walk. If they can't walk, we need to get them under their beds with mattresses on top for protection.'

Poppy nodded. Cecilia ran into the ward where Poppy had been working. Summoning up courage, she smiled brightly at the patients. 'Okay, boys, here's what we're going to do . . .'

If the men could walk themselves, they were directed to head to the beach and the cliffs of Kahlin Bay, about one hundred metres away. One of the patients, an officer who had just been evacuated from Koepang in Timor and survived numerous Japanese air raids there, was shouting orders. 'Lads, hide in the bushes along the shore. Get under cover. Don't stand out in the open on the beach or the Japs will strafe you. Go on, get out of here!'

Nurses ran hither and thither, helping patients out of bed.

Cecilia and Poppy visited each bed in turn. The patients who couldn't walk lay there helpless, faces drawn tight with fear. With the help of a male orderly, Cecilia and Poppy lifted them, one by one, out of bed and carefully placed them on the floor under the bed. Poppy then dragged mattresses off the surrounding empty beds to provide some protection.

Suddenly, a bomb hit the hospital complex, making the walls rock. Windows shattered, showering the ward with shards of dagger-sharp glass. Clouds of dust and plaster wafted through the air. The sound was deafening.

Cecilia shoved Poppy under the nearest bed. Another explosion rocked the hospital. Enormous rocks fell through the roof, crashing into the ward and bouncing off the beds. The aftershock knocked Cecilia off her feet, sending her hurtling across the ward. She crashed into the wall and crumpled to the floor, where she lay motionless.

'Mama,' screamed Poppy, 'are you all right?'

There was no answer. Poppy felt her heart stop, a sob welling up in her throat. *Could she be dead? Could my beautiful mother be dead? Please, God, don't let her die.*

Poppy scrabbled across the floor on all fours, heedless of the falling masonry and debris, to her mother's inert body.

'Mama?' Poppy whispered, gently touching her mother's shoulder.

Cecilia moaned and shuddered, eyelids fluttering. Poppy flung her arms around her mother protectively and kissed her cheek. 'Thank God, you're all right!'

Cecilia rubbed her head and winced, glancing around. 'Oh, the bombs. Poppy, get back under the bed.'

'Not without you,' Poppy replied. They scuttled back across the rubble-strewn floor to the makeshift shelter under the bed.

Cecilia and Poppy huddled together until the dust cleared. Slowly, painfully, they crawled out, checking all the patients. No one seemed to be hurt beneath their mattress protection.

Cecilia limped out, followed by Poppy, and headed next door to another ward. Here, they set to work getting as many patients out of the building as possible. Strangely, Poppy no longer felt afraid — she was too busy lifting, pulling, coaxing and running.

There were two patients, barely mobile, who were trying to help each other shuffle outside. A quick glance around the ward showed that all the patients in this room had either been evacuated or moved under the beds.

'Come on, lads,' said Cecilia with a smile. 'Would you like a hand?'

Cecilia slipped her arm under the soldier's elbow, taking his weight.

'Thanks, Sister,' he replied. 'I think we might be better off outside, don't you?'

Poppy ran to his companion's side and offered her arm, which was already aching from lifting the heavy men. Her legs were trembling as well, but she dug deep inside for strength.

'I don't know about that, sir,' replied Poppy, smiling, remembering her mother's advice. 'They sound really close.'

'Strike me fat! Look at you, missy — not much more'n a tot. What're you doing here in a war zone?'

'Same as you, sir — dodging Japanese bombs,' Poppy joked weakly.

They hobbled outside and stopped. To the west, they had a perfect view of Darwin Harbour. Poppy could see wave after wave of planes darkening the sky overhead, dropping whistling silver bombs. There seemed to be nearly two hundred planes, at a guess.

The scene in the harbour was chaos. Dozens of ships were crowded together, attempting to flee. Black smoke. Roaring flames. Thundering explosions. Men jumped from the shattered wharf into the oil-slicked water. Ships were being dive-bombed, the explosions splitting them in half. The very water of the harbour was on fire.

Halfway along the path, there was another explosion close to the hospital building. Poppy, Cecilia and the two patients were thrown to the ground. Debris and shrapnel hurtled through the air, as dangerous as the bomb itself. Poppy checked that all her limbs were intact, then scrambled to her feet, helping up the wounded patients. She wiped her face which was slick with sweat, and her palm came away coated in crimson.

The Japanese bomber wheeled around, as though to check the damage he'd caused. The pilot spied the group of four standing on the lawn and headed back straight towards them.

'Run!' Cecilia yelled.

Clack. Clack. Clack. Clack.

Poppy looked up. She could see the emblem of the rising sun clearly painted on the underside of the wings.

She could even see the Japanese pilot — impossibly young — looking at her. He smiled and waved, then brought his plane into a low swoop, hurtling towards them.

Cecilia yanked Poppy by the hand, dragging her forward. Fear and adrenaline drove the two patients and together the four raced across the lawns, stumbling down the steep path to the base of the cliffs. The bomber opened fire again with his machine-gun, and they were chased by a hail of bullets until they took cover in the thick scrub at the base of the cliff. Dozens of patients were already huddled there in various states of undress, with crutches, bandages and even intravenous drips.

The bomber wheeled away and strafed the hospital building with machine-gun fire.

Cecilia helped the two patients as they collapsed down in the sand, then realised Poppy was bleeding profusely. She examined Poppy frantically. In addition to the cut on her forehead, Poppy had a deep, jagged laceration down her left arm, caused by flying shrapnel.

Cecilia borrowed a medical bag from one of the doctors, which was packed with emergency first-aid supplies.

'Sorry, darling,' Cecilia apologised, 'this is going to hurt.'

Poppy bit her lip to stop from screaming out loud as Cecilia poured alcohol over the open wound to cleanse it. She carefully dabbed at Poppy's wounds, then bandaged her arm with gauze and an elastic bandage.

When she was finished, Cecilia hugged her daughter to her chest. 'Darling girl,' she whispered, her voice shaking. 'I know it must hurt, but it's just a flesh wound. Thank God you're all right. Have you seen Daddy?'

Poppy shook her head, her mind suppressing thoughts of bombs, falling rocks, shattered glass and machine-gun bullets. Cecilia and Poppy took shelter with the other doctors and nurses among the rocks and held each other in a tight embrace.

At last, the sound of bombs ceased and the drone of aeroplane engines faded.

The all-clear siren sounded from the township. Patients, doctors and nurses crawled out of hiding onto the beach, stretching and chattering, grateful to be alive. Poppy checked her watch. It was nearly eleven; the morning raid had lasted just under an hour. It had seemed like a lifetime. She hurt all over, especially her bandaged arm, but struggled stiffly to her feet.

'Don't go too far,' suggested the patient who had been evacuated from Koepang. 'My guess is that they'll be back for another attack before too long. You might want to change out of those uniforms, too. You sisters are a beacon that the Japanese could spy a mile away. The white gives them something to aim at!'

Poppy shuddered, glancing at her mother's uniform, which had been crisp and pristine earlier this morning. It was now crushed, blood-stained and smudged with dirt.

'You're probably right,' Cecilia nodded in agreement, 'but the nurses can't stay here in hiding — we'll have work to do. There'll be lots of injured people.'

Cecilia kissed the top of Poppy's head. 'All right, sweetie,' she continued, 'you stay here under the cliffs with the patients in case there's another attack. I'm going back to help. You can cheer up the patients and tell them some stories. Whatever you do, stay under cover. You saw what they'll do if they see you in the open.'

Poppy nodded, her hands shaking.

'Look after my daughter now, lads, won't you?' Cecilia asked the gathered men. There were a number of grunts and calls in the affirmative. Cecilia headed up the steep cliff path to the hospital above. Poppy waited a few minutes, took a deep breath and followed — she couldn't bear to wait under the bushes while her parents were possibly in danger.

'Missy, your ma wants you to stay here,' called one of the patients.

Poppy glanced back and smiled. 'They need as much help as they can get up there.'

'God bless you.'

❧

At the top of the cliff she checked the hospital. The pristine white buildings, only completed a few days before, were now battered and scorched, but mostly still standing. The lawn was littered with chunks of concrete, twisted metal and fallen rubble. She picked her way over the wreckage.

Back inside, she leant for a moment against the wall, overcome with shock and pain.

'Poppy, what in the hell are you doing here?' called her father's familiar voice, raised in panic. 'You're hurt. Are you all right? Where's your mother?'

Poppy collapsed against him. His white coat, usually crisp and clean, was rumpled and smeared with blood.

'I've been helping Mama evacuate the patients.' Poppy's voice was husky against his shoulder. 'Then we took shelter down under the cliffs. I was hit by some shrapnel, but Mum says it's only a flesh wound.'

Mark searched her face anxiously, then checked her expertly bandaged arm.

'Go back down to the beach, darling,' Mark ordered. 'The Japs will probably come back. It's not safe for you here.'

Poppy nodded and reluctantly turned to leave.

'Poppet, I have to go back into the operating theatre,' Mark continued, his voice softer. 'Dozens of men are arriving seriously wounded. We don't have enough doctors or nurses or drugs or blood — or anything — to treat them. I want you to get under cover and stay out of harm's way.' Mark held Poppy by each shoulder.

Poppy nodded again and stepped away. Mark kissed her quickly on the forehead and was gone.

Poppy walked slowly back outside. The air seemed eerily silent after the deafening thunder of the raid. Plumes of toxic black smoke billowed up into the sky. In the harbour, the once-proud ships were scattered and sinking. Columns of smoke rose from the shattered buildings of the town.

A huge explosion sounded from the harbour as the ammunition in one of the ships detonated, tossing debris hundreds of metres into the air. Poppy could see distant bodies flailing in the black water and men in rowboats floundering to rescue them.

A car raced up the driveway and stopped near the door. A man jumped out, his face half-shaved and the other side white with soap lather. He wore a steel helmet, singlet and underpants, with boots on his feet, the laces undone.

'Oi, miss,' he yelled to Poppy, opening the back door. 'Give us a hand — I've got a mate here who needs urgent attention.'

In the back seat, Poppy could see a man doubled over and covered in blood. The bottom half of his leg was missing, ending in a crimson stump. Poppy glanced at the path to the beach, then ran to the back of the car.

She smiled at the wounded man in what she hoped was a reassuring way.

'Come along now, sir. We'll have you inside in a jiffy.'

The driver helped carry the wounded man in through the door, where a makeshift emergency area had been set up. Cecilia and Sister Scott were assessing the wounded people who streamed through the door. They sutured, swabbed and bandaged the minor cuts and abrasions, gave tetanus injections and checked for fractures. The more serious cases were directed through to the doctors, who were operating among the dust and debris of the damaged hospital.

'Poppy, what are you doing back here?' Cecilia said, astonished. 'I told you . . . Oh, never mind. We're out of sterile swabs. For goodness sake, can you find some? Also antiseptic . . . Now sir, let me help you through to the surgical ward. We'll fix you up in no time at all.'

Poppy didn't wait for her mother to change her mind. She ran through the wide corridors of the hospital, which were now crowded with patients sitting, lying and moaning on the floor. Nurses bustled among the wounded, washing wounds, dressing burns with sterile bandages and dispensing morphia for pain.

In the first ward, the store cupboard was destroyed, the precious medical supplies smashed on the floor. Poppy ran to the next ward, where she found a supply of swabs, surgical tools and bottles of antiseptic solution. She found a doctor's jacket hanging on a hook and filled it with anything she thought might be useful.

'What's happening, miss?' asked a voice from under a bed, inside a fortress of mattresses. 'Has the bombing stopped? Can I come out now?'

'Yes, sir, the bombing has stopped for now, but they might come back — you'd better stay where you are for a while,' Poppy suggested. Hoisting her sack of supplies over her shoulder, she ran back to her mother's station.

Cecilia was swabbing a man with a jagged, bloody gash down his arm.

'Good girl — can you lay them out on the trolley for me, please?'

Poppy rushed to obey. She had seen her mother do it for her father many times, the instruments, swabs, bandages and bottles laid out in precise rows.

'Sister Trehearne, do you have any sterile instruments over there?' called Sister Scott. 'I'm all out.' She held a bloody pair of tweezers that she had been using to pick shrapnel from a man's face.

Cecilia thrust a bucket of bloody instruments towards Poppy. 'Darling, can you go to the kitchen and scrub these, then boil them up to sterilise them? The sterilising unit was damaged during the bombing. Remember to boil them for at least ten minutes — it's really important.'

'Sure, Mama,' Poppy said, eagerly taking the bucket and darting once more among the bodies of the wounded.

Bewildered men called out as she passed, begging for pain relief or a drink or simply a word of acknowledgement. She smiled and said hello but kept running.

She recognised a patient who had been bedridden this morning. He was mopping the floor of the hallway. Other patients worked to help those who were worse off. Near the kitchens she had to jump over a pile of rubble. *Dad will be distraught*, thought Poppy. *The beautiful new hospital has only been open for seventeen days, and now it's been devastated.*

Coming towards Poppy from the other direction was a handcart piled high with bodies, pushed by two men. Most of them were black with burns. The stench of burnt flesh and fuel filled the corridor.

Poppy averted her eyes and tried not to breathe, her stomach heaving.

'Sorry, miss — excuse us, miss,' apologised one of the men.

Focus, Poppy told herself, fighting back the nausea. *I have to sterilise these instruments so the nurses can keep doing their work.*

In the kitchens she found two more patients who were boiling saucepans of water on primus stoves that they had commandeered from somewhere.

'Hello, love,' one of the men greeted her. 'Need a hand there?'

Together they scrubbed the blood from the equipment and boiled it for ten minutes. Poppy loaded the hot instruments into a sterile container and raced back the way she had come.

The emergency clearing room was more crowded than ever.

The door burst open and two men struggled in, carrying a stretcher. The body on the stretcher, black with oil, writhed in agony.

'We've got another truckload of wounded from the harbour,' the lead stretcher bearer told Cecilia. 'Many of them are badly burnt, but they're lucky to be alive.'

'Okay, put him here,' ordered Cecilia. 'How many do you have?'

Cecilia took the wounded man's pulse and examined his body, checking the extent of the burns.

'We got thirty-odd in this load but there're hundreds of them coming in. Hundreds been killed, too. The town's destroyed. The post office took a direct hit, too, and ten of the workers were killed in the slit trench.'

'The workers?' asked Cecilia, stopping for a moment. 'Do you know who?'

The stretcher bearer rubbed his forehead, which was smeared with oil and dirt.

'Six women. The whole Bald family. The Mullens sisters. Mrs Young and Freda Stasinowsky. Their bodies have just been brought to the hospital morgue.'

Poppy reeled in shock. *The whole Bald family?* she thought in horror. *Gorgeous Iris — Phoebe and Edward's friend? And her mother and father? How could that lovely, vibrant girl be dead?* She thought back to the last time she'd seen Iris just a few days ago when she'd told Poppy that the Administrator had once again urged the women to leave their jobs and escape south.

Cecilia swallowed but completed her examination of the patient. 'I'm so sorry to hear that,' she said. 'All right. This man needs to go through to the surgical ward now. Poppy, can you please show these men where to go? Then perhaps you could check the operating theatre — they might need help topping up supplies.'

Poppy ran from emergency station to ward to operating theatre to kitchens, fetching supplies, directing stretcher bearers, sterilising instruments. The doctors and nurses, volunteers and orderlies worked tirelessly as patients poured in from the harbour, the town and the bases with wounds ranging from gunshots, burns, lacerations, broken bones and blindness.

In the kitchens, two of the patients made hot drinks and food on the primus stoves for the patients and staff.

Around midday, the air-raid sirens sounded again, heralding the return of the Japanese bombers. This time the target seemed to be further south near the RAAF airfields.

Once again, Poppy and her parents took shelter down under the cliffs of Kahlin Bay, together with the mobile patients. The hot sun beat upon their heads, blistering in its intensity. Poppy's throat was parched with thirst. She couldn't remember the last time she had had a drink. They huddled together at the base of the cliffs for over an hour, which stretched out like an eternity.

As soon as the all-clear finally sounded, it was back to the operating stations.

14

The Aftermath

'This is not good, love,' one of the orderlies told Poppy. 'They say this is the softening up by air before a land invasion. The Nips have wiped out all our defences and most of the planes were destroyed at the air-fields. They say they'll be landing tomorrow and we'll be outnumbered twenty to one. I, for one, am heading south before they get here.'

Poppy's gut twisted in fear. It couldn't be true.

As Poppy delivered another container of sterilised instruments to her mother, Mark dashed in.

'Cecilia, Poppy – there's an evacuee train leaving Darwin this evening,' Mark announced. 'All women and children are to be on it. I want you to go home, get your bags and get on that train.'

Cecilia looked around helplessly at the room crowded with wounded men.

'But –'

'No "buts", Cecilia,' Mark insisted.

One of the soldiers took Mark by the arm. 'Sorry, Doctor — the evacuee train left half an hour ago. It was jam-packed to the gunnels. Apparently they had to fire warning shots above the crowd to stop them from trying to stampede onto it. People are absolutely panicking with the rumours that the Japanese will be invading before dawn.'

Mark wiped his brow wearily.

'Doctor, we have another truckload of wounded coming in.'

He smiled at Cecilia and Poppy. Cecilia smiled back.

'You know we can't leave all these patients to look after themselves, can we, Poppy?' Cecilia said.

Poppy smiled too, feeling a wave of pride surge through her. She was part of a team — a motley collection of medical professionals and volunteers who had suffered through a terrifying ordeal but were still achieving amazing things.

'Of course we can't, Mum.'

'Well then, Poppet, you can come and give me a hand in the operating theatre,' Mark suggested. 'Our emergency lamps have died; you can hold up a torch for me so I can see what I'm doing.'

A sister helped her scrub up and she followed her father into the theatre. She had to focus her torch on where the surgeons needed the light, trying not to think that the area she was illuminating was someone's abdomen that had been ripped open by a bomb, or a stump that had once been a leg or an arm.

At five o'clock, the patients in the kitchen came to beg Cecilia, Poppy and some of the other nurses to take a short break to drink hot tea and eat something. Poppy realised she had had nothing to eat since that peaceful breakfast on the verandah nine hours ago. Cecilia sent Poppy on ahead while she finished bandaging up a policeman with shrapnel lacerations.

Poppy collapsed into a chair in the nurses' dining room and closed her eyes. Now that she had stopped moving, her left arm stung painfully, her head ached and every muscle in her body hurt. She opened her eyes gingerly. Then she noticed today's newspaper lying on the table: *The Army News*, Darwin, Thursday, February 19, 1942.

A sentence leapt out at her from the front page — a quote from one of the military experts:

'Australia is safe from immediate attack.'

You must be joking, thought Poppy, remembering the events of the day: two air raids, hundreds killed and hundreds more injured, ships sunk, buildings shattered, planes destroyed. *Explain that we're safe to Iris, to Mrs Bald, to Jean and Eileen Mullen, to Emily Young and Freda Stasinowsky, to everyone else who was injured or killed.*

Tears filled Poppy's eyes; she wiped them away angrily and picked up the newspaper. Prime Minister John Curtin was quoted on the front page:

'Just as Dunkirk opened the Battle for Britain, Singapore opened the Battle for Australia.

'On its issue, depended, not merely the fate of the Commonwealth but in a very large measure the fate of the English-speaking world . . . Protecting this country is no longer a question of contributing to the world war but resisting an enemy which threatened to invade our own shore.

'Our honeymoon has finished. It is now work or fight as we have never worked or fought before.'

Poppy sat up straighter, filled with resolution. *Well, that is exactly what we have been doing*, she thought. *Working and fighting as we have never worked or fought before. We* can *turn the tide*.

Mark came in and sat down beside her, smiling wearily. A volunteer patient brought them both a cup of hot, strong tea. Poppy stirred in a spoonful of sugar and sipped appreciatively. Its warmth flooded her with a sense of comfort.

'How are you holding up, Poppet?' asked Mark, stirring his tea.

'I'm okay,' Poppy replied. 'I'm exhausted, but I feel really good. I feel like I've helped to do something really worthwhile today.'

'I'm so proud of you, Poppet. You've done an absolutely sterling job.'

Just then Cecilia came in, looking pale and drawn. She hobbled a little and winced as she lowered herself into the chair.

'I'd kill for a cup of tea,' murmured Cecilia, closing her eyes and sighing.

Mark frowned. 'Are you all right, darling?'

'Tired and feeling a little knocked around,' Cecilia admitted, opening her eyes and trying to smile. 'I feel a bit bruised from where I fell during one of the explosions, and it's a hard to breathe when I walk.'

'You didn't tell me you were injured,' Mark said, concerned. 'Let me take a look at you. Where does it hurt?'

'My left side and left elbow — I'm sure it's nothing much,' Cecilia insisted, but she winced severely as Mark probed her injured ribs. He took his stethoscope from around his neck and listened to her chest.

'Breathe in slowly,' he ordered. 'Breathe out.'

He frowned and then probed her elbow gently with his long, slim fingers. Cecilia gasped in pain and jerked away.

'I can't be sure without an X-ray, but I suspect you have two fractured ribs and a fractured elbow. Poppy, can you run and get your mum a cup of tea and some hot soup? Make sure you have some as well. I'll go and fetch some bandages and something to take for the pain.'

'I took some aspirin an hour or so ago,' Cecilia said.

'I'll find you something stronger.'

'No — I don't want anything stronger or I won't be able to focus on what needs to be done.'

Mark stood up and smiled. 'What *needs* to be done is for you to rest and drink some tea,' he advised. 'We've got some extra nurses now, who have come over from the Army hospital at Berrimah to help, so we need to look after you.'

Mark returned in a few moments and took Cecilia aside to strap up her ribs and immobilise her arm in a sling. He then made her sit beside Poppy to rest and sip some soup.

'It sounds like most of Darwin is being evacuated, except for men fit for military service,' Mark explained. 'There are rumours the Japanese might arrive at any time, and we are being told to prepare to evacuate the hospital before dawn, even though many of these men are barely out of the operating theatre.'

Poppy rubbed the grit out of her eyes, trying to concentrate on what her father was saying.

'They want us to move the patients to the Army hospital, which is already completely full, or evacuate the worst cases on the hospital ship *Manunda* tomorrow. But the nurses said the army hospital was bombed multiple times today as well, and the *Manunda* was bombed twice and has been severely damaged. I want to get you two out of Darwin as soon as possible.'

'Do you mean the Japanese intentionally bombed both hospitals and the hospital ship?' asked Cecilia.

'Perhaps they didn't see the huge red crosses painted on our white roof,' Mark replied dryly.

Poppy thought of the Japanese pilot who had tried to machine-gun them down outside the hospital. He must have known they were nurses and wounded patients. She picked up her pearl pendant and twisted it in her fingers.

'I think the best plan is for you both to get on the next evacuee train if you can or, if not, go south by road to Adelaide River. It's only seventy-odd miles away,' Mark continued. 'There, you can get on a train south. I wish I could take you, but there are so many wounded and dying men, I have to stay and help them.'

'But, Mark, I can —' began Cecilia.

'Cecilia, I know you want to nurse them, too, but now your responsibility is to get Poppy to safety, and look after Daisy and Charlie. I want you to go home, get them both, fetch your bags and head south. It might be a good idea to take my old rifle.'

Cecilia took a deep breath. 'All right, Poppy. Let's go.'

'One more thing,' Mark said, in a gentler tone. 'Apparently, Myilly Point has been badly damaged during the

159

raids. Many of the houses have been destroyed. I don't know what you'll find at home.'

Poppy caught her breath in pain when she stood — her whole body ached and throbbed. Cecilia and Poppy said their farewells to nurses, orderlies and doctors, both feeling that they were abandoning their colleagues. But the tension in the air was palpable. Everyone was sure it would only be a matter of hours before the Japanese would attack again.

Mark walked them to the entrance of the hospital and hugged them both close.

'Take care,' he begged. 'Leave as soon as you can, and try to send me word. I'll feel better when I know you're safe.'

He whispered an aside to Poppy as he kissed her. 'Poppet, look after your mother. I'm worried about her. Be brave. I love you.'

Together, Cecilia and Poppy hobbled outside into the early evening light. To the west, the harbour was a disaster. Misshapen hulls, still smoking, were partially submerged. Wreckage and vast oil slicks floated on the water. Down on the beach, men were still working to retrieve the bodies washing up on the shore. The gardens around the hospital were decimated with fallen building rubble, wide bomb craters, twisted metal and collapsed walls.

On the short walk back to their house on Myilly Point, they passed several homes that had been destroyed, the water tanks blown onto their sides. In other homes, whose owners had been evacuated, shipwrecked sailors had swum ashore and made temporary camps.

At first glance, their own home appeared intact. Honey sprinted out from under the house and jumped up, her tail wagging madly as she whimpered. Poppy scooped Honey into her arms and wept for joy to find her alive. Honey wriggled out of her arms and ran into the garden, stopping and turning, whining, as though begging Poppy to follow. Poppy walked along the path after Honey, who bolted off towards the slit trench in the garden, pausing repeatedly to urge Poppy along.

Poppy had a terrible sense of foreboding. 'Mum! *Mum!*' she called, her voice rising in panic.

Cecilia came running, and together they walked to the slit trench. Honey jumped down into the hole, whimpering. At the bottom, curled up together, were Daisy and Charlie. At first, Poppy thought they were asleep, with Daisy huddled protectively over her baby. Her once-starched, white apron, now soaked with blood, was tucked around him.

'Daisy!' shrieked Cecilia, her voice filled with panic. 'Charlie!'

There was no answer.

'Don't look,' Cecilia cried, pushing Poppy away. 'Stay back, Poppy. I don't want you to come any closer.' Cecilia dropped into the trench to check the bodies for any sign of life. 'Poppy, fetch me some blankets, please, darling.'

'Are they all right?' Poppy begged, crouching down on the ground, her fingers clutched around her pearl.

'No,' sobbed Cecilia. 'I'm afraid not. They've been shot by a machine-gun.'

'*No. No,*' Poppy screamed. 'Daisy. Charlie.'

Cecilia climbed out and hugged her daughter for many long minutes, both of them sobbing. Poppy felt the grief and panic well up, seizing her throat so that it was so tight she could hardly breathe. She clung tightly to her mother, shutting her eyes against the terrible sight of the open trench and those limp, lifeless bodies.

'I can't breathe,' Poppy panted, struggling for tiny gasps of air. 'I can't breathe.'

Cecilia rubbed her back soothingly. 'You *can* breathe, darling,' she assured her. 'Just concentrate on breathing and nothing else.'

Gradually, her chest loosened up and there were no more tears to cry.

'Come on, Poppy,' urged Cecilia at last, gently mopping Poppy's face with her handkerchief. 'I want to bury them here. I don't want them to go in the mass grave with everyone else at Kahlin Beach.'

Together they fetched some blankets, which Cecilia wrapped around the bodies, Charlie still clutched tightly in his mother's arms. Poppy ran to Daisy's room to find some little treasure she could bury with them. The room, next to the storerooms and kitchens, was simple and bare, a dark-grey blanket pulled up neatly over the bed.

On the chest was a teddy bear that Poppy had given Charlie for his birthday. She took that and carefully laid it in the grave.

Cecilia and Poppy worked hard to fill in the trench with soil from the surrounding embankment. Poppy's mind was filled with visions of Daisy laughing, telling stories of her life on Never-Never Downs; Charlie giggling and holding up his arms for a cuddle; Daisy cooking and baking her favourite lemon cake; Charlie cuddling Coco the cat or chasing Christabel. They were both far too young to die like this.

When the trench was filled with soil, Poppy went over

to the sprawling frangipani tree and gathered a pile of creamy blossoms, which she laid carefully on the grave. Cecilia and Poppy stood together for a moment and said the Lord's Prayer.

'Peace be with them,' Cecilia concluded, drying her eyes on her handkerchief. 'Now, Poppy, it's time for us to go. I promised your father we'd go south as soon as we could. We'll load up the car and drive into town to see what's the best way for us to leave. It'll be sunset soon, so we need to hurry. We need food, water, blankets, toiletries and some essential clothes.'

Poppy trudged to her room in a daze, Honey following at her heels. She felt like a limp rag doll, all feeling and grief wrung out of her. *How could such a terrible thing happen? Why did Daisy and Charlie have to die in such a horrific way? What if the raid had happened half an hour earlier? I would have been at home with Daisy and Charlie, and I would have been sheltering in that trench. I would be dead now, too . . .*

Honey licked her hand and whined mournfully, gazing up at her with sad brown eyes. Poppy hugged Honey, then pulled herself together and set to work.

Her bag had been packed for days. All she needed to grab were her pyjamas and toiletries. She took one last, slow look around her room: the two beds neatly made, the books stacked away on the shelf, the knick-knacks on top of the chest of drawers and Bryony's left-behind cosmetics laid out on the dressing table. She breathed deeply and closed the door.

She knew they were in a hurry but she couldn't help but run into each room to say goodbye, trying to memorise her home.

'Goodbye, Hippocrates,' she whispered to the skeleton in her father's study. 'Goodbye, two-headed calf.'

'*Poppy*,' her mother called from the back of the house. 'What are you doing?'

With shaking hands, Cecilia carefully locked the back door after them.

'Goodbye, Basil,' Poppy whispered to the golden-green coil of snake in the rafters. 'Go and take shelter in the garden. It might be safer.'

Poppy loaded the two bags and blankets into the car boot with her father's rifle, while Cecilia went to the kitchen to pack food and water. Poppy made a nest for Honey on the floor of the back seat.

'Come on, girl,' she urged. 'In you hop.' Poppy covered Honey with a blanket. 'Stay there, girl, and don't make a peep. It's better if no one knows you're there.' Honey thumped her tail and curled up in a ball to sleep.

Poppy prowled around the house, calling out to Christabel and Coco. There was no sign of them. At last, Poppy gave up, guessing they might have been frightened away by the explosions.

In the kitchen, there were signs of interrupted preparations. A cup of cold, half-drunk tea sat on the kitchen table, beside a bowl full of flour and shredded coconut. A saucepan was knocked over onto the floor, its contents of sticky golden syrup spilled in a puddle. Ants swarmed around the puddle, feasting.

The two turtles, Tabitha and Tobias, swam around the fish tank on the sideboard. Poppy lifted the tank and carried it down to the end of the garden where the ground was low and boggy.

'Goodbye, Tabitha. Goodbye, Tobias. Enjoy your freedom.'

Next were the two possums in the fruit box in the storeroom. Poppy carried them out to the mango tree and climbed, setting them carefully on a broad branch. The two possums blinked, round-eyed in the evening light, then scampered away.

'Goodbye, Jessica. Goodbye, Clarissa. Stay away from Basil, or he might eat you.'

'*Poppy!*'

Cecilia had collected a pile of food supplies — tins of ham and baked beans, a tin-opener, two water bottles, a canister of tea, a loaf of bread and some biscuits, which were packed in a wooden box.

'It's time to go, darling,' Cecilia reminded her.

Poppy reached around her neck to twist the pearl that always hung there. But it was gone.

'Mum, I've lost my pearl!' Poppy cried. She dropped to her hands and knees and searched the floor frantically.

'Poppy, we have to go,' Cecilia reiterated. Poppy raced to the storeroom where she had just been to fetch the possums. There was no sign of the pendant.

Cecilia hugged Poppy to her chest. 'Darling, it could be anywhere. You might have dropped it in a million places at the hospital, on the beach, under the cliffs. When did you last have it?'

'I can't remember,' Poppy confessed. 'Maybe . . . I definitely had it at breakfast on the verandah.'

'Poppy, we have to go.'

15

Escape

Poppy stared out the window as they drove through Darwin. The town was shattered and eerily quiet. Rubble, masonry and twisted iron roofing littered the streets. Cecilia drove down the Esplanade, past the Hotel Darwin to Government House. Every building seemed to be damaged.

An army truck was parked outside the Administrator's residence. Two men carried boxes out of the house, past the armed guards, and loaded them carefully onto the back of the truck.

'Mum, that's Bryony's friend, George,' Poppy called. 'He might be able to tell us the best thing to do.'

Cecilia pulled over and Poppy jumped out of the car. George looked nervous.

'Hello, George,' greeted Poppy.

'Oh, um, Poppy, Mrs Trehearne,' George stammered uncomfortably, taking off his hat. 'What are you still doing here? The last women and children were meant to leave by train this afternoon.'

'We've been working at the hospital with Dad, dealing with the wounded,' Poppy replied. 'There're lots of nurses still there. What are you doing here?'

George shifted and glanced over his shoulder to where his companion had gone back inside the residence.

'We are evacuating the Administrator's wine cellar,' George confessed.

'His *wine cellar*?' demanded Poppy. A wave of anger surged through her belly and threatened to erupt. Poppy thought of Daisy and Charlie, of Iris and her parents, of all the hundreds of people who were injured and dying or already dead — and the head of the administration was worrying about his wine cellar.

'Yes — plus all the glassware and silver . . .' George continued.

Poppy glared into the back of the truck. There were dozens of boxes of wine and liquor, plus crates stuffed with crockery, glasses and silverware. Poppy could identify the regal crest on some of the teacups.

'But we have hundreds of wounded men at the hospital who need treatment and help. Surely you should be evacuating *them* before the teacups?' Poppy insisted, her face flushing in her weariness and anger.

'I'm under orders from the Administrator himself,' George said defensively. 'He's pulled several of the police officers off duty to make sure it's done as soon as possible. He's concerned about looting — apparently some of the soldiers helped themselves to food from the Administrator's kitchen this afternoon.'

'Well, shouldn't the policemen be on duty stopping the looting, not acting as removalists?' demanded Poppy, tossing her head. She stamped her foot in frustration.

Cecilia opened the car door, wincing as she climbed out, and shuffled to join them. Cecilia put her hand on her daughter's shoulder to calm her. Poppy bit her lip.

'George, we need to leave Darwin as soon as possible,' Cecilia confided. 'Do you know when the next train leaves or where we can get petrol?'

George scratched his head. 'There's another train due to leave at nine o'clock tonight, but there have been riots down at the railway station. The provosts have been firing over people's heads, trying to deter able-bodied men from stealing places on the train. The advice has been completely contradictory, so who knows what's going on? There's no petrol to be had for civilians without written permission from the Administrator — and he isn't giving that to anyone.

'People have been fleeing south by bicycle, car, foot, horseback — even the sanitary truck,' George continued. 'If I were you, I'd try to fight my way onto that train, though I did hear there was an unexploded bomb on the train line, or just head south however you can.'

Cecilia grimaced in pain, holding her hand over her broken ribs. 'Thank you, George. We appreciate your help. Come on, Poppy.'

Cecilia drove south-east to the railway station at Parap. Crowds of men were huddling around the station, pushing and shoving, begging for a place on the train. A military policeman screamed at Cecilia, pointing his gun at the car.

'Turn off those danged lights before I shoot 'em out. Don't youse know the bleedin' Japs are comin' back?'

Cecilia hurriedly extinguished the headlights and pulled over to assess the situation, leaving the engine running.

'Git back all youse bleedin' low-lives before I lose my dang patience!' shouted the provost, firing his gun over the heads of the shoving crowd. They immediately stopped and retreated, before surging forward again. ''Ow many times do I 'ave to tell youse? The dang train's full!'

'Let us on, sah,' begged a Chinese cook. 'We are civilians — we must get out before the Japanese land. They'll massacre us all.'

'Well, walk, ya yellow-livered scumbags. Youse're not getting on this train!'

The provost let off another round of gunshots. The crowd scattered, with several men running towards the Trehearnes' car, pointing and shouting, demanding a lift.

'Lock your door, Poppy,' called Cecilia, accelerating rapidly and grinding through the gears. The car lurched forward and Cecilia drove back towards town, leaving the unruly crowd behind.

'What shall we do?' asked Cecilia, her voice rising in panic. 'We don't have enough petrol to drive to Adelaide River. That provost is drunk and I don't fancy trying to fight our way onto the train through that crowd.'

Poppy thought carefully, considering their options. *We could wait until morning and try to get on our planned flight, but that might be too late, and for all we know our plane was destroyed today like most of the others. We could head back to the hospital and see what arrangements are being made for the patients — but then when Singapore fell, injured soldiers were left behind to be captured and killed by the Japanese because the civilians had refused to evacuate in time. No — we have to get out of Darwin ourselves.*

'We could harness up Angel and drive down in the cart?' suggested Poppy. 'We could drive for an hour or two, then camp in the bush. We'd be in Adelaide River by tomorrow afternoon.'

Cecilia closed her eyes, then accelerated, smiling at Poppy. 'All right, let's go home and start again.'

Back at Myilly Point, Angel was harnessed to the cart and all the luggage was transferred, as well as Honey and a couple of camping swags. They headed around the outskirts of town and onto the main road going south, bypassing the gun-toting provosts and the noisy crowd at Parap. Cecilia drove, drooping with exhaustion and pain.

Two hours later, they pulled off into the bush.

'We'll just sleep for a few hours and be off before dawn,' Cecilia promised. Angel was tied up to a tree on a long rein so she could crop the wispy grass. Cecilia and Poppy wrapped themselves in their swags and a blanket, side by side, to make a rough bed on the hard, packed earth. Honey crawled in to sleep with Poppy, giving her immense comfort after this unbelievably impossible day.

Poppy had no sooner closed her eyes when she was awoken by Cecilia in the grey half-light before dawn. Cecilia glanced nervously towards the north. Memories of yesterday flooded back: the bombs, the operations, the deaths. Poppy shut them out — she didn't want to think about Daisy or Charlie or Iris or anyone else. She just wanted to focus on surviving.

'We should get going,' Cecilia hissed. 'I don't think it's

safe to light a fire or cook breakfast. Let's just get going and we can eat on the way.'

It only took a few moments to roll up the swags and blankets and throw them onto the cart. Poppy felt disgusting in the dirty clothes she had worn since yesterday morning.

Angel was untied and they were on their way.

The dirt road south was strewn with detritus, relics of a panicked populace in full flight: a bicycle with two flat tyres, a truck run out of fuel, a bag fallen from a roof, a pile of outhouse pans that had fallen off the sanitary truck on a sharp corner, a camp of soldiers sleeping on the side of the road.

This teeth-juddering, bone-shuddering corrugated road was the only overland access to Darwin, meandering for over three thousand kilometres south. During the wet season, much of it was impassable, boggy mud, while in the dry season it was composed of vast drifts of bulldust, potholes and wickedly sharp rocks. The train line was not much better and finished in the middle of nowhere, just over five hundred kilometres south.

After another hour of plodding along, Cecilia handed the reins to Poppy.

'I'm sorry, darling,' Cecilia said. 'Do you think you can drive for a while? This rutted road is jarring my ribs and my elbow – I'm in agony. I might feel better if I lie down for a while.'

Poppy took over and Cecilia burrowed in her medical kit, searching for aspirin. She lay down on her uninjured side on top of the swags and bags, breathing deeply, trying to still the pain. She eventually dropped into an uneasy sleep. Honey snuggled into Poppy's side on the driver's seat, snuffling about at all the unknown smells and sights.

The endless grey-green brush stretched out on either side of the track for hundreds of kilometres, relentless in its sameness. Angel plodded on, hour after hour. The sun rose higher and higher in the sky, beating down on their necks and heads. Honey lay down and slept, snoring softly in the heat.

The kilometres juddered by, one after the other. Poppy could feel her skin burning and her head aching under her straw hat. She swigged water from the water bottle and offered some to Honey in the palm of her hand. Cecilia woke and made them a meal of cold baked beans on stale bread. The day passed in a blur, but Poppy felt safer the further they drove from Darwin. Sometimes they were passed by army trucks or cars or bicycles — even a garbage truck — all heading south, billowing up a cloud of dust on the unsealed road.

It was evening when they finally pulled into Adelaide River. The tiny township was chaotic, with not enough food or water for all the evacuees who had arrived over the last day. The soldiers had little direction and were trying to decide what to do with all these people. Cecilia and Poppy at least had food and could make a welcome cup of tea over a campfire, but there was no water for washing. They camped another night, sleeping on the ground. The next morning they tethered Angel and the cart out the front of the railway station and went inside to enquire about trains going south.

Two soldiers were letting on the wounded and older

men, but turning back a horde of young, fit men, who could be enlisted in the army.

'Let the ladies through,' an old Greek man called out when he saw Cecilia, Poppy and Honey. 'Ladies coming through.'

The men stepped aside to let them pass, tipping their hats.

'There's a train leaving in an hour,' explained the soldier. 'You can get on it, but you won't be able to take your dog, I'm afraid. Our orders are clear: no domestic pets are to be evacuated. You should have destroyed her before you left Darwin.'

'Please,' begged Poppy, her throat closing over in panic. 'Please — I can't leave her behind.'

'Please let her on, sir,' added Cecilia, her hand on Poppy's shoulder. 'The dog won't be any trouble. My daughter's been through so much.'

Honey seemed to sense that her life was in the balance, and she looked up at the soldiers with liquid, golden eyes. Honey leapt up on her back legs and twirled around, performing a perfect pirouette. The two soldiers laughed.

'Isn't she a treat?' asked the other soldier.

'I can't let dogs on the train,' reiterated the first soldier firmly. Then he winked. 'But what I don't know won't hurt me, will it?'

Poppy smiled and bent to pat Honey and hide her tears.

'We'll go and get our bags,' said Cecilia, 'and thank you, sir. You're very kind. By the way, we have a horse and cart. Have you any ideas what we can do with her?'

The soldier pointed across the road to a paddock. 'We have a good collection already across the road,' he explained. 'Put her in there with the other horses and we'll look after her. Park the cart over there and leave the harness in the back. We'll find a use for it. Take care, ladies, and have a good trip.'

Angel was unharnessed and set free in the paddock. Poppy rubbed her nose affectionately and hugged her neck. 'Goodbye, Angel. Thank you for bringing us here safely.' Angel harrumphed, then gladly wandered off to graze with the other horses.

Poppy unpacked most of her bag to make room for Honey, then closed her safely inside, leaving a small gap for air. 'Good girl, Honey. Now stay quiet.' She wrapped the remaining clothes in a blanket.

Cecilia and Poppy made their way onto the train, carrying their belongings. Until yesterday, the trucks had been used to carry cattle to the meatworks in Darwin and, despite being roughly swept out, they still stank of urine and cow manure. They found a corner of the truck to spread out a blanket and make a camp on the filthy floor, where they huddled together. Poppy was too frightened to let Honey out of the bag until the train clanked its way out of the station and they were safely heading south.

The three-thousand kilometre journey from Darwin to Adelaide was to take them a week. It took the whole day just to chug south to the end of the railway line at Larrimah, then they disembarked and joined a convoy of army trucks to take them the next thousand-odd kilometres of rough, unsealed roads to Alice Springs. At least they had a rough bench seat and a canvas canopy to shelter them for the three-day journey. At night, they camped in the bush on the side of the road.

The red dust billowed up and sifted into everything — eyes, nose, mouth, bags, underwear. Poppy's hair was stiff with dirt. Once along the route, the drivers stopped so they could all splash in the creek to rinse off, but within half an hour of driving they were all as dirty as before.

The soldiers on the convoy were kind and tried to make the journey less tedious — singing songs, playing the mouth organ, telling jokes, organising card games and encouraging Honey to do tricks in exchange for titbits. Many of them were wounded and Cecilia busied herself tending to their injuries.

Poppy just felt numb, like something had died inside her. She wondered if she would ever feel happy again — if she could ever feel truly alive again. The tears brimmed just below the surface, threatening to spill over. Cecilia held her close with her good arm.

At Alice Springs they were billeted at the showground until they could get on a train to Adelaide. It was a slow, painful trip. The constant jolting and hard, wooden benches were agony for Cecilia's fractured ribs. At night they could hear dingoes howling in the desert. There was nothing to see but bleak, vast desert. There was nothing to do but worry about Mark and Edward, Bryony and Phoebe, Maude and Jack, and if they would ever see any of them again.

At last, in Adelaide, Cecilia rented a room and they had a long, hot bath to soak the stench and ingrained dust from their skins. They slept in a real bed for the first time in over a week. Poppy felt the cold, hard stone of fear and grief in the pit of her stomach start to soften. The respite was short-lived — they were soon on a train again for another journey of more than two thousand kilometres from Adelaide to Sydney, via Melbourne.

⟨❦⟩

On the softer upholstered seats of the overnight train to Sydney, Cecilia finally seemed to relax, no longer braced against the endless jolting, so painful to her fractured ribs. She began to reminisce, sharing stories from Poppy's child-hood, then she moved on to stories of her own childhood, growing up on the south-west coast of Cornwall, near Penwith.

As Cecilia told her stories, Poppy felt herself gradually unwind, the fear abating.

'Did you know that your great-grandmother, Tamsyn Tredennick, was a Pellar?' asked Cecilia. 'A healer or, as some folk thought, a white witch?'

Poppy was intrigued and sat forward, her green eyes bright with interest.

'A white witch? I know you always said we come from a long line of Cornish healers, but you've never mentioned witchery before!'

Cecilia smiled and stroked Poppy's hair. 'In Cornwall, Pellars were the village wise women,' she explained. 'It was a hereditary occupation, passed down from mother to daughter for centuries. The Pellars would cure illnesses and infertility, heal people and cattle, deliver babies and set broken bones.'

Cecilia gestured to her own fractured elbow nestled in its sling.

'They were very powerful women,' continued Cecilia. 'People would make long and difficult journeys to consult the Pellars in our family. However, they were not only healers. They had a reputation for foresight and making divinations, seeing what the future would bring.'

Poppy immediately thought of waking to her mother's screams, of the nightmares of Edward being injured when Singapore fell. *Does Mum have the power of second sight?*

'The Pellars were also believed to have the power to make curses and to lift ill-wishing,' Cecilia told her. 'One of the skills each daughter learnt from her mother was the skill to make charms. The Pellars would sell small charm bags containing magic powders and written charms. Villagers believed the Pellars had the power to reverse bad luck and even find lost items.'

Poppy laughed. 'Now that *would* come in handy!' she joked. 'Did the charms work? I mean, could your grandmother Tamsyn really do magic? Was she really a witch? And if she was a witch, what about you? Did you learn, too?'

Cecilia closed her eyes in concentration. 'Turn thee into a frog,' she thundered, shooting her finger out at Poppy dramatically. She peered at her daughter, her green eyes sparkling with mischief. 'No? Well, I guess my cursing techniques are a bit rusty!'

Poppy giggled, pushing her mother's curse finger away.

'The Pellar power had a lot to do with the magic of suggestion,' Cecilia explained. 'It's a little like the way an Aboriginal is said to fade away and die if a medicine man points a bone at him. The mind is so powerful that if people truly believe something, it often comes true. I think my grandmother's charms often worked the same way.'

Cecilia gave Poppy a hug and said, 'My grandmother did pass her knowledge on to my mother, but by late last century, people no longer believed in witches and curses in quite the same way. My mama was the village midwife and healer, but by the time I was growing up, science had taken sway. My mother taught me all she knew, but to work as a healer I had to train as a nurse at Penzance, just like Phoebe is doing now in Sydney.'

Poppy gazed out the window at the rolling farmland of New South Wales whizzing past.

'I just want to say how proud I am of the way you worked in the hospital in Darwin during the bombing,' Cecilia said, her eyes bright with emotion. 'You were brave, steady and calm. I think you would make a wonderful healer, too, if you want. The Pellar gifts flow in your veins.'

Poppy bent down to stroke Honey, who was asleep on the floor, to hide her discomfiture.

'What about the second sight?' asked Poppy with a flash of mischief. 'Do you think we have the Pellar gift of foresight?'

Cecilia frowned, thinking. She ran her fingers through Poppy's curly hair. 'I believe I do have the gift of foresight sometimes,' she confessed.

'I knew it,' said Poppy. 'You felt something about Edward the night Singapore fell, didn't you?'

Cecilia paused, then nodded. She took Poppy's hand in her own.

'Let me foretell your future, my gorgeous girl,' Cecilia

offered, her finger gently tracing the lines on Poppy's palm.

Poppy leant forward, fascinated.

'Let me see,' began Cecilia. 'The war will be over soon. You will study and learn and work and grow up into a beautiful young woman with the world at your feet. You will fall in love with a handsome young man — dark, no . . . Let me see, fair.'

Poppy's heart pounded faster.

'You will marry him, and one day you will have beautiful, mischievous children full of life, like their mother. I'd like to say that you both live happily ever after, like in the fairytales, but of course life will throw happy times and sad times at you. But I know that you will face the hard times with toughness and courage, and you will revel in the happy times with joy and thanksgiving. You will have a good life.'

Cecilia kissed Poppy's palm and closed her fingers over the kiss. Poppy sighed, snatching her hand away. 'You didn't really see all that,' she complained. 'You just made it up.'

Cecilia laughed again. 'Well, with all my power as a mother, I wish you a charmed life! Now, I think we should get some sleep — it's still a long way to Sydney.'

Cecilia tucked a blanket around Poppy, then herself. Poppy fell asleep to the rhythmic *clickety-clack* of the train rumbling over the tracks, dreaming of a life full of love and joy.

16

Journey's End

In the gritty dawn light, the size of Sydney overwhelmed Poppy. Its suburbs seemed to stretch forever. It felt drab, dirty and crowded as the train crawled through the inner-city slums. Poppy's heart sank. Where was the beautiful Sydney that Maude had raved about? The golden buildings of sandstone, the stunning harbour and gorgeous beaches?

From Central Station, they changed trains to the north of the city, then lugged their bags down to Circular Quay. The streets were littered with rubbish, the paint of the buildings cracked and peeling. The final leg of the journey was by ferry to Manly, on the north side of the harbour.

At last, Poppy could see what Maude meant. She sat back, completely exhausted, soaking in the spectacular views of the sparkling blue harbour, the towering grey arch of the Harbour Bridge, the grand waterfront buildings, and then, as they moved away from the city, the picturesque islands, the soaring sandstone cliffs and the grey-green bushland.

Cecilia had sent a telegram from Melbourne so that, when the ferry pulled into the wharf at Manly, they were greeted by the welcome sight of Bryony, Phoebe and Maude waving madly from the jetty.

There were hugs, tears and laughter. Everyone helped carry the luggage as they walked up the steep Eastern Hill of Manly to Maude's Victorian terrace in Addison Road, high above the harbour.

A huge Moreton Bay fig stood out the front, with massive, spreading branches and tangled roots. The house itself was a substantial two-storey terrace, painted pale cream with a verandah across both levels, trimmed with white lace ironwork. The front garden was cobbled with mossy bricks and surrounded by box hedges. In the centre, a riot of dark-green foliage clung to a sandstone birdbath. Poppy could see a wisteria vine curling over an archway that led around the side of the house.

'Mrs Trehearne, Miss Poppy, welcome to my humble home,' said Maude proudly, waving them through the brick gateposts.

'It's beautiful, Maude,' Poppy replied, gazing up at the graceful old house.

Maude winked. 'I *told* you Manly was beautiful,' she teased.

Maude knocked on the ornate front door, using its wrought-iron knocker. Mrs Tibbets opened the door and ushered them in, exclaiming over their long journey and offering them tea and scones.

Mrs Tibbets boiled the kettle and they all sat down for what must have been the best cup of tea of Poppy's life. While the girls had chattered and laughed about trivialities all the way up the hill, now their thoughts turned to the calamitous events that had occurred since they had last seen each other.

'Tell us what happened in Darwin?' asked Phoebe. 'The newspapers told us nothing. The first reports said that there were hardly any casualties and minimal damage, but that's not what we've heard through gossip. They say the Government tried to cover up the true figures to avoid panic.'

Cecilia shifted in her seat to ease her aching back and ribs. 'I don't think anyone will ever know how many people died,' she replied, grim-faced. 'I heard some reports suggesting the death toll might be as high as a thousand people, but I think that's unlikely. Others estimated that it might have been about three hundred. I don't know, but it was terrible.'

Cecilia and Poppy took it in turns to describe that terrible day in Darwin. Poppy struggled to find the words to describe what it had really been like. The girls all wept together when they heard about Daisy, Charlie and Iris. However, when the story was done, Poppy felt better, as though she could now lay the whole horrible experience to rest and move on.

Then it was Phoebe's and Bryony's turn to share their news. Phoebe was still working hard at the hospital and studying at night for her exams. Bryony had successfully joined up with the Australian Women's Army Service by fibbing about her age and was studying stenography, typing and signals with women from all over Australia. She was now living in the barracks with the other new recruits.

While they shared their stories, Poppy took a good look at her sisters. She hadn't seen Phoebe for almost a year and was surprised at how much she'd changed. She was taller and thinner, more mature. Even Bryony had changed in a few, short weeks. They were no longer carefree girls — they were serious, responsible young women.

'Mrs Trehearne, Maude and I are so thrilled that you have come to stay with us,' said Mrs Tibbets. 'I want you to know that you are welcome to stay as long as you want. Harold will be stationed in Alice Springs for a while, so there's plenty of room. Maude and I will enjoy the company.'

'That is so kind of you, Mrs Tibbets, but I must insist that we pay you some housekeeping money and rent,' replied Cecilia.

'No,' said Mrs Tibbets firmly. 'You and Poppy were so kind to us in Darwin — I would be delighted to repay your hospitality.'

'Thank you, but we couldn't stay here without contributing,' Cecilia persevered. 'Otherwise, Poppy and I could stay in a hotel until we find a little flat.'

Maude flashed Poppy a look of deep alarm.

Mrs Tibbets gave in gracefully. 'Well, thank you. That would be a great help.'

Poppy and Maude exchanged a secret smile of relief.

❧

After taking a week to recuperate from their strenuous journey, Cecilia made an appointment for Poppy to meet the headmistress of Maude's school. On Tuesday, they dressed in their smartest clothes, perfectly pressed and starched, and made the journey by tram to Woodfield in North Sydney. Cecilia wore a navy suit, hat, gloves and stockings, despite the late-summer warmth. Poppy wore her white summer dress with short, sheer sleeves, white socks and black Mary Janes. A long, red, puckered scar ran down Poppy's forearm, an ugly reminder of her ordeal. She rubbed it self-consciously.

The school term had started weeks before and Poppy was acutely aware that she had only attended the tiny Darwin primary school until sixth class, where many of the children were barefoot and dressed in patched, hand-me-down clothes. The teachers had struggled to teach children from a vast range of ethnic backgrounds, many of whom settled their cultural differences with fist fights in the schoolyard. Then Poppy and Bryony had worked at home with a governess. Miss Grey had hated the steamy, hot climate and returned to civilisation after just a few months, leaving the girls' education somewhat neglected.

As the tram groaned up the steep hill away from the Spit towards Mosman, Poppy felt sick with nerves, her mind jumbled with thoughts. *What if the girls think I'm a country bumpkin? What if I'm so far behind the other girls and I have to repeat with the twelve-year-olds? What if they all think I'm stupid?*

'Do I look all right, Mum?' Poppy asked anxiously, fiddling with her white gloves.

Cecilia appraised her daughter, noting the carefully brushed curls, usually so unruly, the white Panama hat and spotless gloves. Poppy looked different. She looked more serious, a little thinner, somehow older than she had just a few weeks ago.

Cecilia stroked Poppy's forehead with her gloved hand. 'You look beautiful, darling. The other girls are going to love you.'

The school was housed in several gracious Federation houses, surrounded by playing fields. Poppy could see girls in navy gym tunics playing cricket on an oval, and another group playing tennis. They all seemed to be laughing and enjoying themselves, like the girls Poppy had read about in her English boarding school stories.

Poppy felt her stomach clench again with nerves as they waited outside the headmistress's office. A secretary eventually showed them in.

The office was panelled in dark wood and contained a huge oak desk and shelves crowded with books. Sunshine glowed through the stained-glass window. Gilt-framed oil paintings of former headmistresses gazed down at them from the walls. A red tabby cat lay sleeping on the window seat among the cushions.

A stern-looking, middle-aged woman sat behind a desk piled with neat towers of paper. She rose to greet them, holding out her hand. She was wearing a grey suit, with her steel-grey hair pulled back into a bun.

'Good morning, Mrs Trehearne. Good morning, Poppy. My name is Miss Edith Royston. Welcome to Woodfield.'

'Good morning, Miss Royston,' Cecilia replied, shaking hands. 'Thank you for seeing us.'

'Hello, Miss Royston,' added Poppy, also shaking hands.

'A nice, firm handshake,' Miss Royston noted with approval. 'If the girls don't have a good handshake, I usually send them to the back of the line to try again. I believe a firm handshake is a sign of a strong character.'

She examined Poppy closely. A smile lit up Miss Royston's somewhat stern face so that she no longer looked so forbidding.

'Your mother tells me that you have recently come from Darwin after the bombing raids, Poppy? It must have been rather frightening.'

Poppy thought back to her experiences. 'Yes, I suppose it was, Miss Royston,' she replied, 'but at the time we were so busy trying to help the patients at the hospital that we didn't have much time to think. We were all at the hospital when the Japanese planes arrived, and many of the men couldn't walk.'

Miss Royston nodded thoughtfully. 'We have made numerous preparations for air raids here, including digging slit trenches in the playground and building an air-raid shelter in the cellar,' she said. 'However, I would be interested to know if you have any suggestions, Poppy, having experienced Japanese air raids firsthand?'

Poppy thought back to that terrible day of death and destruction. She saw the image of Daisy and Charlie huddled in the trench, Daisy's white apron signalling to the Japanese where they were hiding.

'In Darwin, all the nurses were wearing white uniforms, which makes them more visible to the bombers,' Poppy explained. 'I noticed that all the girls here wear white shirts and white hats, so you might want to do something about that.'

Miss Royston frowned, pulling a piece of paper towards her and scribbling down a note. 'Good point. I'll make sure the girls are briefed to leave their hats behind if there is an alert, but to take their blazers to cover themselves up.'

Miss Royston asked Poppy a number of questions about her experiences in Darwin, then smiled warmly. 'I think you are exactly the sort of young lady we want at our school, Poppy. At Woodfield, we aim to raise young women of spirit and resourcefulness. Strength of character is the one thing that can never be taken away from you. I believe that it is just as important for young women to serve their community and their country as it is for their brothers.'

Poppy felt a surge of pride at the compliment. 'Thank you, Miss Royston.'

The headmistress turned to Cecilia. 'At Woodfield, we aim to provide the girls with a rigorous education in literature, mathematics, history, French, Latin, natural science, art, music and games. Many of our girls sit their Leaving Certificate examinations and go on to university, and we are very proud of their scholastic achievements.

'I know Poppy has had a patchy education over the last few years, but she seems like a bright girl, so I'm sure if she works hard she will catch up easily. We will put her in second year with the other girls her age and see how she goes.'

Poppy felt a sense of relief — Miss Royston wasn't going to make her start in a lower grade.

'I'm sure Poppy will study hard,' Cecilia concurred. 'We are very grateful that you are prepared to take her in the middle of the school term.'

Miss Royston leant forward. 'Since the war began, our motto has been "business as usual",' she explained. 'We have made the decision not to evacuate the students to the country. The girls have all been working hard to do their bit for the war effort — knitting socks and rugs, raising money for the Woodfield Comforts Fund, rolling bandages, collecting scrap metal for recycling and preparing care packages for soldiers. Poppy, you will be expected to join in with these activities on top of your schoolwork and games.'

'Yes, Miss Royston,' agreed Poppy. 'I've been doing many of those things in Darwin.'

Miss Royston handed a typed list to Cecilia. 'The girls need to wear an identity bracelet and have a survival kit in a calico shoulder bag with them at all times,' she continued. 'The kit should contain basic first-aid equipment: a whistle, a tourniquet, earplugs, gas mask, malted milk tablets and a rubber bit to place between your teeth in case of explosions. There is also a comprehensive uniform list that you will be able to buy at David Jones department store in the city.'

Poppy's gaze drifted around the room as Miss Royston listed the details of all the things she would need to start school. Her gaze fixed on the ginger tabby cat curled up on the window seat. He stretched and yawned, revealing a pink tongue and needle-sharp teeth. The cat reminded Poppy of Coco back in Darwin.

'His name is Winston Churchill,' Miss Royston said with a smile. 'Winston is a great comfort to me.'

Miss Royston rose, her back ramrod straight. 'I hope you will be very happy here at Woodfield, Poppy. I'm sure you will make many friends — and make the most of the opportunities we have to offer.

'I regularly remind all my girls that we are going through tough times and none of us knows what the future will hold. It is important to remember that it is not what you get out of life that counts, but what you put into it.'

Poppy nodded as she rose to her feet, unconsciously standing tall like the headmistress.

Cecilia and Poppy shook hands once more and followed Miss Royston back to reception. Here, Poppy was shown into an empty classroom where she had to complete a number of examinations to test her proficiency in English, mathematics and general knowledge.

To her great relief, she learnt that she had performed reasonably well, despite her unorthodox schooling to date.

Afterwards, Cecilia and Poppy caught a train into the city and walked to David Jones, where she was fitted for her summer school uniform — a white, short-sleeved poplin shirt, a box-pleated tunic with a belt, stockings, black buckle-up shoes, a straw Panama hat, navy serge blazer, gloves and sports tunic.

Laden down with boxes and bags, Cecilia led them to the cafe for coffee and a celebratory chocolate milkshake.

'Woodfield seems like a lovely school, Poppy,' Cecilia commented, sipping her coffee. 'Miss Royston is a truly inspiring woman. I hope it will be a wonderful opportunity for you, darling.'

Poppy felt a twinge of excitement mixed with nerves. 'I hope so, too.'

17

Telegram

March 10, 1942

Perth

My dear Cecilia and Poppy,

I hope this letter finds you well. It seems like such a long time ago, Poppy, that you and I were standing in the sunshine outside the hospital — a moment of peace before the nightmare of the bombing began. Despite the horror of that day, I feel honoured to have been part of that wonderful Darwin Hospital nursing team. Pat Davis wrote and told me that you had finally managed to escape Darwin and should now be in Sydney. I'm now in Perth, working at the hospital here. Our trip from Darwin on the *Manunda* was slow and nerveracking, as we expected to be attacked by Japanese planes or subs at any time. The ship was quite badly damaged during the Darwin bombing but managed to sail us safely to Fremantle.

Sadly, another twenty of our patients died on the journey south and were buried at sea. Still, we were able to save a great many. I feel it was a stroke of extreme good fortune that a fully equipped hospital ship was in harbour when the Japs attacked – many more would have died if we'd tried to evacuate the worst cases by road.

We had no sooner arrived in Perth and transferred all our patients to hospitals here when we were inundated with more patients from the Japanese attack on Broome. I'm not sure if the newspapers are reporting on it in the eastern states, but it's a terrible story. On 3 March the Japanese attacked Broome, which was being used as a staging post to evacuate thousands of refugees from the Dutch East Indies by flying boat.

According to one of the Dutch pilots I nursed, he thought the Japanese were trying to destroy the airfield to close the escape route. The flying boats, crowded with refugees, mostly Dutch women and children, were moored in Roebuck Bay for refuelling. The Japanese attacked at about nine o'clock in the morning. They destroyed fifteen flying boats and over twenty aircraft, including shooting down an American plane loaded with wounded servicemen.

The survivors said it was terrible – the water was aflame with burning fuel. Many of the Dutch refugees couldn't swim. More than one hundred people, mostly women and children, are said to have died – some taken by shark, while others were incinerated or drowned. It's so sad because if the Japs had attacked just an hour later, the flying boats would have already flown south and the refugees would have been safe.

There were stories of great bravery: a young Aboriginal man, Charlie D'Antoine, saved a woman and child by swimming through the burning oil with both of them on his back, while an Australian pilot relayed many of the refugees to Port Hedland in his damaged ten-seater plane.

One of the most intriguing parts of the story, though, is that one of the planes was rumoured to be carrying a package of diamonds worth hundreds of thousands of pounds!!! The diamonds disappeared when the plane went down. Wouldn't it be nice to find that little package washed up on the beach?

Anyway, hope you are both well and recovering from your ordeal.

Best wishes
Minnie Scott

March 23, 1942

Adelaide River

My Dearests,

I was overjoyed to hear that you made it safely to Sydney, and that at least the girls in our family are reunited. I miss you all so much.

After the bombing, we evacuated all the remaining patients south to Adelaide River, where we have established a new hospital to deal with the wounded coming in from the Pacific. The hospital is really just a collection of tents and huts in a sea of mud. You should see our operating theatre here — primitive, to say the least.

All the nurses have dyed their white uniforms a muddy khaki. It seems completely odd to have a hospital where all the medical staff are mud-coloured!

Not long now until the dry season, which will be much easier for everyone, especially the nurses. It is so frustrating to think of our beautiful new hospital abandoned after just a few days, but we did manage to salvage some equipment and supplies from Darwin before we left.

It is just as well we moved, for the Japanese have bombed Darwin on multiple occasions since you left. One raid caused significant damage to the hospital again, which strengthens my belief that it must have been a deliberate target. On some days there have been several air-raid alerts and numerous reports of reconnaissance planes. The town of Katherine was also bombed yesterday, but not as severely as Darwin — thank goodness.

There has been a steady stream of injured soldiers coming in from various areas of the Pacific. Many are also suffering from tropical diseases such as malaria, dysentery and beri-beri, and unfortunately these are more difficult to treat than they should be. Because of the Japanese occupation of the Dutch East Indies, we are having trouble obtaining drugs such as quinine.

Did you hear that the Aborigines on Melville Island captured a Japanese pilot? His plane was shot down and he was discovered by a group of Aboriginal women. One of their young men captured him by sneaking up from behind and pressing a tomahawk into his back, pretending it was a gun. The Aborigines quickly disarmed the pilot and turned him over to the mission on Bathurst Island. This was the first Japanese prisoner-of-war, taken on Australian soil.

Poppy, you will be pleased to know that before I left Darwin I went home and found Coco looking hungry, bedraggled and very sorry for herself. I've brought her with me to Adelaide River, where she has been adopted by the nurses. They are spoiling her rotten. She sends you a huge miaow and a cuddle.

Good luck starting at school, Poppy. My love to you all with many hugs and kisses.

Your loving father and husband,
Mark

March 28, 1942

Addison Road, Manly

Dear Edward,

We have no way of knowing whether you are dead or alive, but Mama insists her heart tells her you must still be alive. I don't know if you will ever even get this letter, but it makes me feel better to write to you anyway.

Mama, Bryony and I are now in Sydney. Mama and I left Darwin the day after the Japanese attacked it the first time. We are staying with our friends, the Tibbets, renting a couple of rooms at their house in Manly. We had planned to get our own place but housing is very short here. So many people have moved to Sydney to get work at the munitions factories, and with petrol rationing everyone wants to live close to public transport.

Manly is lovely. On weekends we swim at the beach,

although it is starting to get cooler now. It is sometimes quite alarming because the army uses the beach to practise manoeuvres, so they are forever firing mortar bombs out to sea or simulating battles on the beach. We can hear the thunder of the guns right up on Eastern Hill. It makes Mama and me feel quite nervous, as though we were back in Darwin during the air raids. The first time it happened, I moved so fast and was huddled under the kitchen table, quivering, waiting for the house to start falling down. Boy, did Maude give me a ribbing – she said it was the funniest thing she'd ever seen.

Last week, we helped Mrs Tibbets dig up her rose garden and plant a 'victory garden' of vegetables. I thought Mrs Tibbets might cry when we dug up all her beautiful rose bushes. We sowed broccoli, cabbage, carrots, silverbeet, cauliflower, leek, beetroot and lettuce. The garden looks very pretty, all in neat rows and mulched with straw. Mum is going to try to find some chickens for the back garden as well, to give us eggs. Next spring we will plant potatoes because they have been quite scarce. I'd love some of Mum's crispy baked potatoes with roast beef and gravy. Instead, it's liver and onions for dinner again – yick!

I started school two weeks ago at Woodfield at North Sydney, which is where Maude goes to school, so at least I know someone. The first week has been a bit of a blur trying to work out all the new faces, names and teachers, but it is gradually falling into place. Everyone seems really friendly, which is a relief. I thought they might be snooty. There are even a couple of girls boarding who were evacuated from Singapore earlier this year, so they know what it's like to be a long way from home and finding your new life strange. I like to ask them questions about Singapore so that I can imagine you there. Their father was captured by the Japanese, so he's a prisoner-of-war also. I wonder if you know him? His name is Aubrey Jones.

Once I am settled at school and Mum has recovered from her injuries, she plans to apply to work at one of the local hospitals. Dad says she mustn't do any heavy lifting for at least another few weeks.

We no sooner arrived in Sydney than Phoebe was transferred to Townsville to work at a new Army hospital that has been built there. Mum is worried that Phoebe will be too far north in the event of another Japanese attack. There are rumours that the Government has plans to abandon the far north if the Japanese invade, and focus on defending the industrial areas around Sydney, Newcastle and Wollongong. Phoebe, however, is quite excited at the thought of travelling somewhere new and being close to the action.

You wouldn't recognise Bryony – she's training with the Australian Women's Army Service as a signals operator. She wears a uniform and tie, with a little peaked hat. We only get to see her on her rare days off, but she's having fun. A lot of her work is hush-hush, apparently, so she doesn't talk about it much. I'm sure she's just doing deadly boring officework.

There's been a terrible fuss in Sydney because the American Government has sent black soldiers to Australia, contrary to the White Australia Policy. Australian customs refused to let them land. It's ridiculous – these men have come to fight to save us, putting their lives on the line, and some silly old politicians want to send them home!

Anyway, Honey sends you a big lick and a woof. Hope they are treating you well. We miss you so much and think of you every day. We are all praying that this war will end soon and you can come home to us.

Your loving sister,
Poppy

RECEIVED TELEGRAM — MARCH 26, 1942
PRIVATE TREHEARNE MISSING.
I REGRET TO INFORM YOU THAT PTE
EDWARD MARK TREHEARNE HAS BEEN
REPORTED MISSING. THE MINISTER FOR THE
ARMY AND THE MILITARY BOARD EXTEND
SINCERE SYMPATHY.
MINISTER FOR THE ARMY

April 8, 1942

Townsville

Dear Mum, Bryony and Poppy

Sorry I haven't written for so long, but the days just seem to whirl by.

I have arrived safely in Townsville, which is more like a massive tent city with thousands of American and Australian troops. In many ways, it is like Darwin – hot, muggy and tropical. It is the tail end of the wet season so there's still red mud everywhere, almost up to my knees. We wear khaki overalls and wellington boots most of the time – my Matron in Sydney would be horrified!

Our accommodation is in tents in a big paddock. Privacy is almost non-existent, but they promise us that they will build huts soon.

The hospital is likewise cobbled together from tents, hastily erected huts and requisitioned buildings. The locals are in shock at having their tiny, sleepy town turned into a military camp. The food is dreary – cold baked beans, cold diced pork, bully beef, sliced fruit – but we can't really complain. It must be much worse for the boys overseas.

We have to take quinine every day and sleep under mosquito nets to avoid malaria. This is the greatest health problem up here, along with dengue fever and dysentery, although of course we are getting evacuated soldiers with battle wounds and injured airmen. There are also so many automobile crashes at night-time from people trying to drive without lights.

I have made some lovely friends up here and we are all very protective of 'our boys'. We work very long days but most of us are happy that we can do something useful. We feel like we are making a real difference. It's good we're so busy – it means there's no time to think much about the war and how it's all going.

I have been asked out by a few of the American GIs – there are dances every night, concerts and films, but most of the nurses are just too exhausted to kick up their heels. The Americans are very generous, buying us chocolates and stockings as presents. The stockings are especially welcome. I'm not sure if they are doing this in Sydney, but up here some of the girls have taken to painting their bare legs to look like they are wearing stockings, even down to drawing a dark seam down the back of their calves!

The Americans make us laugh. They just _love_ ice-cream – I'm sure they'd eat it every day for breakfast given half a chance! They are much better paid than the poor Aussies, and they definitely get superior food. It's no wonder this causes some resentment, but I have to say I am incredibly grateful that the Americans are here to help defend us. Without them, I hate to think what would happen.

Hope you are well. Write soon.

All my love,
Phoebe xxx

18

Austerity

Cecilia walked into the sitting room, where Poppy was gazing out the window at the view.

'Poppy, I'm just going down to the Corso to . . .' Cecilia paused and gazed at Poppy critically. 'Oh dear, I think you've grown again overnight. That skirt is indecently short, Poppy Trehearne!'

Poppy glanced down at her hemline and shrugged. It was rather short, but all her clothes were shrinking. Other than her school uniforms, she hadn't bought any new clothes for over a year — there had been too many other important things to think about.

'Come on,' Cecilia ordered. 'Let's go and see if we can buy you a new dress.'

Together, mother and daughter wandered down the hill to the Corso — the main shopping street in the village of Manly. There were several shops purporting to sell clothes, but wartime shortages meant that the shelves were pitifully bare. There was hardly anything that would fit Poppy, and definitely nothing remotely pretty. Most clothes were utilitarian overalls and clothes for factory work in drab shades of khaki, brown and grey.

'Perhaps we should check the haberdashery and make you something,' suggested Cecilia at last. The haberdashery was also sparsely stocked, but Cecilia was determined to find something useful. At last, she purchased two matching floral tablecloths, a bolt of blackout material, thread, ribbon, needles and two dress patterns.

Poppy looked dubiously at the tablecloths and heavier blackout material as the sales assistant wrapped them up.

Back at home, Cecilia took Poppy's measurements then lay out the patterns and started cutting. Cecilia seemed very secretive that week, working late into the night. A few days later, she triumphantly brought Poppy a package wrapped in brown paper and tied with green ribbon.

'Surprise, darling!' Cecilia called.

'Thanks, Mum — but it's not my birthday.'

'Let's call it a *belated* Christmas present,' Cecilia replied. 'Goodness knows there wasn't much to celebrate at Christmas time.'

Poppy grinned with delight. It had been a long time since she had received a present or a surprise. She untied the ribbon and undid the paper, careful not to tear it.

Inside was a pile of folded clothes. There were two dresses: one a pretty floral with a nipped-in waist, short sleeves and a slightly flared skirt, the other a sleeveless black cotton dress with a longer, fuller skirt and a tight-fitting, ruched bodice. Underneath were a pair of black shorts and a floral halter top.

'Mum, you are truly astonishing. These are beautiful.' Poppy held the dresses up against her, one after the other.

'Try them on. I hope they fit well.'

Poppy skipped to the bathroom and tried on the floral dress first, the one cut from the two tablecloths and trimmed with green ribbon. She slipped on Bryony's silver dance shoes and whirled and twirled, flaring out the skirt with delight.

'You look gorgeous,' Cecilia told her. 'Absolutely gorgeous.'

Poppy curtseyed graciously and then skipped away to slip on the black dress created from the blackout material. The dress, with its slim shoulder straps and beaded belt, instantly made Poppy feel glamorous and sophisticated. This was not a little girl's dress. It was a French film star dress.

Cecilia smiled triumphantly. 'You look beautiful.'

'Thank you, Mum. It must have taken you ages to make these! I love them.'

'It's a pleasure, darling, and I really couldn't have you walking the streets looking like an orphan! I also added a thick black band to the bottom of your white skirt. Thank goodness for blackout curtains!'

Poppy was just dancing around the sitting room in her new dress when the bell jangled down below. Cecilia and Poppy ignored it, more interested in the success of the new dresses. The bell jangled again.

Poppy flew to the window and leant out. A young man stood below, twisting his hat in his hands.

'Who is it?' she called. 'Oh . . . no, it can't be . . .' Poppy flew down the stairs and threw open the door. 'Is it really you?'

Jack stood on the doorstep, smiling. Lovely, familiar Jack, so far from Alexandra Downs. Poppy threw herself at him in a hug.

'Jack, it's so good to see you. What on earth are you doing here?'

'Hello, Midget,' Jack replied with a crooked smile. 'Now it's my turn to ask if it's really *you*? You look far too glamorous to be the grubby Miss Poppy Trehearne, the famous croc hunter and adventurer, who I know from faraway Myilly Point.'

Poppy blushed.

'Yes, of course it's me,' retorted Poppy with mock indignation. 'I'm just wearing a new dress that Mama made for me from blackout curtains. Well, don't stand there like a stunned mullet — come in! Tell me what you're doing in Sydney.'

Cecilia and Maude were also delighted to see Jack, a familiar face to remind them of the good old days in Darwin. He was soon seated on the couch, sipping on a cup of steaming, fragrant sweet tea that Cecilia had made using her precious ration of tea leaves.

'Well, I'm here because your father sent us,' Jack explained.

'You've seen Mark?' Cecilia asked longingly. 'How is he? Did he look well?'

'Yes, Dr Trehearne was fine but busy. He was at the new hospital at Adelaide River. You see, my father had a nasty fall while we were mustering. We took him to see your father, and he insisted that we bring him to Sydney to see a specialist. My mother didn't want to leave me alone at Alexandra Downs, and she didn't want to leave

Father, either. So, we organised a manager to look after the property and came to Sydney. I think Mum was glad to see the back of the Territory after the bombing and the talk of a Japanese invasion. Although, of course, she'd never admit to it.'

Jack grinned at Poppy before continuing. 'We brought a letter of recommendation from Doctor Trehearne, so Father is at Royal North Shore Hospital. Mother is with him now, and we are staying at a hotel in North Sydney so we can be close to him.'

Poppy felt a rush of excitement — Jack would be staying here in Sydney while his father was in hospital. She fought to quell the selfish emotion.

'That's terrible, Jack. Will he be all right? Will he be in hospital very long?' Poppy asked.

'He's a tough old thing,' Jack admitted, smiling. 'The Germans couldn't get him in the last war, and I don't think he'll be beaten by a cranky old horse. Anyway, he's seeing an excellent surgeon, who thinks that with the right care he'll be back on his feet in a few weeks. However, he won't be back on a horse for at least a year. The manager has agreed to stay on for twelve months, so Mum thinks we should rent a little flat near the sea where he can have a long recuperation.'

Cecilia nodded and smiled with relief. 'That at least is good news. And what will you do, Jack?'

Jack frowned at his boots and then glanced quickly at Poppy. 'I'm planning on going to university and studying engineering,' he confessed. 'I'll need to do one more year of school in Sydney to complete my Leaving Certificate, then I'll apply to Sydney Uni.'

A wave of sorrow crossed Cecilia's face. Poppy guessed she was reminded of Edward and wondering where he was and if he was alive.

'How are your brothers?' Poppy asked, changing the subject.

'They are training near Ingleburn and are due to go overseas in a few weeks. Mum is hoping to see them before they go. She's trying to be brave, but she's clearly worried.'

Poppy jumped to her feet, feeling restless with all the thoughts of distant loved ones. 'Come on, Jack. It's too nice a day to be sitting inside chatting. Why don't Maude and I take you for a walk and a swim? It would be lovely.'

Jack agreed, so they all separated to change clothes and find towels. Poppy wore her new shorts and floral halter-neck top over her swimming costume. Maude found Jack some swimming trunks that had belonged to her father.

They walked down the hill towards the harbour. It was a glorious day, the autumn sun beaming down and glinting off the bay. From the harbour they cut through the centre of the village, past the school with its large brick air-raid shelter dominating the playground, towards the beach.

A couple of the famous Norfolk pine trees had been cut down to make way for machine-gun emplacements, while sandbags reinforced some of the buildings along the Steyne. The white sand of the beach was fortified with barbed-wire entanglements, concrete barriers and tank traps, with only small gaps where people could access the surf and sand. A group of soldiers marched past on their way back up to the Army station at North Head.

'Let me take a photo of you girls,' suggested Jack, taking his Brownie camera from around his neck.

Maude and Poppy obligingly posed, slinging their arms around each other and laughing, the sparkling sea behind them.

'Beautiful,' Jack said. 'A perfect autumn day.'

They continued on, chatting, joking and laughing.

'If you are going to stay in Sydney for a while, you might want to become a volunteer lifesaver,' suggested Maude, gesturing towards the surf club at the southern end of the beach. 'All the lifesavers have joined up and are fighting overseas, so they've had to recruit from the local school boys. I'm sure they'd love a strong, practical country boy! You should learn to surf while you're here, too. It's lots of fun.'

Poppy and Jack looked at the large breakers crashing a little way out. To their eyes, the waves seemed huge and powerful compared to the gentle waves in Darwin. Maude led the way down onto the beach. The sand between the fortifications was crowded with mothers and children, servicemen on leave, and workers enjoying a well-earned Saturday afternoon.

The trio stripped off their clothes, lay down their towels and raced to the surf. The autumn seawater felt freezing to Poppy after the tropical climate of the Top End. She shivered as the water washed over her toes and retreated hastily.

'Come on, Poppy,' shrieked Maude, grabbing her friend by the hand and dragging her back. Jack waded out to join them in the knee-deep water.

'I agree with you, Poppy,' retorted Jack, laughing. 'It's icy.'

Maude retaliated by splashing them both. Poppy squealed and ran, scooping up a handful of water and flinging it at Maude. Jack roared and chased Maude, picking her up and throwing her out into the deeper water. Maude spluttered and giggled. Jack turned for Poppy and sprinted after her.

'No, don't you dare!' Poppy screamed. Jack had a dangerous glint in his eye, so Poppy turned and fled up the beach towards the towels. Jack overtook her and scooped her up in his arms, running back towards the surf. Poppy squealed, half in trepidation and half in delight. Jack jumped through a wave and they both went under, arms and legs flailing.

Once they were all wet, they soon adapted to the temperature of the water and spent ages swimming and splashing. Maude taught them how to bodysurf, surging like a dolphin on the powerful waves. They staggered out at last, tired and exhilarated, and collapsed on the towels in the sand. Poppy shook her dark curls to dry them and sighed with contentment.

'Why don't we go to Burt's Cafe for a milkshake?' Maude suggested. 'He does the best chocolate milkshakes you've ever tasted.'

'Sounds like a great idea,' agreed Poppy, sitting up. 'My treat — Mum gave me some pocket money last week.'

The three dressed, sand freckling their bare legs and feet, and wandered back up to the esplanade. Poppy felt content, walking along between her two best friends, the crust of salt on her skin and the warmth of the sun on her back.

As they neared the wharf, a group of servicemen on leave milled around, laughing and chatting.

One young man caught sight of Poppy and Maude and wolf-whistled. The other servicemen turned to stare at the girls, nudging each other and whispering. Poppy blushed and avoided their gaze, embarrassed by the attention.

'Hey, little lady,' the wolf-whistler drawled in a strong American accent. 'Would you like to join me for an ice cream?'

Poppy tried to ignore the serviceman, but he strolled along beside them, hands in his pockets. 'Hey, honey, I won't bite.' Poppy smelt a waft of alcohol on his breath. 'Why don't you ditch your brother and come have some fun? Bring your friend along, too, if you like. I have plenty of friends who'd like to meet a pretty Aussie like her.'

Poppy looked up and shook her head. 'Thanks, but we're busy,' she replied, hurrying forward.

'Awww shucks, don't be shy.' He smiled, keeping pace. 'What'll it be — chocolate or vanilla? How about a double cone?'

'Thanks, mate,' Jack said firmly, 'but we're on our way somewhere. She's not interested.'

An Australian soldier passing the opposite way overheard the exchange and stopped. He leant in and pointed his finger threateningly at the American soldier. 'Why won't you drunken Yanks ever listen?' he yelled. 'You seppos think you own the blasted place! Leave our Aussie girls alone.'

The American puffed his chest out, stepping up to the challenge. Poppy thought they looked like two bantam roosters fighting over the kitchen scraps.

'It's none of your business, buddy,' the American retorted. 'I was just asking the young lady if she wanted an ice cream.'

Maude stepped back, frightened by the aggression in the two men's stances.

'It's okay,' Poppy muttered, dragging both Jack and Maude forward by the arms. 'We have to go.'

Jack put his arm around Poppy's shoulder and drew her away.

'Can't you see she already has an Aussie sweetheart?' demanded the irate Australian. 'You Yanks are all the same — over*paid*, over*fed* and over *here*!'

'If you Aussies weren't such softies, we wouldn't need to be here covering your backsides,' retorted the American. 'We're here to save your bacon, buddy.'

The Australian bristled and charged at the American.

Jack stepped towards the soldiers, determined to calm them down. 'It's okay, fellas. Thanks for your concern, but there's just been a small misunderstanding.'

The American shoved Jack out of the way, swinging a punch at the Australian soldier. Jack stumbled and nearly fell. The Australian retaliated with a blow to the American's nose. The other soldiers swarmed over to protect their friend and pull the two brawlers apart.

'It's all right, buddy,' soothed another American. 'He's just had too much to drink and a touch of the sun. Come on, Hank, let's take you home.'

Poppy, Jack and Maude hurried away, feeling quite shaken.

'I don't feel like a milkshake anymore,' Poppy confessed. 'Let's go home.'

19

The Apparition

Later that week, Poppy and Maude arrived home from school to find the sitting room crowded with local ladies sitting in a circle, knitting socks, drinking watery tea and gossiping.

Honey whimpered and pranced around on her hind legs, delighted to see the girls again after the long school day. Poppy patted her head, careful not to make too much fuss. Mrs Tibbets had only recently relented and allowed Honey to come inside during the day. If she became too excited, she was banished outside to the garden again to be tied up. At night-time, Poppy would sneak down and let Honey in to curl up and sleep on the foot of her bed.

'Come in, girls,' Mrs Tibbets said, gesturing welcomingly. 'There's some hot tea in the pot. Help yourselves. Why don't you join us in knitting a few socks for the lads overseas?'

Poppy and Maude exchanged glances. Poppy hated

knitting, especially boring, khaki socks. She knew Maude hated it, too, and was mentally rolling her eyes in disgust. But both girls smiled dutifully, poured a cup of watery tea and picked up a ball of dull-green wool and some knitting needles.

'Sorry, we're out of sugar, but there's some honey if you'd like it,' Cecilia invited, smiling sympathetically at the girls.

'How are you enjoying your new school, Poppy?' asked one of the local ladies. 'It must be a big change for you going to a proper high school. I sent my Sally away to boarding school in the country. She moans that it's boring, but at least she's *safe*.'

'Thank you, it's fine,' Poppy replied politely.

Poppy frowned as she concentrated on the rhythm of the knitting, swearing under her breath as she dropped a stitch and had to waste minutes trying to unpick it. While Maude hated knitting, her stitches were neat and dainty, producing perfect ribbed socks.

'Bert says we should move away from the coast — it's too dangerous,' said Mrs Morris, her needles flying. 'If the Japanese invade Sydney, Manly would be a prime landing spot. I have a sister who lives in the Blue Mountains, so I think we might move there for a few months.'

Maude passed around the platter of dry, tasteless scones. It was hard to make a good scone with margarine. The knitting needles clicked and clacked rhythmically.

'It might not be too dreadful if the Japanese invaded,' replied another older woman, who lived in one of the original grand mansions on the ridge. 'It would stop these awful shortages, and at least that might solve the servant problem. I hear the Japanese make excellent men-of-all-work.'

Poppy had to pretend to sneeze to repress a guffaw. Cecilia glanced at Poppy warningly.

'Mrs Gibbs, I don't think the Japanese who invade will be interested in becoming servants,' reproved Mrs Tibbets. 'I think they might be more interested in taking over your beautiful house and making *you* the servant.'

'Oh,' Mrs Gibbs replied. 'Of course . . . I mean . . . Well, I'm sure it won't come to that — our boys will teach them a lesson they won't forget in a hurry.'

Poppy thought about the steady Japanese advance through Malaya, Singapore and the Dutch East Indies. It didn't sound like they would be easy to defeat at all. She put aside her knitting, finished her cup of tea and dry scone, then rose to leave. 'I have some study I have to do for school,' she explained. 'We have a Latin test tomorrow.'

'Latin?' asked Mrs Morris. 'Wouldn't you be better off learning sewing and cooking? Perhaps a little typing? You'll need to know how to manage a household when you're married.'

Poppy and Maude glanced at each other. Poppy's mouth twitched in a little smile.

'At our school, girls are expected to perform just as well scholastically as boys,' Maude replied. 'Our headmistress believes girls are capable of tackling anything they set their minds to.'

The two visiting ladies glanced at each other. Mrs Morris coughed.

'My, what strange notions they teach girls at school these days,' said Mrs Morris. 'I'm glad my daughter's school doesn't teach them such nonsense. She's being educated to make a fine wife and mother.'

'Don't worry, Maude,' Mrs Gibbs assured her. 'This war will be over in a couple of years, and you'll be keen to marry a nice young man, keep house and raise a big family.'

❦

The weather started to turn colder. During the week, Poppy's life was a busy whirl of school, sport and homework, helping in the house and garden, knitting and weaving camouflage nets. On the weekend, she had more free time to take Honey for walks along the beach, meet Jack and Maude to go to the cinema or hang out at Burt's Cafe, drinking icy-cold, frothy chocolate milkshakes.

Cecilia was thrilled because Poppy soon caught up with her other classmates and managed to top her class in her English test.

In late May, early one Friday evening, Poppy was walking Honey west along Addison Road when she saw a young boy, about seven years old, who lived in a block of flats there. He was playing fighter pilots, zooming and droning up and down the patch of lawn. Poppy often saw him on her walks and stopped to chat.

'Hello, Ian,' Poppy called. 'Glad it's the weekend?'

Ian stopped swooping and bent to stroke Honey, who promptly rolled over and offered her tummy for a tickle.

'Sure am,' he replied, obligingly scratching Honey's belly. 'Mum says we can go to the cinema tomorrow afternoon if I get all my chores done.'

Poppy heard a low droning coming from the north-east. Ian stopped scratching Honey's tummy, distracted by the sound of the plane. Honey pawed his hand. When Ian still ignored her, she jumped up on her hind legs and begged, paws pressed together in supplication.

'Oh, Honey,' Poppy complained, 'you are such an actress. Ian doesn't want to pat you anymore.'

The sound of the plane drew closer. Poppy scanned the sky. From the garden's elevated position, she and Ian had a close view of a bottle-green seaplane flying close to the ground, nearly skimming the trees with its fat, boat-shaped floats. It was only about one hundred and fifty metres away from them.

'That plane's flying unusually low,' Poppy observed.

'It sounds different, too,' Ian added, his brow furrowed in concentration. Poppy remembered that Ian, although only seven, was a passionate plane-spotter. He could rattle off the make and type of almost any aeroplane passing overhead, and his greatest ambition in life was to be a fighter pilot when he grew up.

'I wonder what it's doing?' asked Poppy. 'It looks like some kind of war manoeuvre.'

Ian shook his head. The plane continued heading south-west and was quickly out of sight.

'It's not one of ours,' Ian decided firmly.

'Maybe it's American,' suggested Poppy nonchalantly, not really caring one way or the other.

Ian shook his head again more certainly.

'No, it's definitely not American,' replied Ian.

'Oh.' Poppy shrugged her shoulders and picked up Honey's lead, preparing to continue her walk.

'I think it's a Japanese float plane.'

Poppy felt like Ian had punched her in the stomach. 'Japanese?' she cried. 'Are you sure? How could a Japanese plane get all the way down here?'

'I don't know, but we better tell someone,' Ian replied over his shoulder as he sprinted towards the flats. Poppy followed at a slower pace.

'Mum, Mum,' Ian yelled. 'I just saw a Japanese plane.'

Ian's mother came running out the front door, wiping her hands on her floral apron.

'*What?*'

'A Japanese float plane just flew by, heading towards Sydney Harbour,' Ian insisted.

'Are you sure?' asked his mother, her voice raised with anxiety.

'Yes, it definitely wasn't one of ours.' Ian's mother glanced at Poppy, frowning. Poppy shrugged – she had no way of knowing whether the plane was an ally or a foe.

Ian's mother paused, pondering what to do. 'Let's go and see the army sergeant next door,' she suggested.

❧

The army sergeant was obviously looking forward to a relaxing night at home. He opened the door with his collar open, shirt sleeves rolled up and slippers on his feet.

'Sorry to disturb you, sergeant, but Ian thinks he just saw a Japanese plane flying low over the harbour.'

The sergeant looked at the young boy before him and smiled. 'Now, Ian,' he began kindly, 'I know you love planes, but I think your imagination must have been playing tricks on you. It's absolutely impossible for you to have seen a Japanese plane. An enemy aircraft would require a Japanese-occupied airstrip, and there's not one of those for thousands of miles. A Japanese plane would never make it this far.'

Ian straightened his shoulders and looked the army sergeant in the eye. 'Or a Japanese aircraft carrier, or even a submarine,' he insisted.

'Yes, yes,' agreed the sergeant impatiently, 'but our defences would detect a Japanese vessel long before it came close to Sydney. It must have been an American plane.'

Ian pouted and shook his head. 'It was a low-wing float plane, very unusual looking, with a radial engine. It didn't look or sound like any plane I've ever seen before.'

The sergeant sighed and glanced at Ian's mother, then at Poppy.

'Did you see it?' he asked Poppy.

'Yes, it was bottle-green.'

'Do you think it was a Japanese aircraft?' asked the sergeant.

Poppy thought back to the Zero fighter planes she had seen in Darwin, with their distinctive rising suns painted on the underside of the wings, dropping those lethal silver bombs. She shuddered at the memory, her stomach clenched in fear.

'I . . . I don't know,' she admitted. 'I didn't see any identity markings.'

'It was Japanese,' Ian insisted. 'I'm sure of it.'

The sergeant sighed once more and clapped Ian on the shoulder. 'Okay, son,' he said. 'Thanks for telling me. I'll look into it.'

Ian, his mother and Poppy said their thank-yous and goodbyes. Poppy continued her walk with Honey, her eyes following the path the mysterious plane had flown.

It was now nearly dark and, from the top of the hill, she could see the harbour spread out below, dotted with strings of navigational lights. On the southern side, houses glowed, golden and welcoming, and the horizon gleamed with lights from the city and naval dockyards beyond Middle Harbour.

It's so beautiful, thought Poppy. *Could it really have been an enemy reconnaissance plane scouting over Sydney? Could the Japanese really be so close?*

She shuddered, pulling her collar up around her ears, and hurried home in the darkness.

20

Sydney Harbour

Sunday, 31 May 1942

The weekend was chilly, with squally rainstorms. Several large ships, including the USS *Chicago*, had come into Sydney Harbour for repairs following the battle of the Coral Sea a couple of weeks before, and crowds of young people were flocking to the city to join in the celebrations, everyone rejoicing in what they felt to be a turning point in the war.

Cecilia reluctantly agreed that Poppy could catch the ferry into Circular Quay with Maude and Jack to meet Bryony on Sunday afternoon. The city streets were bustling with people – Australian, American, New Zealand, French and Dutch servicemen, many on leave for the first time in weeks, as well as locals.

The four friends wandered the streets around the city, drinking in the carnival atmosphere. In Martin Place, three black American soldiers were playing improvised jazz on saxophones and trumpets, sitting on wooden crates. A group of US naval men danced with young Australian girls, who laughed and flirted, wooed by the exotic accents and polite manners of the foreigners.

One of the Americans asked Bryony to dance, and she was swept up into a lively jitterbug. Poppy tapped her foot to the jazz musicians' swinging beat. It would be fun to join in the swirl of dancers.

They explored the city, people watching and window shopping.

At dusk, they bought crispy battered fish and chips, liberally sprinkled with salt and wrapped in newspaper. They sat down near the Quay and crunched on the delicious fish. Squawking seagulls squabbled and swooped. A busker played a mournful tune on his harmonica, the notes warbling and bending. To the west, beyond the graceful grey arch of the bridge, the sky was stained vibrant golds, pinks and crimsons as the sun sank behind the clouds.

'Delicious,' sighed Poppy, tossing a chip to the flock of greedy seabirds.

'Not quite as good as charred barramundi, freshly caught and cooked on a campfire at Mindil Beach, but not bad,' added Maude, raising up a morsel of fish for observation, then popping it in her mouth.

'A lot safer, though,' Jack suggested. 'No risk of a crocodile leaping out of Sydney Harbour.'

He held up a long, thin chip and bit its head off with a snap.

'That's one thing I don't miss about Darwin,' agreed Bryony. 'Crocodiles.'

'And mud,' added Maude.

Poppy glanced at Bryony, a glint of mischief in her eyes. 'Don't tell me you miss Darwin?' she joked. 'I thought you'd never look back now that you are living in sophisticated Sydney again, with all the shops, dance halls and cinemas.'

Bryony snorted, tossing her head.

'As if I have time to shop,' she said. 'Speaking of which, I suppose I'd better get back. I'll get a terrible dressing down and be confined to the barracks for a week if I'm late.'

'We'll escort you,' Jack said.

'Thanks for the offer, but there's really no need,' replied Bryony. 'I'll be fine heading back on my own.'

Jack crumpled up his pile of greasy newspaper into a ball. 'The city's full of drunken servicemen. I don't want to be the one to tell your mother that we left you to make your way back to Paddington all by yourself. Besides, I'm freezing, so a good walk will warm us up. It won't take long.'

Jack was wrong. Between the crowds in the city and the trams overflowing with people, it took ages to walk up to Oxford Street. By the time they delivered Bryony to the barracks in Paddington, it was getting late.

The return trip took even longer after they missed a tram back to the city, then the following tram was cancelled. They huddled together at the tram stop, their coat collars turned up against the chilly wind, their frozen hands buried deep in their pockets.

When a tram finally trundled along, it was crammed with people and they struggled to squeeze on.

'We'd be better off walking,' suggested Maude. 'This is hopeless.'

'Mum is going to be cross,' Poppy sighed. 'I promised her we wouldn't be back late. She'll think something terrible has happened.'

'Nooo.' Jack grinned. 'She knows you're both with me and that I'd never let anything terrible happen to you, Midget.'

Poppy cuffed him lightly on the arm. 'It's more likely Maude and I will have to look after you, Jacko.'

When they finally reached Circular Quay, they just missed another Manly ferry and had to wait half an hour for the next one. It was with great relief that they finally made their way onto the dimly lit ferry and sat down near the starboard windows. It was now about 10.30 pm and there were only about twenty people on board.

The crew stowed the mooring ropes and the engines chugged, propelling the ferry away from the pontoon. Poppy leant back against the seat and closed her eyes.

'I'm so tired,' she murmured.

The gentle rocking of the ferry felt soothing as it gained speed, heading around Bennelong Point towards the sandstone fortification of Fort Denison. Bright moonlight flooded the water with a silvery, shimmering glow.

'Isn't it pretty?' asked Maude, pressing her face against the window. 'It must be the most beautiful harbour in the world.'

Poppy gazed appreciatively at the view. The black hills on either side of the harbour were dotted with golden lights that glimmered on the water.

'It looks so peaceful,' Poppy agreed.

Suddenly, a loud explosion reverberated through the cabin, making them all jump. They peered nervously out the window towards Rushcutters Bay.

'What was that?' asked Maude.

'Navy training?' suggested Jack. 'They must be firing blank shells.'

A siren sounded, wailing through the chilly air. The ferry slammed into reverse and veered aside; passengers were sent sprawling. The internal lights switched off, plunging the cabin into darkness.

There were screams and groans as the ferry rocked wildly. Jack, Maude and Poppy picked themselves up, rubbing bruised elbows and knees. They crowded around the grimy window and stared out into the night. A shell whizzed by, sending a spout of water metres into the air.

'I don't think they're blanks,' Poppy whispered. Her stomach knotted with anxiety and her throat was so tight she could hardly breathe.

Within moments the serene harbour had transformed into a battle zone. Searchlights blazed across the sky and water. Navy ships zipped back and forth, searching the harbour's murky depths. Red tracer bullets zinged through the air like shooting stars. Alarms sounded. Huge pillars of water erupted into the air.

'Look,' cried Jack, pointing out into the night.

A searchlight swept over the ferry and across the water. In its intense white light they could all see the periscope and snub conning tower of a small submarine, black against the silver water.

To the right were the floodlights of the Garden Island dockyard and the glow of dozens of troop ships moored in the harbour. The huge hull of the US battleship *Chicago* was silhouetted against the dockyards. The black shadows of naval personnel swarmed on the docks.

A nearby minesweeper opened fire on the submarine with a machine-gun. Stray bullets pinged off the side of the wallowing ferry; another explosion thundered right in front.

Poppy, Maude and Jack dived for cover under the bench seats, huddling together.

'Who are they firing at?' asked Maude.

'The Japanese,' replied Poppy, her heart sinking to the bottom of her stomach. 'They're attacking Sydney.'

'They couldn't be,' Jack insisted. 'How on earth would a tiny sub like that get all the way down here? The war's up in the Coral Sea, thousands of miles away.'

'Not anymore,' whispered Poppy, covering her head as another mortar shell detonated close by. 'Not anymore.'

Jack put his arms around both Poppy and Maude, trying to shield them with his body. 'We'll be okay,' he assured them. 'We'll be fine.'

An enormous explosion sounded, followed by answering machine-gun fire. The ferry tossed wildly, buffeted by massive waves. Red flames illuminated the cabin with an eerie, flickering light.

The three ducked and clung tightly to each other. Wild thoughts swirled through Poppy's head as she huddled with her friends under the seat. *Will we survive this? Will I ever see my mother, father, sisters, brother, dog or home ever again? Is this the start of the invasion?*

Poppy found herself praying over and over, 'Please, God, help us get out of this safely.'

At last the ferry threw its engines into full speed ahead and raced towards Manly. An anxiety-filled half hour later, the vessel drew up against the wharf, thudding into the pylons. Relief spread through Poppy's body like a physical warmth. She hugged Maude then Jack, clinging to her friends like a life raft.

'We made it,' she whispered. 'Thank God, we made it.'

As the passengers shuffled off the vessel, they glanced at each other and grinned, strangers united by giddy relief at still being alive.

On the wharf, Poppy was met by a hurricane welcome as Cecilia and Honey rushed towards her, her mother enveloping her in a tight embrace, while Honey jumped and licked and whined.

'Thank God, you're all right,' Cecilia whispered, her face red, puffy and streaked with tears. 'I was petrified that you were caught up in the raid. Are you hurt? What happened? *Where have you been?*'

Poppy did her best to answer the barrage of questions. When she had explained the events of the last hour, she realised that Mrs Tibbets was also there, alternately scolding and squeezing Maude. Cecilia broke her grip on Poppy to give Jack a quick hug and check that he was all right.

The harbour was now in complete darkness, with most of the lights finally extinguished. Over the black water, they could still hear the distant sound of erratic gunfire and explosions, while the sky towards the city glowed red.

'Come home and I'll make you all a hot cocoa,' suggested Cecilia. 'It's nearly midnight. Whatever happens, we'll all feel better for a hot drink and a good night's sleep.'

❧

The next day, Cecilia and Poppy searched the newspapers for an explanation of what had happened in Sydney Harbour the night before. There was no mention of an attack in the paper or on the wireless news bulletins. Yet, throughout the early hours of the morning, muffled explosions and gunfire could still be heard rumbling in the distance.

Cecilia snapped off the wireless in irritation. 'It's just like Darwin all over again,' she announced. 'The censors are trying to suppress any details of the attack. It seems ridiculous when most of Sydney could see or hear what was going on. Don't they understand that people will be more frightened of their own imaginings than if they knew the truth?'

With no official information, wild rumours abounded throughout the city, passed from neighbour to neighbour as swiftly as a bushfire: there was a huge Japanese force, anchored just off the coast of Sydney, preparing to invade. The Japanese survivors were hiding out in the bush at North Head or meeting with enemy spies, ready to attack. The Japanese officers had already picked out which lavish harbour-side mansions they would inhabit once Sydney was conquered.

Many families packed up their valuables and prepared to flee to the country, as far from the coast as possible. Those who remained set to work digging air-raid trenches and building bomb shelters. Windows were blacked out with black curtains or cardboard and secured with tape. Preparations were made in case the Japanese came knocking on the front door.

Poppy discovered that Cecilia had hidden a kitchen carving knife under her pillow.

Finally, the Government decided to release limited details of the raid in order to control the rumours, carefully worded to underplay the threat, reduce panic and praise the heroic action of Sydney's defence force.

On the evening of Sunday, 31 May, three Japanese midget submarines had entered Sydney Harbour undetected. One had become entangled in the partially constructed anti-submarine boom net and, after being discovered, the two Japanese submariners had committed suicide and set off a detonation to scuttle the craft.

Two other midget submarines had entered the harbour soon after, possibly following the Manly ferry through the boom net. The submarines had been detected by various vessels and fired upon. One of the submarines had fired torpedoes at the USS *Chicago* but missed, instead destroying a former ferry, the *Kuttabul*, which sank killing twenty-one sailors. The search for the two remaining enemy submarines had continued through the night, with depth charges being dropped throughout the harbour. Only one of these submarines was discovered the next day. The Japanese crew had also committed suicide when they realised their mission had failed.

What the newspapers *failed* to say was that there had been numerous warnings of Japanese activity in the days leading up to the attack, including the reconnaissance plane witnessed by Ian and Poppy in Manly, which the authorities had ignored. Several enemy submarines had been detected off the east coast of Australia, including one that attacked a Russian merchant steamer, the *Wellen*, fifty kilometres east of Newcastle, and an enemy submarine detected by a New Zealand aircraft only forty kilometres from Sydney.

In addition, Sydney Harbour was supposedly protected from submarine attack by indicator loops on the harbour floor, which record the passing of vessels overhead, and by the incomplete boom net. On the night of the midget submarine attack, two of the six indicator loops were out of action, while the readings of the submarine crossings over the other loops were misinterpreted as being other legitimate vessels.

This audacious attack in the very heart of Sydney had a massive impact on the morale of Australians. Until then, the authorities had not believed it was necessary to have a blackout in Sydney due to the low threat of attack. Until then, Sydneysiders had considered themselves safe.

❧

On Tuesday night, Poppy heard someone at the front door. Honey barked loudly at the dark outline of a male through the stained glass window, standing on the front verandah in the gathering dusk.

Cautiously, she opened the door a crack on its safety chain. 'Oh, Jack, hello,' she said, unfastening the door. 'Come in out of the cold. What are you doing here?'

Jack shuffled on the tessellated tile floor, twisting his hat anxiously in his hands. Behind him, the great branches of the Moreton Bay fig spread into the sky.

'No, I can't stay more than a minute,' he replied. 'Poppy, there's something I want to tell you.'

By the look on his face, Poppy could tell it would be something serious. She smiled nervously. 'Oh?'

'I've decided to join up.'

Poppy clenched her fingernails into her palms. 'No. You can't. What about school? What about studying engineering at university? You've only just turned seventeen.'

Jack squared his shoulders and gazed at Poppy. 'After what happened on Sunday night, I don't think I can just stay here pretending to live a normal life, as though there's not an enemy on our doorstep threatening to take it all away from us. My brothers are sailing overseas this week, probably heading to New Guinea. I want to go, too.'

'But Jack, what if something terrible happens? What if you're *killed*?' Poppy pleaded. Her eyes were filling with tears and she fought to keep them down. 'What if you and your brothers are all killed and your parents are left with nobody?'

'Poppy, what if we'd been killed on Sunday night? Or when the Japanese bombed Darwin? We all have to do what we think is right.'

Poppy swallowed hard. She surreptitiously rubbed her eyes as though they were itchy. 'Aren't you scared?' she asked.

'Weren't you scared on Sunday night, or up in Darwin? Of course I'm scared, but I think I'm doing the right thing, doing whatever I can to help stop this terrible war.'

Poppy looked at her feet. The toes of her school shoes were scuffed. She'd need to clean them or Miss Royston would be annoyed. The headmistress hated untidiness and tardiness.

'Poppy?' Poppy looked up at Jack again. 'I came to say goodbye, Midget. I'm leaving tomorrow morning to start training. Will you say goodbye to your mum for me — and to Maude and Mrs Tibbets? Will you write to me?'

Poppy flung her arms around Jack's neck and sobbed onto his chest.

'Of course I'll write to you, silly,' Poppy cried. 'Please, please look after yourself — and don't do anything stupid.'

Jack hugged her back. 'Who are you calling silly, Midget?'

After a moment, Jack reluctantly pulled away. 'I have to go and see Dad and Mum. Look after yourself, Midget. And don't forget to write.'

Jack strode off down the darkened street. Poppy watched him recede until he was nearly swallowed up by the shadows. He stopped at the corner and looked back, raising his hat in a silent salute. Then he was gone.

Honey whined, licking Poppy on the leg. Poppy scooped the dog into her arms, crept upstairs to her room and turned on the record-player. She sat on her bed in the dark, hugging Honey and listening to the melancholy tones of Vera Lynn singing, as tears ran down her face.

'We'll meet again,
Don't know where, don't know when,
But I know we'll meet again some sunny day.
Keep smiling through,
Just like you always do,
'Til the blue skies
Drive the dark clouds far away . . .'

It was much, much later when she could face going downstairs to tell her mum and Maude that Jack was going away and had dropped by to say goodbye to them all.

❧

Maude knocked on Poppy's door and found her friend seated at her desk, doing mathematics homework, surrounded by a pile of open books.

'Poppy, can I talk to you for a minute?' Maude asked.

'Sure, come in,' Poppy said, standing up and stretching. 'Have you finished your arithmetic already? It's taking me ages.'

Maude strolled in and sat on the middle of Poppy's bed, her legs crossed. Poppy turned her desk chair around and plopped down again.

'No, I can't concentrate on arithmetic,' admitted Maude. 'Mother wants us to pack up and move to Bathurst. We have friends with a farm out there, and she wants to move as far from the coast as possible in case the Japs come.'

Poppy nodded slowly. Her shoulders drooped and her heart felt like a lump of grey stone in her belly.

Maude is leaving again. Will we have to run away, too? I don't want to run anymore. I don't want to start all over again in a new place. Why should we be forced to leave our home again?

'I wish you didn't have to go,' Poppy said. 'I feel like I've just settled in here. I'm really enjoying going to school, too. I love living here with you — it's so much fun.'

'Do you think your mum will want to move away?'

asked Maude. 'Perhaps you can come to Bathurst, too? Mother wants to sell the house.'

Poppy thought back over all that had happened in the last few months. Shinju and Mrs Murata being arrested and interned. Edward going missing in the fall of Singapore. Bryony, Maude and all her friends and neighbours being evacuated by ship. The terrifying bombing of Darwin. Iris Bald and her mother and friends being killed at the post office. Daisy and Charlie being shot in the air-raid trench. Leaving her father behind in the war zone to escape south by horse and cart. Being caught up in the Japanese raid on Sydney Harbour by the midget submarines. Jack joining up to be a soldier at the age of seventeen.

I've experienced and survived so much, thought Poppy. *I'm not going to give up now. I'm not going to let them take anything more away from me.*

Poppy felt a well of confidence and courage swell inside her. 'I don't want to leave Sydney,' Poppy said with deep conviction. 'I want to stay here and finish school — and make sure I make the most of my life.'

She paused and looked at Maude, worried her friend might take offence or think she was being melodramatic. Instead, Maude nodded her encouragement.

'Mum and I can get a room somewhere close to the hospital and school,' Poppy continued.

'I know it might be hard, but one day the war will be over and things will get better. Life might never be the same again, but I want to feel like I've done my best. It's just like Miss Royston says: we all have a responsibility to help in any way we can — no matter how small — even if it's just trying hard in a horrible arithmetic test.'

The two sat in silence for a few minutes, thinking everything over.

Maude frowned. 'I can't see how trying hard in an arithmetic test is going to help win the war,' she teased.

Poppy picked up the nearest weapon — a cushion — and threw it at Maude's head. 'You know what I mean.'

'You're right, Poppy,' Maude said. 'I don't want to leave Sydney either. Mother can sell the house and move to Bathurst if she wants — I'm staying here, too. I can board at school, or live with you and your mum. I don't want to run away and skulk in Bathurst, terrified of every shadow in case it's the enemy.'

Poppy smiled at Maude in relief.

'Good — there has to be someone at school that's worse at hockey than me!'

21

Epistles

8 April 2012

'Nanna, you were so brave!' exclaimed Chloe. 'I don't think I could ever be so courageous.'

Nanna shook her head with a smile. 'Of course you could. We didn't think of ourselves as brave — we just tried to do the best we could in difficult circumstances. Everyone did.'

Nanna shivered. The sun had moved around to the west and their bench was now in shade.

'Shall we go back upstairs?' Nanna suggested. 'I think I could do with another cup of tea. My throat is parched.'

'Sure.' Chloe jumped to her feet and gathered up the cushions. 'Can we read some more of the letters, Nanna?'

Nanna smiled as she packed up the tin once more. 'You can read them out loud to me while I drink a cup

of tea and give my voice a rest. I haven't read them for
years — I found lots of the family letters when I packed
up the old house in Darwin after my mother died and
I couldn't bear to throw them out.'

Upstairs, Nanna settled into her favourite chair with a
cup of steaming hot tea, her eyes closed. Chloe took a sip
from her own tea, then started to read.

Addison Road,
Manly

June 30, 1942

Dear Dad,

Hope you are well and enjoying the dry season. It's
freezing down here!! Mum says I'll get used to it. I used
to think that Maude carried on and on about how hot
and humid it was up in Darwin, now I'm exactly the
same but moaning about the cold and shivering over
the tiny heater.

Good news! Mrs Tibbets has given in about selling
the house and moving to Bathurst. Maude just flatly
refused to go, and then Mrs Tibbets agreed that she was
only going to the country to keep Maude safe. Maude
said they would both die of boredom — at least in Sydney
we can do something to help. We have knitted another
five million socks, not to mention thousands of mittens
and caps. I'm sure none of the soldiers would want my
socks, but still we keep knitting.

Still no news from Edward. Mum tries to be brave, but sometimes she gets this faraway look in her eyes and I know she is thinking about him and worrying and hoping he's all right. Then she throws herself into working long days and nights at the hospital. I think she can only sleep when she's completely exhausted. Her ribs are still troubling her somewhat but she rarely complains.

The Japanese seem to have given up on terrorising Sydney for the moment, which is a small relief. Japanese subs have been attacking and torpedoing ships up and down the coast between Newcastle and Wollongong. They also shelled Newcastle and the eastern suburbs of Sydney on 8 June. Several houses and shops were destroyed, but miraculously no one was killed. It could have been far, far worse.

The papers were full of amazing stories of escape — like the little boys in Newcastle who were watching the 'fireworks' from their bedroom window when their mother dragged them down to the bomb shelter. A moment later their bedroom was shelled and they would almost certainly have been killed.

There was a lot of anger in Sydney because the Government decided to cremate the four bodies of the Japanese midget submarine crews with full military honours and return their ashes to Japan. Some people say this is to encourage the Japanese to treat the Australian prisoners-of-war well. Others say it makes their blood boil when they think how many of our boys were killed on the Kuttabul and the merchant ships that have been sunk since.

Two of the midget submarines were pulled up from the harbour floor, and one of the subs has been on display to raise money for the war effort. Maude and I went to see it. Apparently, these subs are designed to attack large warships with little hope that the Japanese crew will ever survive. Can you imagine setting off on a mission knowing it means almost certain death?

The shortages are getting worse. Maude and I are doing all the cooking and housekeeping now because Mama is too tired after a long day at the hospital and Mrs Tibbets is volunteering at the Red Cross. We do our best to implement the principles of Austerity House-keeping – as advocated by the Australian Women's Weekly – a thousand-and-one ways to cook brains, livers and kidneys without spices!! Thank goodness for fresh herbs, the vegie garden and the chooks. The house and garden, together with schoolwork and games, keeps us really busy.

We are soon to lose Bryony, too. She is being trans-ferred to Brisbane with the Royal Australian Corps of Signals, leaving in two weeks, together with many of the other AWAS personnel. I'm not quite sure what she'll be doing – I don't think she really knows either.

Spirits are much higher in Sydney after the Battle of Midway. Up in Townsville, Phoebe nursed lots of the wounded men after the battle, many of whom had terrible burns. It was incredible that our men could be so outnumbered and yet inflict such great losses on the Japanese. It finally looks like the tide might be turning in our favour. We can only pray.

We are all missing you so much. Mama is hoping

we will see you at Christmas – surely the war can't go on much longer. Mama sends her love.

Your loving daughter,
Poppy

Ingleside Army Camp

July 2, 1942

Dear Poppy,

How are you going at school? I'm settling in to training. We have eight men crowded into a tent, which can be a little uncomfortable, but we don't spend much time in them anyway. One of my mates snores like thunder, which at first kept us all awake – at least now we are so exhausted we can sleep through anything! The food is awful, of course, but there is a great sense of camaraderie among the lads.

The ages range from 'eighteen' to forty-five, from all over Sydney and a few from country areas. There are lots of 'eighteen-year-olds' that look a lot younger than me. There are a few brothers who have joined up together, and even a few father-and-son teams. Not sure if it is the father joining up to keep an eye on the son or vice versa! Many of the married men have their wives living close by, so they can see them when they have time off.

Training is tough with long route marches along the country roads every day. They get progressively longer and harder every day to build up fitness. Marching in the cold, soaking rain is miserable! Some of the city lads find this difficult, especially the office workers – it's easier for the country lads like me who are used to spending long days out of doors and being physical.

Of course, we spend hours learning to march and stand on parade. It's tedious but is supposed to teach us discipline, obedience and teamwork – or something like that! At first, some of the men just used to keel over in a faint from standing at attention for so long. We are also excellent trench diggers now. If you need a few slit trenches built in the backyard, I'm the lad for the job!

Our colonel is a hard taskmaster and is very good at finding us tough jobs to do – like spending the night in the trenches in the pouring rain. Sometimes it's hard to see the purpose of it all. I'm guessing we'll get plenty of practice doing that when we're up in the Pacific somewhere. It will be at least six months of training, though, before I get to face the enemy. I hope the war isn't over before I get a chance to do my bit.

Please give my regards to your mother and sisters, and Maude and Mrs Tibbets, and of course Honey-dog. Give my mother a hug if you see her.

Kind regards,
Jack Shanahan

Kuran Street, Chermside, Queensland

July 20, 1942

Dear Mum and Poppy,

I am now settled in my new home – the dusty AWAS camp in Chermside, surrounded by a high barbed-wire fence. Not sure if the fence is to keep the women in, or to keep the four thousand soldiers from the army camp out!! The barracks are all temporary buildings set up in a huge paddock, including mess hall, ablutions block and sleeping quarters. Much of the land around here is farmland, and most of the locals get around in horse and sulkies, which means the roads are a mess of manure!

Most of the women here are working at Central Bureau with me. We work at Ascot, a few miles away near the Brisbane River, so army lorries take us to and from work. There are twelve women rostered on each shift, round the clock, working in a cramped garage, listening to and recording radio transmissions for hours every day. The work requires high levels of concentration, so I've been getting a few migraines.

The garage belongs to the most beautiful old mansion, which is where the men work. I even met US General MacArthur last week. He has moved his headquarters from Melbourne to Brisbane to be closer to the action, and closer to the American troops up north.

I work with a lovely bunch of people. We all got to know each other very quickly since we work, sleep, eat and play together seven days a week. When we are not working, we chat, write letters, read books, play cricko (a type of cricket) or go swimming. On Friday nights we go to dances at the School of Arts, or watch films at the Dawn Theatre. There is a nice Aboriginal girl I work with called Kath, who has two brothers who are both POWs in Singapore.

I will write again soon.

Love to you both,
Corporal Bryony Trehearne
(yes – I've been promoted!)

July 30, 1942

Townsville

Dear Mum and Poppy,

Don't be alarmed – I am quite safe! The Japanese have bombed Townsville several times over the last few days but fortunately no one was killed and the damage has been minimal. Everyone hurried down to the air-raid shelters and we entertained our- selves by singing songs and playing music. I watched one of the raids and it was quite an eerie sight, seeing the 'Emily' bombers flying in and dropping their payloads. For some reason, most of the bombs fell harmlessly into the sea. Presumably, the blackout helped and they couldn't see what they were aiming at.

According to the Japanese propaganda broadcasts, most of the military installations in Townsville were smashed, but from where we are sitting, only a coconut palm was decapitated by a daisy-cutter bomb, and the chickens at the poultry farm were terrified and now refuse to lay eggs!! I know it could have been so much worse, as it was in Darwin and Sydney, but it helps us all to look at the lighter side of things.

Speaking of amusing stories doing the rounds, we are all giggling over the airman who, when the air raid sounded, raced to report for duty but had forgotten to put on his trousers! Of course he has been the subject of much ribbing from everyone over the last few days.

Life in the hospital continues much the same as ever – long days under intense pressure. The influx of American servicemen has put a huge strain on the food resources in Townsville and, even worse, the water supplies during the dry season. We have to be so frugal washing ourselves that I'm afraid a hot bath is a dim, distant memory.

One of our great pleasures, though, is to go for moonlight swims after work at one of the many waterfalls and creeks around Townsville. Just a small group of the girls go at a time and we are all sworn to secrecy – the last thing we want is for our haven to be discovered. It is absolute bliss after a hard day to soak under the ice-cold water. Of course, we stay right away from the estuaries where the crocodiles are.

I went to a fun army dance on Friday night with one of the American soldiers, from New Orleans, named Henry Worth. He is a real gentleman, always bringing me lovely presents, and he has the most charming accent. We've been to the pictures a couple of times, and on my next day off we're going for a picnic up into the mountains.

I have seen General MacArthur up here a couple of times when he has been visiting the US troops. He looked like he had the weight of the world on his shoulders – which I suppose he does. I guess on him rests the future of Australia and the whole Pacific.

Anyway, much love as always,
  Phoebe

Dear Bryony,

Here's a poem we studied at school by Mary Gilmore.
I thought you might enjoy it.

Love,
Poppy xxx

No Foe Shall Gather Our Harvest

Sons of the mountains of Scotland,
Welshmen of coomb and defile,
Breed of the moors of England,
Children of Erin's green isle,
We stand four square to the tempest,
Whatever the battering hail -
No foe shall gather our harvest,
Or sit on our stockyard rail.

Our women shall walk in honour,
Our children shall know no chain.
This land, that is ours forever,
The invader shall strike at in vain.
Anzac! . . . Tobruk! . . . and Kokoda! . . .
Could ever the old blood fail?
No foe shall gather our harvest,
Or sit on our stockyard rail.

So hail-fellow-met we muster,
And hail-fellow-met fall in,

Wherever the guns may thunder,
Or the rocketing air-mail spin!
Born of the soil and the whirlwind,
Though death itself be the gale -
No foe shall gather our harvest
Or sit on our stockyard rail.

We are the sons of Australia,
of the men who fashioned the land;
We are the sons of the women
Who walked with them hand in hand;
And we swear by the dead who bore us,
By the heroes who blazed the trail,
No foe shall gather our harvest,
Or sit on our stockyard rail.

Townsville

September 13, 1942

Dear Mum and Poppy,

It is with great sadness that I am writing to let you know
that my American friend Henry Worth was killed up in New
Guinea recently. One of his friends wrote to tell me.
    Henry and I had hoped to be married after the war.

Love,
Phoebe

Bathurst

December 15, 1942

Dear Poppy,

Hurray! Training is finished at last and we are coming back to
Sydney. Our unit will march through the streets on Tuesday
next week. Then we get a couple of weeks' leave to spend Christmas with our folks.

Would you like to come along to see the march? I am really
looking forward to seeing you all before we head off overseas in
January. I wonder where we'll go?

Best wishes,
Jack

Adelaide River,
Northern Territory

June 21, 1943

My Darling Cecilia and Poppy,

The Japanese air raids on the Northern Territory continue
with monotonous regularity, but fortunately they seem to
have less and less impact. The troops seem to be inflicting
more damage on the raiders than we are receiving. We have
calculated that there have now been nearly sixty air raids
on Darwin and its surrounding airfields.

I am due for some leave soon. I only wish it was long enough to come and see you, but Sydney is such a long way away. I miss you all terribly and long to see you.

On a sad note, I recognised one of the wounded boys who came in last week. It was Harry Shanahan. Unfortunately, we were unable to save him. The Shanahans will be devastated; by now they will have received the dreaded telegram. When you see them, could you please pass on my condolences? It is so sad to see such a tragic waste of a young life. I feel so helpless not being able to do more to save them.

Much love as always
Mark

Addison Road, Manly

August 30, 1943

Dear Jack,

Are you all right? You haven't replied to my last three letters. Maude says she hasn't heard from you either.

I hope everything is okay. I saw your parents the other day, so at least I know you are alive. Perhaps you are just too busy? Everything continues here, same as ever — schoolwork, chores, study, tennis, war work . . . We don't do archery at school anymore — all the arrow heads have been donated to the war effort. Mrs Tibbets has even donated the beautiful wrought iron from the verandahs, so the poor old house looks quite forlorn.

You may have heard that Prime Minister Curtin survived the election with a landslide victory, which is a great relief, after all the kerfuffle over whether there was ever a plan to abandon all of Australia north of Brisbane to the Japanese. The very first women representatives were also elected to the Australian Parliament, which is an astonishing first.

Please write soon.

Kind Regards,
Poppy

IMPERIAL JAPANESE ARMY

Date 15-1-44

I am interned in Thailand

Your mails (and love) are received with thanks.
My health is (~~good~~, usual, ~~poor~~)
~~I am ill in hospital~~.
I am working for pay (~~I am paid monthly salary~~)
~~I am not working~~.

My best regards to everyone much love Edward

September 20, 1944

Townsville

Dear Mum and Poppy,

I am off to New Guinea! The nurses were asked for volunteers to go up and work in the hospital near Port Moresby. We have been assured there is absolutely no danger from the Japanese there now. Most of the patients we'll treat are not battle casualties but men suffering from tropical diseases, like malaria and dengue fever.

We will be flown up in a couple of weeks. I'm really looking forward to it. Sorry I won't have time to come down and see you before I go. Anyway, you probably wouldn't recognise me – I am now a glamorous shade of yellow, thanks to the atabrine tablets we take for malaria. At least it tastes better than the quinine.

Keep up that study, Poppy! Good luck in your Leaving Certificate exams – I know you'll do us proud!

Much love, as always,
Phoebe

August 16, 1945

Dear Edward,

Can you believe it? What joy! The war is over. I wonder if you know yet? The news that the Japanese had

247

surrendered was announced on the radio in the morning, then the whole of Sydney took to the streets to celebrate.

Maude and I caught the ferry into the city. George Street to Town Hall was jammed with thousands of people. You should have seen it. There was dancing in the streets. Complete strangers hugging and kissing each other. Music playing. People crying.

It is a day I will never forget. We took in bags of confetti we cut up ourselves, which everyone was tossing in the air. Martin Place was nearly knee-deep in shredded paper. It looked just like snow.

We all linked arms, swaying, and sang song after song after song – all the war favourites – 'We'll Meet Again', 'The White Cliffs of Dover', 'As Time Goes By'. We didn't want the night to end.

The only sad note is that Prime Minster Curtin didn't live to see this joyful day that he has worked so hard for. He died six weeks ago, worn out by care and worry, and has been greatly mourned.

I hope you have been receiving our letters. Mum had a batch returned, which worries her greatly.

We hope and pray that you are all right - and that you will be coming home to us soon.

All my love,
Poppy

Addison Road
Manly

September 19, 1945

Dear Phoebe,

It's come. We received notification this week that
Edward is alive and coming home! It's the first news
we've received in nearly two years — a month since the
war ended! — and the best eighteenth birthday present
ever. Oh, the celebrations in our house — it was better
than V-J Day. Maude and I were dancing and singing
in the kitchen, while Mum just sat down, pulled her
apron over her face and cried as though her heart would
break. I swear she had four years' worth of tears to shed.

Mum is making plans for us all to be reunited in
Darwin for Christmas. She hopes you will be back from
overseas and that Bryony can get leave. Please, please
write and say you can come. It would mean the world to
her. It will be nearly four and a half years since we were
all together as a family.

I just can't believe the war is over and we can finally
go home. We will stay in Sydney for the next few weeks
while we pack up and I resign from my mindless, horrible
job. I'll be so happy if I never see the inside of a munitions factory again. Then we will travel by ship back to
Darwin. It will be strange to leave Maude and Mrs
Tibbets after all this time - Maude is like a sister to me
now. Of course I adore you and Bryony, but I haven't
seen you for such a long, long time. Please write at once

and say you'll come!! I can't wait to see you both. Can you imagine how wonderful it will be to have Christmas all together in our very own home?

Much love to you,
Poppy

Singapore

September 20, 1945

Dear Mum, Dad, Phoebe, Bryony and Poppy,

Thank you all so much for your letters and cards over the last four years. I truly believe that it was those letters that kept me going when things got really bad. That and the mateship of all the Aussie POWs looking out for each other.

This is the first real letter I have written since Singapore fell in February 1942 (not counting those phoney cards the Japanese forced us to write). And here I am again, back in Singapore after all this time. We caught the train to Bangkok, then were flown by DC3s to Singapore yesterday. The Red Cross has been wonderful.

They are urging us all to be patient. It could take weeks to repatriate all the POWs. Many of us will need to stay here in Singapore until we are fit enough to travel home by ship. The very worst cases are being flown back by plane. We are all terribly thin — don't be too shocked when you see me. We have been advised to eat only small meals for some time because our digestion cannot cope with too much after three and a half years of nothing but a tiny serve of rice and boiled-up weeds.

I need to warn you of something more serious: I had my left leg amputated in the camp a couple of weeks ago. Tropical ulcers were a major problem. I had five ulcers and, unfortunately, our medical officer decreed that the leg would need to come off at the knee. Dad, you would have been proud to see our operating theatre created from nothing more than what we could scrounge in the jungle — an operating table built from bamboo, a saw from the work parties, sterilised in half a fuel drum of boiling water over an open fire. Unfortunately, no anaesthetic — and I've been pretty sick — but now we're getting proper medication and good food. I'm sure I'll be on the mend soon.

You wouldn't believe the ingenuity of the doctors in the camps. They made vitamin brews from boiled grass, weevils, snails and weeds, used broken glass for scalpels, and treated dysentery with burnt rice scrapings and charcoal. Their greatest medicine was humour, making prisoners laugh under the most dire conditions. Still, despite their very best efforts, so many of us won't be coming back.

Good news — I've just been informed that I'll be sailing home in a few days on the Highland Chieftain, which should call into Darwin by the end of the month, then Sydney by about the tenth or eleventh of October. I can hardly believe that I'll be seeing you all again so soon.

All my love to you all,
Edward

October 11, 1945

Internment Camp 4

Tatura, Victoria

Dear Dr and Mrs Trehearne,

I hope that you and your family have been blessed to survive this terrible war.

My name is Asami Murata. I hope you remember me. I worked for you until four years ago in Darwin, when my family was interned and taken to Tatura Camp, near Rushworth, in Victoria. Your daughter Poppy saved the life of my granddaughter Shinju at Kahlin Bay.

I am writing to ask you a large favour. We have been told that the Japanese internees are to be repatriated to Japan now that the war is over. Yet none of my surviving family has ever been to Japan – we were all born in Australia. My father came to Broome sixty-five years ago and died here in the camp three years ago. My husband also died last year from pneumonia. While life has been very hard in the camp, we do not wish to be taken to Japan.

One of the officers, a kind man, suggested that I ask you to write a reference for my family so that we might be allowed to stay together in Australia. He has warned us that it will be a long, slow process.

While we have experienced the sadness of losing my father and husband, we have also had the joy of three more grandchildren born here in the camp. Shinju now has a baby brother called Jiro and a sister called Hoshi. My second son, Takazo, has also married and has a newborn son.

Shinju has grown into a beautiful nine-year-old girl. She barely remembers life outside the barbed wire fence that surrounds this camp. She goes to the school here and is a good student who works hard. She also helps her mother and me at the sewing factory and looks after the younger children. We have a family hut and are lucky to all be together.

I hope that you do not find my request too presumptuous. We would be very grateful for any help you may be able to give us in presenting our case. I have also written to the minister of the local church, who has promised to help me find work as a housemaid if we are allowed to stay.

Enclosed is also a letter for Miss Poppy from Shinju. We would have written earlier; however, we were not allowed to have any contact with people outside the camp.

Please give my warmest regards to your family, especially to Miss Poppy, who is always remembered in our prayers.

Yours sincerely,
Asami Murata

Dear Miss Poppy,

I hope you are well. I go to school here but there are only Japanese children at the camp, not like in Darwin. I remember your kindness to me the day the soldiers came to Darwin school to take us away.

We do lots of activities and work to keep busy: craft, gardening, sport and music. I like to draw pictures of dragons and Naga maidens swimming in their palaces deep under the sea. I thought you might like one of my pictures.

I have a new brother and a new sister. We all live together in an iron hut. It is freezing in winter and sometimes the babies get sick. In summer it is very hot. The guards are kind to us but we can't ever leave the camp. One day I hope to swim in the sea again. My grandmother says when we are free she will teach me to swim like a Naga maiden.

Yours sincerely,
Shinju Murata

October 18, 1945

Internment Camp 4

Tatura, Victoria

Dear Mrs Trehearne and Miss Poppy,

Thank you so much for your letter and your kind reference. We pray it will make a difference and the authorities will let us stay. I'm told it may be many months before we know. They say that the Australian people are very angry with the Japanese and that life will be hard for us here. But Australia is our home. I hope Shinju and the other children will be able to grow up here in a land of peace.

I'm glad that Miss Poppy enjoyed the letter and drawing from Shinju. Thank you so much for sending the parcel of books and art supplies for her, along with the toys and clothes for all the children. Shinju was so excited when the huge parcel arrived. They were the first real presents she has received since we came here four years ago.

I will let you know as soon as we have any news about whether we will be allowed to stay.

Yours sincerely,
Asami Murata

22

Homecoming

It was late November 1945 when their ship chugged into Darwin Harbour. Poppy and Bryony stood by the rails, straining to catch a glimpse of their hometown — their first for nearly four years. Honey was lying on the deck, one fluffy ear cocked while she slept, her muzzle now grey about the whiskers.

The early summer heat was still and oppressive, building up to the wet season. Poppy couldn't believe how lethargic it made her feel and how much she had teased Maude when her friend complained constantly about the heat.

'Look,' she cried, 'there's Government House and the jetty.'

'At last — we're nearly there,' Bryony added. 'I can't wait to get home.'

Bryony and Poppy flung their arms around each other, performing a little jig of excitement. Honey woke up with all the noise and woofed with pleasure. Cecilia, Mark and

Edward came over from the bench where they had been sitting to get a better view.

'The Japs sure did a thorough job on those ships, didn't they?' Edward pointed to the rusty wrecks still littering the harbour.

It seemed to take forever for the ship to dock and the passengers to be allowed to disembark at the new jetty. Edward had had a prosthetic leg fitted in Sydney, and he was still a little wobbly on the moving gangway. They gathered all their baggage and hailed a taxi to drive them the short distance home.

The family approached Myilly Point with mounting apprehension. Darwin still looked like a war zone. They saw skeletons of bombed-out houses, mounds of debris and rubble overgrown with brown grass. On the side of the road was the scorched wreckage of a crashed fighter plane.

The taxi pulled up outside the Trehearnes' home on Myilly Point.

'Good luck — and welcome home.' The driver took his coins and reversed away, leaving them surrounded by a pile of luggage.

The house looked like it had been abandoned for decades. The corrugated roof was riddled with machine-gun bullets. The main water tank was empty and turned over on its side. The garden was overgrown with long, dry grass and littered with empty petrol drums. The back door had been kicked in, and was now hanging from one broken hinge.

'Oh,' croaked Cecilia, her hand held to her throat.

They climbed the steps to the verandah slowly and peered inside. Everything was gone. Every room was empty. The furniture, books, pictures, curtains, rugs, clothes, saucepans, refrigerator, shelving — everything had been taken.

Cecilia collapsed to the floor. Poppy and Bryony huddled beside her, shocked and distressed.

'It's all gone,' Cecilia cried, her bitter tears welling up and overflowing. 'Everything we owned.'

Mark rubbed Cecilia's shoulders soothingly. 'We heard there was looting,' he admitted, his voice hoarse. 'First the shipwrecked sailors made camps, using what they could find, then the army took over and requisitioned what it needed. Then we heard that some of those left behind just helped themselves to what they wanted and sent it back to Adelaide and Melbourne by truck. There was no one here to stop them.'

Edward stood by the window, gazing out at the view. 'I fought and gave up years of my life in a stinking hellhole so they could do this to us?' His voice was low and angry.

'What will we do?' asked Bryony. 'We've come all this way for nothing.'

Cecilia looked up at her family gathered around her. She wiped the tears from her face and stood up, squaring her shoulders. 'We start again,' she announced. 'We work and we clean our house and we fix what's been broken. I am having Christmas with my beautiful family — in my home — and *nothing* is going to stop me.'

Poppy laughed through her tears. 'That's the spirit, Mum. We didn't let the war beat us, so we're not going to give up now.'

Mark gave Cecilia a hug. 'Okay, boss,' he joked. 'Where do we start?'

Cecilia looked around at the filthy room and ticked the list off on her fingers. 'Well, first we need a nice cup of hot tea — so we need water, a fire, some timber and a spade.'

'Why a spade?' asked Edward, intrigued.

'Because I buried a box full of my best china and silver under the house, and we'll need some teacups.'

Everyone laughed, suddenly feeling much better, and set off to scrounge whatever they could find that might be useful. Honey accompanied Poppy, exploring all the old, familiar scents with her nose.

While Poppy was on her way to fetch a bucket of water from the remaining tank at the back of the shed, she paused beside the filled-in trench where Daisy and Charlie were buried. She gathered a big pile of hot-pink bougainvillea and laid it on the mound, saying a silent prayer for them. Honey pawed at the ground and whined.

'I know, Honey,' Poppy whispered. 'I miss them too.'

When Phoebe arrived home a week later, the house had been scrubbed from end to end. Edward and Mark had made furniture from wooden crates, flour sacks, recycled building materials and iron camp beds from the abandoned army barracks. The cooking was done over an open fire in a cut-down fuel drum, while the house water tank had been righted and repaired to catch the first of the early rains.

Cecilia and Bryony had scoured the stores in Darwin for basic supplies. Mark bought a bolt of unbleached calico that the girls sewed into curtains. When the house was in order, they had started on the vegetable garden — weeding, hoeing, digging and planting.

It wasn't their gracious home from before the war, but it was a start.

❦

On a warm morning in early December, Poppy was scything the overgrown grass in the garden. She was wearing a pair of Edward's army shorts pulled in tightly with a belt and an old, ragged shirt belonging to her father. Her hair was tied up with a scrap of calico. On her forearm shone the thin, silvery-pink scar of the shrapnel wound from the day the first bombs fell.

The scything was hot, heavy work, but it was rewarding as the garden was gradually transformed.

Honey snoozed in the freshly cut grass, occasionally cocking an eyebrow to check on Poppy's progress. Poppy was sweeping the scythe in large semicircles under the frangipani tree when she sensed someone behind her. Honey jumped to her feet, tail wagging furiously.

'Hello, Midget.'

Poppy dropped her scythe and swung around. 'Jack!'

She rushed forward to hug him, then checked herself, feeling self-conscious. She hadn't seen Jack for three and a half years, not since he went off to war, and now here she was — sweaty, dirty and dressed in rags. She swept the piece of calico off her head, wiped it over her face, then quickly fluffed out her hair.

'Jack, how are you? When did you get back? Are you all right?'

She quickly scanned him, checking for missing limbs or injuries. Jack looked just the same as ever — tall and fit, tanned and healthy, fair hair swept back off his forehead, blue eyes dancing with laughter.

'Glad to see you're still a hoyden, Miss Midget,' joked Jack. 'I thought all those years in Sydney might have turned you into a glamour puss.'

Poppy swiped at him with her calico rag. 'Don't be mean,' she protested. 'I'm not a hoyden. I'm just working hard, unlike *some*.'

'Aren't you going to invite me to take a seat?' asked Jack, motioning to the freshly mown grass under the frangipani tree. 'Is that any way to welcome home a poor, exhausted Aussie digger, who's spent his youth fighting for his country?'

'Excuse me, poor exhausted Aussie digger, would you care to take a seat?' Poppy plopped down under the tree, glad for the chance to take a break. Jack moved the scythe and sat down beside her.

Jack looked at her, now serious. 'I'm glad to see a flash of the old Poppy. It's been a long time. I thought you might have forgotten me.'

'*Forgotten* you?' demanded Poppy. 'You're the one who stopped writing.'

Jack had the grace to look discomfited. 'Your letters seemed so full of your schoolwork and friends – it was such a distant world from the one I was fighting in up in New Guinea,' confessed Jack. 'Then my brother died, and that was terrible. I was just too sick and tired of it all to write. There didn't seem to be anything to say.'

Poppy touched his hand. 'I'm sorry.'

They sat in silence for a moment. Honey pawed Jack's arm, begging for a pat. Jack obliged and scratched her between the eyes. Honey woofed with pleasure.

'Well, to answer your questions, I was demobbed in October, so I came straight back to Alexandra Downs,' Jack said. 'We fared better down there than you did here because we were a long way from the bombing, plus we had a manager to keep an eye on the place. Mum and Dad moved back a few months ago, so the house was still intact. I had to come to Darwin to deliver a mob of cattle to the meatworks, and I heard in town that you were back, so I thought I'd just pop by to see how you all were.'

Poppy asked Jack about his family, and he said his dad had recovered from his operation and was back running the station. His mum was devastated after the loss of her son, but was thrilled to have her other two home safely.

'But what about *your* family?' asked Jack. 'I heard your brother had a rough time?'

Poppy nodded, her eyes growing misty. 'He's up and down but getting better,' Poppy explained. 'Working on the house has really given him a project to throw himself into, and he's good with tools. He lost his leg in the last weeks of the war, so he had to have a lot of rehabilitation in Sydney. He was emaciated when he first came back — they'd all been starved and terribly mistreated. He told me he had several bones broken from beatings, not that he likes to talk about it much.'

Jack winced. 'I've heard it was absolutely dreadful — he's lucky to be alive. And your sister Phoebe? She's just arrived back in Darwin?'

'Phoebe went overseas as a nurse, firstly to New Guinea, but then she got really sick,' Poppy explained. 'She caught malaria and dengue fever and had to come home for a few months to recover. Mum nursed her — she was desperately ill and terribly sad. She had fallen in love with an American soldier who was killed up in New Guinea.'

Poppy paused and picked up a frangipani blossom, which she spun between her fingers.

'Then, when the Japanese surrendered, they needed nurses experienced in tropical medicine to go up and look after the rescued prisoners of war at the medical camps in Singapore,' Poppy continued. 'Phoebe went in a flash — she says it was heartbreaking, seeing all these British, American, New Zealand and Australian soldiers reduced to shuffling skeletons. Many of them couldn't walk up the gangway to get on the ships home.'

'I saw some of them when the ships came into Darwin a few weeks ago,' Jack said. 'It'll take the poor blokes a long time to get over the horror of it all. But you should have seen the joy on their faces when they set foot on Aussie soil for the first time in years. It was indescribable.'

The two lapsed into silence, lost in thought.

'Do you still see Maude?' asked Jack. 'Last time you wrote, you were still living at the Tibbets's place in Manly.'

Poppy's face lit up. 'Maude is great. She's studying art at university and having a marvellous time. All the boys think she's gorgeous.'

Jack pulled a battered piece of paper out of his wallet. 'I have this photo of you and Maude that I took in Manly that day I first came to Sydney,' Jack confessed. 'I carried it with me all through the jungles of New Guinea. It used to remind me why I was up there fighting.'

The photo was dog-eared and soiled from so much handling. It showed Maude and Poppy as fourteen-year-old girls, their hair salty and windblown, arms around each other, laughing into the camera.

Poppy felt a wrench in her stomach. Jack had carried a photo of Maude in his wallet all through the war. He had obviously looked at it often. Was Jack sweet on Maude?

'We look so young and carefree then,' said Poppy wistfully. 'That was a wonderful day — at least until you were nearly beaten up by the American.'

Jack laughed, stroking the photo with his finger. 'Well, if you weren't such a flirt, we would never have got into such a fix.'

'Flirt?' exclaimed Poppy indignantly. 'I was not a flirt!'

Jack tucked the photo back into his wallet. 'No, but that Yank was certainly determined to buy you an ice cream! So I know Bryony was with the AWAS, but what about you? What have you been doing for the last three years?'

Poppy shrugged and smiled. 'I did my Leaving Certificate last year and scored pretty well, especially in English,' said Poppy. 'My headmistress wanted me to go on to university and get my degree. She said I would regret it my whole life if I didn't take the opportunity to go to uni.'

Jack nodded, encouraging her to continue.

'But by that stage I was seventeen; I wanted to get out there and do something useful for the war.' Poppy smiled at Jack. 'I was sick of knitting socks and hearing about everyone else being heroes. All the men, like you, were off fighting, and so the girls were encouraged to take over male jobs. I worked in an aeroplane factory out in the western suburbs of Sydney where we built components for Beaufort bombers — fuselages, undercarriages and stern frames. I was a riveter.'

Poppy pulled a wry face and laughed at herself. Jack grinned at Poppy in her sweaty men's clothes and tried to imagine her scrambling over a bomber fuselage with a riveting gun.

'Actually, it wasn't heroic at all,' Poppy confessed. 'It was deadly dull and repetitious shiftwork, day and night, twelve hours a day. I thought I'd go mad, my brain was so dead. The noise and heat were incredible and the work was tough and exhausting.'

'Poor Poppy,' sympathised Jack. 'I don't like to think of you working in some horrible factory.'

'Of course, being females, we were being paid a lot less than the men doing the same job,' Poppy complained. 'That really annoyed me, and it was made quite clear that as soon as the real workers came back from the war we women would no longer be required.'

Jack laughed at her contradictory emotions. 'I thought you'd be glad to get out of there, Midget,' joked Jack. 'It doesn't sound much fun.'

Poppy pursed her lips in thought and then laughed as well. 'Well, some of it was enjoyable. I shared a flat with a couple of the other girls who worked there. While the work was ghastly, we did make up for it socialising and going out with some of the boys who worked there.'

'Oh?' commented Jack, glancing away, his voice flat. 'That does sound more amusing . . .'

Poppy gazed at his profile, his clenched jaw. What was wrong with Jack? Had she said something to upset him?

A glint of gold caught her eye, glimmering in the gnarled roots of the frangipani tree, half-buried in the soil. She stared at the object curiously, leaning over to examine it more closely.

'Jack, look!' she shrieked with excitement and picked up the object with shaking hands. 'It's my pearl! It's the pearl Mrs Murata gave me, the one I lost on the day Darwin was attacked.'

Poppy polished most of the dirt off with her fingers and held out the perfect silvery-golden teardrop hanging from a fine gold chain for Jack to admire.

'An angel's forgotten tear,' Poppy explained softly. 'Mrs Murata told me it was a magic jewel of good fortune that would keep me safe. A jewel of wisdom, wealth and healing. I thought it was lost forever.'

Jack leant in closer and stroked the shimmering pearl nestled in the palm of Poppy's hand. 'Well, they are definitely good powers to have,' he agreed. 'Would you like me to put it on you?'

'Yes, please,' replied Poppy, handing it over. Jack took the pearl and carefully polished it on the hem of his shirt, removing the remaining dirt. He untangled the chain, letting the pearl dangle in the sunlight.

Poppy turned around and pulled her hair off her neck. Gently, Jack placed the chain around her neck and fastened the clasp. Poppy could feel his fingertips on the back of her neck and shivered.

Jack stood up. 'Well, I suppose you should get back to massacring the grass. Would you like me to help?'

Jack offered his hand and pulled her to her feet.

'That would be great, but come and say hello to the rest of the family first,' Poppy said. 'Mum is making preparations for an amazing Christmas feast. She wants it to be the best Christmas ever.'

23

Christmas Feast

Christmas Day dawned, fair and bright. Edward and Mark set up a long trestle table that had been used at the barracks by the army, under the spreading branches of the mango tree. Seats were made from crates and petrol drums cut in half and padded with fabric, enough for all the family, friends and neighbours that Cecilia had invited.

Phoebe had made a tablecloth from a white sheet. Bryony and Poppy set the table with the best silver and crockery, dug up from under the house, and decorated it with frangipani blossoms. Edward set up Phoebe's record-player on the verandah with a stack of records that she had brought from Sydney.

'It's sweltering in here,' complained Bryony, mopping the perspiration from her forehead. Cecilia opened the new oven to check on the roasting meat — a leg of pork with crackling and two chickens provided from the Shanahans' farm.

'Mmmm. You won't mind the heat when we get to eat real roast pork and chicken,' Poppy reminded her. 'I can't remember the last time I ate roast pork!'

Poppy and Bryony were chopping baby cucumbers and avocados for the salad. Honey was asleep under the table, her nose twitching at the wafting scents. Phoebe leant against the doorjamb, observing the action.

'You could help, Phoebe,' complained Bryony, scraping the sliced greenery into a bowl.

'I haven't cooked a meal in *years*,' Phoebe admitted. 'The nurses always ate in the canteen, or went out for dinner. I wouldn't know where to start.'

'You can start by peeling those potatoes,' Cecilia suggested, handing Phoebe a sharp knife. 'It's nearly time for them to go into the oven.'

Soon the preparations were all completed and the girls disappeared to freshen up for lunch, touching up powder and lipstick, and tidying their hair. The Shanahans arrived along with the other friends and neighbours Cecilia had invited.

Everyone mingled in the garden under the shade trees, sipping on icy-cold lemonade or beer. Cecilia's Christmas present had been a new gas oven and refrigerator, bought at the army disposal auction, along with many other practical items to replace those stolen during the army occupation.

The girls fluttered like butterflies, wearing colourful floral sundresses, their hair soft and curled. The men sipped on beer, trading stories from their experiences during the war. Cecilia sat on a deckchair, chatting with old friends she hadn't seen for years. Phoebe and Edward kept a continuous stream of records playing.

'The Red Cross was wonderful,' Edward explained. 'They regularly sent in parcels of food, medicines and mail, but the Japanese would rarely let us have them. Well, one day the parcels included these massive seven-pound tins of Vegemite. The Japanese had no idea what it was, so they asked us. One of the fellows had the brilliant idea of telling them it was paint, because if they'd known it was food they would have kept it for themselves.

'So the Japs set us to work painting the barracks with Vegemite,' continued Edward. 'Little did they know we were licking it straight off the brush and making sure all the sick blokes in the hospital had plenty, too. I'm sure that Vegemite paint saved a few lives and kept us going for weeks. The guards were furious when they realised the trick we'd played on them — but by that stage the Vegemite had gone.'

Everyone laughed, then Jack's brother told a light-hearted tale of mateship, laughing in the face of danger and endless mud on the Kokoda Trail — and being looked after by the 'fuzzy-wuzzy angels' — the New Guinean villagers who saved the lives of countless injured Australian soldiers by nursing them and carrying them to safety.

Cecilia called everyone to sit down at the table, with Mark at the head and Edward at the place of honour at the other end. The older generation sat at one end, gossiping together, while the younger generation gathered at Edward's end. Honey stayed under the table, hoping to catch some fallen scraps.

Bryony and Poppy laid multiple dishes down on the table — green salad with avocados and baby cucumbers from the garden, baked potatoes and pumpkin, a jug of gravy, tiny truss tomatoes with chopped spring onions and basil, a huge tureen of apple sauce, mustards, sliced cold ham and minted green peas with butter. Mark carved the huge leg of pork with crackling, while Edward carved the chicken and stuffing.

Everyone helped themselves to whatever took their fancy, passing the plates from hand to hand, then Mark said grace.

Everyone filled their glasses and Mark made a toast. 'Here's to a wonderful celebration of family and friends, returned safely home again.' Everyone clinked their glasses, smiling.

'And to those who won't be coming home again,' Cecilia suggested.

'To my brother Harry,' said Jack, exchanging glances with his parents and Danny.

'To Daisy and Charlie,' said Poppy, her voice choked.

'To Iris,' said Edward.

'To Henry,' said Phoebe with a muffled sob.

'To all our friends and family who sacrificed their lives so we could enjoy this day,' said Mark.

There was a moment's silence, and a few tears as everyone thought of those who had died.

'Now let's enjoy the afternoon,' suggested Mark, picking up his cutlery.

Then everyone shared in the best meal that any of them had eaten for many years, smiling and talking and laughing and joking and sharing stories.

After lunch, Jack and Edward began a game of backyard cricket, which everyone joined in, including Honey, who snatched the ball more often than anyone.

Then the oldies sat in the shade and rested while the younger generation walked down to Mindil Beach for a swim. Poppy was relieved to see that the barbed wire had been rolled away.

≈≈≈

Salty and sandy after their afternoon swim, everyone strolled back to the house along the dirt track in pairs and in groups. Jack and Poppy dawdled together at the rear, catching up on three years of news and thoughts.

As they drew closer to the house, the strains of a Vera Lynn record could be heard on the breeze, singing many of her greatest hits from the war years.

'I love this song,' Poppy confessed, and began to sing along to the lyrics of 'As Time Goes By', swaying to the slow music, eyes closed.

'You must remember this
A kiss is still a kiss
A sigh is just a sigh
The fundamental things apply
As time goes by.'

'May I have this dance, Midget?' asked Jack with mock formality. They danced to the song under the frangipani tree with bare, sandy feet. Jack swung her around and out, and back in again. Then he kissed her. The song and the dance and the kiss seemed to go on forever, and then it was over. With hearts pounding, they joined the others in the garden.

Much later in the afternoon, Cecilia served the plum pudding, made with carefully hoarded sugar, served with mangoes from the tree and vanilla ice cream.

'Ice cream always makes me think of the Americans,' joked Jack. 'Their favourite breakfast food!'

'Thank goodness for the Americans,' said Phoebe. 'If we'd left it to the British we'd be speaking Japanese now.'

'No,' Edward disagreed. 'The Poms were right beside us at Singapore, and over seventy thousand British soldiers were taken prisoner with us. They made mistakes, but they didn't abandon us.'

'Children, no arguing on Christmas Day,' Cecilia pretended to scold. 'All right, let's change the subject. The war is over, we have a whole new future ahead of us — what are you all going to do with it?'

Everyone thought for a moment.

'I'm going to rebuild our surgery here in Darwin, alongside my beautiful wife, and never leave her again,' Mark declared. 'What do you think, darling?'

'I second that,' Cecilia agreed, squeezing his arm.

'I'm going to *find* a beautiful wife and take her to Alexandra Downs,' said Jack's brother Danny. 'It's time Mum and Dad had a rest from all that hard work.'

Everyone laughed and raised their glasses in a toast. Cecilia glanced at her eldest daughter, a small furrow of concern between her brows. A wave of sorrow passed over Phoebe's face, but she shook it off and smiled brightly.

'I've been offered a job as matron of a small private hospital in Brisbane,' confided Phoebe. 'It's offering good money for a nurse, and it will be easy after the work I've been doing.'

'Oh, well done, Phoebe,' Cecilia said. 'That's a huge achievement.'

Phoebe twisted a gold ring she wore on her left hand, and turned to Jack.

'I'm going back to Alexandra Downs as well, and working out what it is I really want to do,' said Jack. 'I think it will be nice to have a rest for a while. Then I might follow Danny's lead.' He flashed a shy smile at Poppy.

'Well, now might be the time to make an announcement,' said Bryony. 'I'm engaged to be married. I met a lovely man in Queensland called Joe, and we are saving up to buy a house and get settled. We worked together at Ascot and he asked me to marry him just before I left Brisbane.'

There were loud cries of congratulation and more chinking of glasses.

'Why didn't you tell us, Bryony?' asked Poppy, thumping her on the shoulder.

'You didn't ask till just now!'

Phoebe stood and hugged her sister. 'I'm so happy for you.'

'I don't know what I'm going to do,' Edward admitted. 'Not much good for anything with this leg.'

'You are going to stay home for a little while and rest,' his mother assured him. 'You've been through a lot, and you need to heal. You'll be sick of recuperating soon enough, and then you'll be raring to start a new project.'

'And what about you, Poppy?' asked Mark.

Poppy thought carefully, tucking a stray curl behind her ear. She glanced at Jack, then looked away, biting her lip.

'I'm going back to Sydney to apply to university,' announced Poppy. 'I'm going to study English literature, but I'd like to do teaching as well. It seems to me that good teachers can make a big difference in the world, just like our headmistress, Miss Royston.'

Cecilia nodded, encouraging her to continue.

'When the war came, I didn't want to leave Darwin. But being forced to go actually gave me an opportunity I might not otherwise have had — to get a good education. One day I'd like to come back to Darwin and teach. It seems a crime that there is no high school here, nowhere that children can learn. I'd like to change that.'

Poppy paused and looked around the table.

'Go back to Sydney?' asked Bryony. 'Go to university? I thought you couldn't wait to come back *here*.'

Poppy raised her chin defiantly.

'You'll make a wonderful teacher, Poppy,' said Jack.

'I think it's a fine idea,' agreed Cecilia. 'You'll be the first woman in our family to get a university degree. Now that would make me very proud.'

Mark raised his glass once more. 'To my beautiful family, who fill me with delight,' he said, his voice filled with emotion. 'And to the best Christmas for many a long year.'

'Merry Christmas!' shouted everyone.

Epilogue – 8 April 2012

'So, did you go to Sydney to study at university?' asked Chloe.

Nanna was silent for a few moments, lost in her reverie. 'Yes, I did Honours,' Nanna sighed. 'And I did become a teacher, and helped to get a high school started in Darwin.'

'But what about Jack?' asked Chloe. 'Couldn't you see he was in love with you?'

Nanna laughed, putting her teacup down on the table beside her. 'Oh, yes – but I didn't realise it for a while. Not until he came back to Sydney to study engineering at university. For a while I thought he was in love with Maude.'

Chloe shook her head in disbelief. 'Nanna, for someone so clever, you really were a bit thick.'

Nanna smiled. 'Well, in those days people weren't quite as forthright as they are now. Plus, things were more complicated.'

Chloe couldn't believe that things were more complicated in the 1940s than they were now. She had always imagined life was much simpler in the past.

'You see, married women often weren't allowed to work back then,' Nanna explained. 'If you were a teacher, you were expected to resign as soon as you married. Thankfully, it did eventually change, but I knew teachers who had to pretend they weren't married just so they could keep working in a career they loved. I certainly wasn't prepared to give up my career just as soon as I'd discovered what it was!'

'So Grandad came to Sydney, too?' asked Chloe.

'He followed me within a month,' Nanna said. 'We started to go out, but we were both studying very hard. Then I graduated and started teaching at a country school, so we only saw each other occasionally.

'When I was twenty-four, Jack asked me to marry him,' said Nanna. 'He wrote *Will you marry me?* in foot-high letters in the sand at Manly. We kept the engagement a secret, and were married a year later. Phoebe, Bryony and Maude were my bridesmaids.'

Nanna waved at an old black-and-white photo on the sideboard of her wedding day. She wore a billowy white silk dress with a lace veil on her dark, curly hair. The bridesmaids all glowed with youth and happiness.

'That sounds romantic,' said Chloe with a smile. 'And then you lived happily ever after . . .'

Nanna looked seriously at Chloe. 'Life always has its ups and downs, Chloe, but yes, on the whole, life was very good to us,' she agreed. 'It's like the old saying — you have to decide if your cup is half-full or half-empty.'

Chloe nodded. Her mother had often reminded her that things seemed much better if you thought of your cup as being half full.

'As you know, your poor aunt Phoebe never married — her heart was broken when her fiancé was killed,' continued Nanna. 'Bryony married Joe, and it was only years later that we discovered they had both worked for Central Bureau Intelligence for General MacArthur during the war, decoding intercepted Japanese air traffic. I never realised she had such an important role.

'Bryony said it was very stressful — a simple mistake, a typo, might mean death for the men in the field. Many of the women cracked under the pressure and had nervous breakdowns. I think Bryony found it very lonely and traumatic, not being able to talk about what she was doing.'

Nanna stared out the window at the autumn sky as though gazing through the mists of time.

'Apparently the Japanese didn't realise that the Allies had cracked their codes, and so the Central Bureau was able to decipher many of the Japanese radio messages. Bryony and Joe had to sign confidentiality agreements, promising they wouldn't talk about their work for years afterwards.'

Nanna picked up the box that had held the letters and bundles of photos. She fished around among the objects in the bottom of the box.

'Look, here are your grandfather's war medals,' said Nanna, showing Chloe a collection of service medals. 'And here it is — I haven't seen it for years.'

Nanna held up a fine gold chain with a silvery-golden teardrop pearl.

'Your pearl!' cried Chloe with delight. 'The one Mrs Murata gave you?'

'Yes.' Nanna smiled. 'The angel's tear. I'd forgotten all about it until today. Here, Chloe — I want you to have it.'

Chloe's face lit up with excitement. 'Really? I'd love it.'

Nanna fastened the chain around her neck and kissed Chloe's cheek.

'Remember, the pearl is the jewel of good fortune, wisdom, healing and protection, just like Mrs Murata told me all those years ago,' Nanna said. 'It can't stop bad things happening to you, of course, but perhaps it will remind you that you have the strength deep inside you to deal with whatever happens.'

Chloe's heart swelled with pride and excitement. 'Whatever happened to Shinju and Mrs Murata?' she asked, stroking the pearl with her fingertips.

Nanna frowned. 'Many of the Japanese internees were sent to Japan after the war, even those who had been born in Australia. But the Muratas stayed. They were eventually released but had a very hard time here after the war. Japanese children were often beaten up at school or had stones thrown at them.

'They moved back to Darwin in the 1950s. I saw them there when I was teaching. Mrs Murata was overjoyed because I gave her back her great-grandmother's tea set that I had buried under our house. I still write to Shinju every Christmas.'

'And of course Maude is still one of your best friends,' said Chloe.

'Yes,' replied Nanna with a warm smile. 'Her friendship has been one of the great joys of my life.'

Chloe thought about her own friends — would she still be close with any of them in seventy years?

As though she could read her thoughts, Nanna smiled and took Chloe's hand. 'A good friendship is something you should cherish and protect. You'll make many friends in your life. Some will come and go, and others will stay with you for a lifetime. But a good friendship is worth fighting for.'

Chloe thought about everything that had happened at school recently. How could she fight for her friendship with Brianna? Could she go and ask her what had gone wrong? Had she unintentionally done or said something that caused the rift? Did she have the strength to face her friends and solve the problem?

Chloe squeezed Nanna's hand in return.

The front door opened and Chloe's grandfather came in, carrying a large bunch of white roses. 'Here you go, Midget, I brought you some roses. Oh! Hello, Chloe . . . How's my beautiful girl?'

'Great, thanks Grandad,' replied Chloe, standing up to kiss his rough cheek. 'Nanna's been telling me about her life during the war. She told me a wonderful story of friendship and sisters, grief and love, and about growing up . . . I'll never forget it.'

Her grandfather placed the roses on the sideboard and cupped Chloe's cheek with his hand.

'You know, Chloe, you remind me so much of your grandmother when she was a girl — strong, determined, clever and brave — and the prettiest girl I knew.'

Chloe grinned, her heart warmed. 'Thanks, Grandad. I think that's the best compliment anyone's ever given me.'

'And how's school going?' he asked.

'Oh, it has its ups and downs, but nothing I can't work out,' Chloe said, stroking the pearl around her neck.

'That's my girl,' said Poppy. She took up Chloe's hand and turned it over to read her palm, like a gypsy fortune teller, tracing the lifeline with her forefinger. 'You will face the tough times with strength and courage, and you will face the happy times with joy and love. You will grow up into a beautiful young woman, with the world at your feet.'

'And meet a handsome young man?' joked Chloe.

'And fall truly, madly, deeply in love.'

Author's Note

In the 1940s, many Australians regularly used disparaging terms to describe people of other races and cultures, particularly those belonging to the enemy nationalities. Many of these terms are now considered racist. I have used some of these terms in dialogue, not with the intent to offend any readers but to provide a reflection of attitudes prevalent during the Second World War.

Fast Facts about Australia and the Second World War

- John Curtin became Australia's prime minister on 3 October 1941, leading a Labor government. He was Australia's leader for the duration of the war, dying six weeks before the Japanese surrender.
- Australia declared war on Japan on 8 December 1941 after the surprise bombing of Pearl Harbor. At Pearl Harbor, more than 2400 people were killed and a further 1280 were injured.
- Following the Japanese attack on Pearl Harbor, approximately 2000 women and children were evacuated from Darwin by ship, road and air between 19 December

1941 and 15 February 1942. All Aboriginal women and children were evacuated to camps further south, such as those near Katherine. Approximately 500 part-Aboriginal women and children were evacuated to the southern states. Only sixty-three white women remained in Darwin, mostly employed in essential services. There were also about thirty-five part-Aboriginal girls from Bathurst Island who were in transit on the day of the attack, waiting for evacuation.

- There were more than ninety-seven bombing raids on Australia by the Japanese. Darwin and its surrounds were bombed on sixty-four occasions. Other Australian targets included Broome, Townsville, Mossman, Katherine, Wyndham, Port Hedland, Derby and Horn Island.

- The first and most devastating Japanese attack on Darwin was at 9:58 am on 19 February 1942, followed by a second attack later that day. In the first two raids, more than 243 people were killed and almost 400 wounded, eight ships sank and most of the civil and military facilities destroyed.

- There were more bombs dropped on Darwin on 19 February 1942 than were dropped on Pearl Harbor. Two hundred and forty-two Japanese aircraft were involved in the attack — the same force that attacked Pearl Harbor several weeks before.

- Approximately 540,000 Australians served in the military during the Second World War, out of a population of about seven million, and approximately 40,000 Australians died.

- About 22,000 Australians were taken as prisoners-of-war by the Japanese — of these approximately thirty-four per cent died of starvation, disease and cruelty. This compares to the 8000 Australians taken prisoner by the Germans, where the death rate was only three per cent.

- The Second World War profoundly changed women's role in Australian society. Prior to this, most married women didn't work in paid employment. During the war, women were encouraged to work to free up men for active service. Approximately 66,500 women served in the armed forces.

- A higher percentage of the Australian population was in the military forces than in either the US or UK. When Japan entered the war in December 1941, all men between eighteen and thirty-five (and single men up to forty-five) were called up. Depending on medical fitness and skills, these men were then allocated to the militia or to essential war work.

- Many teenagers from as young as fifteen or sixteen, both boys and girls, lied about their age to join the war effort. They were supposed to be at least eighteen to join the armed services or the women's auxiliary services.

- Rationing was introduced for many items during the war, becoming progressively stricter as the war went on. For example, petrol rationing was introduced in 1940, clothing and food in late 1942, and butter in 1943. Paper rationing meant no new textbooks and no wastage of paper.

- Almost one million US troops passed through Australia during the war. About 7000 Australian women married American servicemen and went to the US as war brides.

- While the Japanese air raids on Australia were destructive and killed hundreds of people, the bombing of Australia was nowhere near as devastating as that in Europe. For example, during the German bombing raids over the UK, 18,000 British civilians were killed during the first five months of 1941, with a further 21,000 people injured.
- The Germans surrendered in Europe on 7 May 1945 after six years of war; however, the Japanese refused to surrender. On 11 July, the Allied leaders met again at Potsdam and reiterated their demand for the unconditional surrender of the Japanese forces. The alternative was 'prompt and utter destruction'. The Japanese again refused. On 6 August 1945 the Americans dropped an atomic bomb on Hiroshima with catastrophic results. Another atomic bomb was dropped on Nagasaki on 9 August. These nuclear bombs resulted in at least 150,000 Japanese people, mostly civilians, being killed either immediately or in the weeks that followed. Japan surrendered on 14 August 1945.
- A total of about sixty million people died during the Second World War, many of those civilians.

Acknowledgements

When my family spent eighteen months travelling around Australia, we stayed about three months in the Top End of the Northern Territory, including Darwin. During this time, we stayed on vast, remote cattle stations and visited some incredibly beautiful places. As well as the sheer beauty of the Territory, we were overwhelmed by its history. Despite studying Australian History at university, I had very little knowledge of the bombing of Darwin during the Second World War and how widespread and lethal the Japanese attacks on Australia were. It was this adventure that inspired me to write the story of Poppy.

A huge thank you goes to my intrepid husband, Rob, for introducing us to many of the Second World War historic sites in the Northern Territory, from airstrips, bomb craters and bunkers to the deeply moving Adelaide River War Cemetery where over four hundred Australians who died defending our country are buried. The youngest was only sixteen years old. Also buried here are civilians such as Iris Bald and her parents, along with the other post office workers and thirty-one Indigenous Australians whose death was due to enemy action. Among these is Daisy Martin, a part-Aboriginal servant who died in the first bombing attack on Darwin.

A big thanks to my daughter Emily for being, as always, my first and most enthusiastic reader.

I am so lucky to have a brilliant publishing team, with an incredible passion for books, who work tirelessly through weekends, holidays and late into the night. A huge thank you to Pippa Masson, Dorothy Tonkin, Nina Paine, Nanette Backhouse and Sarana Behan, but especially to Zoe Walton and Brandon VanOver. You are truly wonderful!

Writing this book required much research, including reading letters, diaries and memoirs by Australian nurses, children and women evacuated from Darwin, soldiers and POWs, as well as articles from newspapers and magazines such as *Army News*, *The Sydney Morning Herald* and *Australian Women's Weekly*. Some of the books that I found invaluable were *Australia's Pearl Harbour, Darwin 1942* by Douglas Lockwood; *Singapore and Beyond* by Don Wall; *Olive Weston: The heroic life of a World War II nurse* by Peter Fenton; *No Place for a Woman*, the autobiography of Mayse Young; *Heroic Australian Women in War: Astonishing tales of bravery from Gallipoli to Kokoda* by Susannah De Vries; *Ut Prosim*, a history of Wenona School by Denise Thomas (which included stories of school life during wartime and anecdotes of their inspirational headmistress, Miss Ralston); *Brave and Bold*, a history of Manly Village

Public School by John Ramsland; *An Awkward Truth* by Peter Grose; and *Australia's Greatest Peril 1942* by Bob Wurth, which included the story of a young Manly boy who spotted the Japanese spy plane. As always, there are family stories and reminiscences told to me by members of my own family, including Lee and Jan Murrell; my mother, Gilly Evans; my father, Jerry Humphrey, who spent several months as a veterinarian working on Northern Territory cattle stations; and my great-aunt Clarice, who told me stories of her brother Aubrey Jones, an Australian soldier taken as a prisoner-of-war by the Japanese. He had his leg amputated in a POW camp on the Burma Railway. It was Auntie Clarice who told me the story of the Vegemite used as paint. Jenn Wall — your lemon cake is truly inspiring.

Finally, for everyone who loves my books, thank you!

About the Author

At about the age of eight, Belinda Murrell began writing stirring tales of adventure, mystery and magic in hand-illustrated exercise books. As an adult, she combined two of her great loves — writing and travelling the world — and worked as a travel journalist, technical writer and public relations consultant. Now, inspired by her own three children, Belinda is a bestselling, internationally published children's author. Her titles include four picture books, her fantasy adventure series, The Sun Sword Trilogy, and her six time-slip adventures, *The Locket of Dreams*, *The Ruby Talisman*, *The Ivory Rose*, *The Forgotten Pearl*, *The River Charm* and *The Sequin Star*.

For younger readers (aged 6 to 9), Belinda has a new series, Lulu Bell, about friends, family, animals and adventures growing up in a vet hospital.

Belinda lives in Manly in a gorgeous old house overlooking the sea with her husband, Rob, her three beautiful children and her dog, Rosie. She is an Author Ambassador for Room to Read and Books in Homes.

Find out more about Belinda at her website:
www.belindamurrell.com.au

THE LOCKET OF DREAMS

When Sophie falls asleep wearing a locket that belonged to her grandmother's great-grandmother, she magically travels back to 1858 to learn the truth about the mysterious Charlotte Mackenzie.

Charlotte and her sister, Nell, live a wonderful life on a misty Scottish island. Then disaster strikes and it seems the girls will lose everything they love. Why were the sisters sent to live with strangers? Did their uncle steal their inheritance? And what happened to the priceless sapphire — the Star of Serendib?

Sophie shares in the girls' adventures as they outwit greedy relatives, escape murderous bushrangers, and fight storm and fire. But how will her travels in time affect Sophie's own life?

**Shortlisted for the 2011 KOALA awards
OUT NOW!**

THE RUBY TALISMAN

When Tilly's aunt tells her of their ancestress who survived the French Revolution, she shows Tilly a priceless heirloom. Tilly falls asleep wearing the ruby talisman, wishing she could escape to a more adventurous life . . .

In 1789, Amelie-Mathilde is staying at the opulent palace of Versailles. Her guardians want her to marry the horrible old Chevalier to revive their fortunes. Amelie-Mathilde falls asleep holding her own ruby talisman, wishing someone would come to her rescue . . .

Tilly wakes up beside Amelie-Mathilde. The timing couldn't be worse. The Bastille has fallen and starving peasants are rioting across the country. The palace is in chaos.

Tilly knows that Amelie and her cousin Henri must escape from France if they are to survive the Revolution ahead. But with mutinous villagers, vengeful servants and threats at every turn, there seems nowhere to run. Will they ever reach England and safety?

OUT NOW!

THE IVORY ROSE

Jemma has just landed her first job, babysitting Sammy. It's in Rosethorne, one of the famous Witches' Houses near where she lives. Sammy says the house is haunted by a sad little girl, but Jemma doesn't know what to believe.

One day when the two girls are playing hide-and-seek, Jemma discovers a rose charm made of ivory. As she touches the charm she sees a terrifying flashback. Is it the moment the ghost was murdered? Jemma runs for her life, falling down the stairs and tumbling into unconsciousness.

She wakes up in 1895, unable to get home. Jemma becomes an apprentice maidservant at Rosethorne — but all is not well in the grand house. Young heiress Georgiana is constantly sick. Jemma begins to suspect Georgiana is being poisoned, but who would poison her, and why? Jemma must find the proof in order to rescue her friend — before time runs out.

A CBCA Notable Book
OUT NOW!

THE RIVER CHARM

When artistic Millie visits a long-lost aunt, she learns about her family's tragic past. Could the ghost girl Millie has painted be her own ancestor?

In 1839, Charlotte Atkinson lives at Oldbury, a grand estate in the bush, with her Mamma and her sisters and brother. But after her father dies, things go terribly wrong — murderous convicts, marauding bushrangers and, worst of all, a cruel new stepfather.

Frightened for their lives, the family flees on horseback to a hut in the wilderness. The Atkinson family must fight to save their property, their independence and even their right to stay together. Will they ever return to their beautiful home?

Based on the incredible true-life battles of bestselling author Belinda Murrell's own ancestors, the Atkinsons of Oldbury.

OUT NOW!

THE SEQUIN STAR

Claire finds a sequin star among her grandmother's treasures. Why does she own such a cheap piece? The mystery deepens when the brooch hurtles Claire back in time to 1932.

Claire finds herself stranded in a circus camp. The Great Depression has made life difficult, but Claire befriends performers Rosina and Jem, and a boy called Kit who watches the show every night.

When Kit is kidnapped, it's up to Claire, Rosina and Jem to save him. But Claire wonders who Kit and Rosina really are. One is escaping poverty and the other is escaping wealth — can the two find happiness together?

OUT NOW!